ELIZABETH STEPHENS

MONSTER IN THE OASIS

POPULATION SERIES: BOOK TWO

Table of Contents

To the scarred.
Scars prove you lived.

E.S.

Chapter One

Listening to the sound of voices, I wonder if I'm dead or asleep. It's the same question I've been asking myself for days now. Or has it been weeks? It doesn't much matter. Time doesn't exist. There's only pain. A bright, effulgent agony. It cuts across my skin, burrowing deep into my flesh, finding home near my brittle bones. The wind whistles through them these days, sounding like sand pattering against paper. I'm just dissolving away.

The hurt hurts worse against my face and chest…but also across my back and shoulders…and also, mostly my right leg, which has been partially flayed.

The bastard enjoyed doing this to me. I wonder if I was wrong in thinking that I'd escaped. Maybe Jack let me get away. Just so I could die like this. *Of course I did, Diego.* Fucker. His voice is all I can hear as I lay dying. That low, demonic chuckle.

My mouth is dry, lips cracked and bleeding, but I can't taste the blood. There's only ash as I lie on the side of the road like something discarded, the slow wheezing of my breath and Jack's ringing laughter keeping me conscious.

I wish I wasn't.

Wish I wasn't alive, either.

I want to die. I've wanted to die from the beginning, but instead, I clawed my way across this wasteland, moving from one water source to the next.

I thought finding the highway might lead me to some town where I could find medical supplies and recover but in the middle of the crumbling asphalt was where my body stopped working and I decided I'd rather let the crows and the carrion take whatever trash Jack left.

The brutal way my body was built was the only part of me with any purpose anyway, and there's no saving it. So there's no point to salvaging something worthless. Fuck it. Let the carrion creatures come out to hunt.

That's the spirit.

A sound in the distance grows louder as everything else begins to fade. Sounds like thunder. A lady once taught me about thunder. Said it was the cough of some great big man who lived up in the clouds. She called him The God. She also called herself mother. I didn't believe her when she said it, and I didn't believe her about that big man either. Nobody treats their kids like that.

Not her.

Not *him.*

How could you think that, my sweet, sweet Diego? I loved you. I love you still.

Another stretch of time passes before the coughing starts up again…then continues, pulling me out my drunken stupor and into the world of pain I thought I'd been lucky enough to leave behind.

The sound persists, forcing memories on me. Memories of big, fat trucks on heavily trafficked roads while me and the other kids running under Jack try to lift merch from them. We succeeded more than we didn't. Jack gave us each fat cuts. I was thirteen? Ten? Younger than that, maybe. But I was a prince to Jack's king. And he's right, I did love him. *Do, Diego, you do love me.*

Maybe he's right now, too.

But here and now, it's the sound that's wrong. I can't be hearing the groan of an exhaust pipe. The last time I heard that sound was a decade back, when eighteen-wheelers still ran. They're too big and too slow for Population though, because they present a moving target for gangs — gangs like Jack's. The one I joined sometime after the one called Mother.

When he found me, I'd been on the streets and I was convinced that he was The God she'd spoken about.

Shouting words sound over the thrum of the truck. Some of the voices are deep and distinctly male, but others are lighter, operating at too high a pitch. Kids or women? And that's surprise number two, because kids don't exist out here and the women that do wish they didn't.

I remember the last woman I'd seen on the road, strung up in a kill box. She'd been bloodied worse than anybody I'd seen in a long while, but she held out. She kept fighting. It'd been hard to watch — not the torture, but her spirit slowly evaporating into the sky. With those injuries, she wouldn't have lasted more than a few hours after I cut her down and let her loose. Whatever Jack didn't do, Population woulda done the rest. She'd a died just like I'm doing now. Broken and bloody and in pain. Alone on the side of the road. Road kill. Wearing her insides on the outsides.

Except I'm not alone. Not anymore. Because there are murmurs belonging to voices that belong to the people whispering them. Distinct words peel apart from the whooshing sound that's filled my ears. I hear "can't" and "Sandra" and "save him."

Don't, please don't.

Wishing I had enough strength left to slaughter one last person — whoever talking about trying to save my skin — I try moving my arms. My left hand twitches, but my right is numb, paralyzed up to the shoulder. It's been that way since I swallowed mud two days ago. The closest I could get to water. I'm just rotting now…rotting from within.

"Hey, hey!" Fingers slap my left cheek, the one that isn't a raw, pus filled lesion, then pull up on my eyelids.

Colors blur and swim, making it impossible for me to see the face looming above me as more than just a muddy smear against a darker light. The sky. It's hideous. But that doesn't matter, because I've seen the sky everyday, but I've only heard that voice twice.

"I know you," she shouts, voice too loud and too close and too fucking impossible. The woman from the kill box. The one who I cut down. The one who's dead.

"I know you and you saved my life. Remember? You fought your brothers for me."

I remember. How could I forget? The one halfway decent thing I've done in the past thirty-two years was what landed me here, strung out on the side of the road wearing my insides as a blanket. The irony is as tragic as it is hilarious.

Good men die in this world. Brutally. In piles of piss and shit and blood.

I'm a bad man, so how is it that I'm here, dying like one of the good ones?

My senses grow distant, numbing out into numbness, until I feel pressure on the open wound that rips down the right side of my neck. I hiss, my body writhing, trying to distance itself from the pain. I can't get up. I can't get away. My chest constricts as I push stale air out and I can tell this will be one of my last breaths. Finally.

"Hey!" The voice roars. "You're not allowed to die yet. I won't let my debt go unpaid. Just hold on. I've got a doctor here and she's going to work her magic. Isn't that right?"

I redirect the last seconds of willpower I've got to my eyelids and blink once to clear them. A brown woman sits at my right side, watching the dead one. Forehead wrinkled, lips turned down at the corners, her expression isn't one I've seen a lot, but I'm still human enough to understand it. She's sorry. She can't help me. Thank fuck.

"Abel," the woman speaks quietly, but I can hear her just fine. I'm dead, not deaf. "The most I can do for him is ease his transition."

"No no no no no." The dead one shakes her head, looking just as fierce as I remember. Just as obstinate, too. Her will to live must be stronger than mine because I don't understand how she could have survived the beating and the lashing and the smoke from the Other's immolation unless she had their blood in her system. A lot of it.

"There has to be something you can do," the corpse says to the breather. "You're a healer. *Heal* him."

The woman doesn't respond right away. After a moment, she coils a piece of rubber around my left bicep and inserts a needle somewhere in my arm. Not that I can feel it. I can't feel anything at all. "Ashlyn, bring me the morphine."

I feel her hand on my skin as if there are layers of dirt separating us. Rick told me that when you die, you hallucinate in your final seconds due to a lack of oxygen in the brain — that was a few days before I killed him. Is this an atrophy of the mind? Am I already six feet under?

A small blonde child comes up behind her, but the specter called Abel holds her back. "No! No, fuck that. Sandra, that's too much." Abel grabs the Sandra woman by the wrist. Clear globs of liquid drip from the needle's delicious tip.

Sandra meets my gaze. I stare up at her listlessly. She whispers, "I can end his suffering."

"No. Don't you fucking dare disobey me." Abel points a finger threateningly at Sandra's nose and shoves her shoulder. "I'm the *Notare*, goddammit! If I can't exercise my power to save this one man then how am I supposed to save the rest of humanity?" A Notare? Sounds like Other speak. I wonder if I'm not hearing her incorrectly.

"Relinquish the few to save the many," Sandra counters diplomatically. But that's fine. I'm happy to be a statistic.

Abel surges forward when Sandra raises the needle a second time and shoves the woman's shoulder. Seated on top of her heels as she is, Sandra falls onto her ass. There are people — men *and* women — standing in the background, watching. None intervene.

"Don't give me that battlefield triage bullshit. I wouldn't be here right now if it weren't for him."

Sandra doesn't seem to rise to Abel's challenge, but instead retreats further into herself. Her hooded gaze looks off into the distance, anywhere but at my face. "If you had been as injured as he is now, then it is likely, Your Grace, that I wouldn't have been able to save you either. It was the blood."

My eyes close and open and behind Abel's frustrated expression I see the tops of heads and above them, spindly boughs crawling up the grey mist, looking like desiccated fingers desperately seeking salvation.

Abel turns to me, places her hand on my good cheek and says, "I'm going to give you my blood."

I gargle up blood and saliva when I mean to attack her. The hell she is. I've lived this long without their shitty alien blood in my body. I'm human. *All* human. One of the few left.

Her wrist comes towards me and I writhe — in my head — because outwardly, I'm not sure I move at all. Castrated by blood loss and incapable of rebelling, I'm grateful when a man steps up behind this dead bitch and grips her shoulders. For a moment I hallucinate Jack. How the fuck did Jack find me? But then I blink.

This guy's not Jack. He's bigger than Jack was — than Jack *is* because it's clear that fucker won't ever die. This guy's bigger than any human I've seen. He's got Jack's dark hair and Jack's green eyes but there's a slight orange pulse around the collar of his shirt that makes it look like he's smuggling a flashlight under his black tee. Huge? Glowing? Nah, he's definitely not human.

So he's a fucking alien Jack. How ironic. All of my favorite fucking things. *You know you could never get rid of me, sweetie.*

My outside shell is immobile though my insides scream as Abel says, "What's the point of *this*, if I can't save him?" She yanks down on the neck of her own black thermal and I see an orange glow pulsing in time to a quick, steady beat. I thought she was human. I was *sure* of it.

I must already be dead and already dreaming.

The other Jack — the Jack Other — shakes his head. "As my Sistana, I can't let you give him your blood. It puts us both at risk."

His voice is even though his eyebrows are pulled together, as if concerned. He watches the human with the glowing golden heart with a fondness that makes me think that he somehow *cares* for her. Jack would never wear an expression like that. He would slice that expression off of any of his dogs' faces if he saw it. He did once.

"Come, Abel. Let Sandra help him." He pulls Abel gently to her feet.

A second male that I recognize as equally inhuman steps into my line of sight. My optic nerve has all but incinerated with the effort it takes to keep my eyes open. I want to close them and fucking die, but curiosity holds my attention just enough to keep me anchored to the hard concrete at my back and the cold breeze nipping at my front like the cruel edges of small, sharp teeth.

"This is the guy?" The blonde Other. His chest doesn't glow, or if it does, I can't see it underneath his sweatshirt. He's got on black basketball shorts and his hair is tied up in a knot on top of his head. He looks fucking stupid — aside from being nearly too big to take.

"Yes," Abel says, voice pleading and haunting. Not the melody I wanted to die to.

Her fists are wrapped in the glowing Jack Other's shirt. She's pulling. He's staring. They're all fucking staring. "He's the one who cut me down. I thought I was dying — hell, I thought I was already dead. But he fought off Jack's men — his war dogs, or whatever he called them. I was all by myself and *he* was the one who protected me before Mikey showed up." She looks to the blonde. "Before *you* showed up and carried me into the river."

But I'm still stuck — protected her? Is that what I did? Evidently in unknown coordination with this big, blood-sucking idiot.

Confusion puts a clamp on my throat. I'm not breathing. And then I'm seizing. My teeth clench together and my eyes roll back. Pain stabs its fingers into my wounds, whittling down through the diseased and rotten flesh until it scrapes bone with its nails. This is it.

I'm covered in pus and mud and blood and a shadow appears before my eyes where that fated fabled tunnel should have been. I'm dying until I feel a hard, warm object against my mouth and pungent heat dripping down the back of my throat that tastes like metal and eggs. A hand shifts behind my neck, tilting my head up at an angle and I cough as my tongue swells up in my mouth, fighting not to swallow.

"Come on man, you want to live or not?" The blonde fucker speaks to me in a low growl.

No, I don't. I really fucking don't.

But I can't speak and he doesn't hear me and the smell of piss is suffocating and the taste in my mouth is like sucking on pennies and shit. When he withdraws a few moments later, a tingling sensation sweeps my body and is followed closely by an unnatural euphoria. Drugs. Other blood and human drugs. They're working together to fuck me over by keeping me breathing.

Death was so close. I was almost there...

"Thank you, Mikey." Abel's voice whispers as sleep and I war with one another. Her low pitch and the Mikey Other's burn and blur together, becoming a thick haze. "Thank you so much."

"I owe him. The debt you sought to pay was mine."

I've never met the alien, but he sure as shit owes me now. He owes me a death. Because as air comes more easily to my scorched lungs, I understand that I'm not in hell but somewhere much worse. Instead of that easy slip into nothingness, I've been condemned to life.

Chapter Two

"Diego...Diego, can you hear me?" The words are faraway but coming closer, like a train from the World Before and I'm tied to the goddamn tracks. She calls me Diego. How in the hell does she know to call me that?

As if I asked the question out loud, she answers, "I remember your name from before. The murdering asswipe from your gang called you that, so I'm going to assume it's correct. You'll have to tell me if it isn't."

Her hand touches my forehead. I want to get out from under it. So hot and heavy and disgusting in the comfort it tries to provide. I don't need comfort. I don't need anything or anyone.

Suddenly another voice cuts in. I know it too. Sandy or Sana or Sancha something. "Diego, if you can hear me we've stopped moving for the night. I'm going to put you under again. I need to keep you sedated and tied down so that I can work on cutting out the scar tissue.

"Mikey's blood has rid your body of infection but the wounds were severe and, left to fester, his blood won't be able to heal your face so that it looks like it did before."

She doesn't apologize, but instead says stiffly, "I am going to see what I can do to minimize the damage."

I say nothing and relish in the numbness that creeps over me in the seconds before I pass out. It's as close to good as I've ever felt, so I take it without complaint once, twice, a dozen more times until finally I wake and somebody that isn't the blessed Sammy hovers over me.

The corpse is back.

The dead woman that is definitely no longer dead is sitting up, looking down her nose at me. Infrequent shafts of light hit the right side of her face. It's brown, like the skin on the backs of her hands and her throat. Darker than mine is. The same color as Santana but just…different.

Her hair is dark, maybe black, unlike the medium brown fuzz that grows out of my head and that I usually raze down to the root. Her hair is clean, too.

I don't see clean hair a lot in Population, so it distracts me. Little feathery wisps touch her jaw in curls. I think it might even be a little longer than it was the last time I saw her.

Now, definitely not dead, I find the way her dark blue eyes watch me annoying, but perhaps it's only because she reminds me of someone I knew once. Someone I liked. Or maybe hated. Is there a difference?

I think about Jack. I wanted him dead — to die suffering — but at the same time, I'd have done anything for him. I loved him with the entirety of my black, withering soul.

Corpse scoots towards me until I feel the warmth of her hip against mine. The first time I've been made aware of my own body in days. As she moves, something beneath her rattles. Metal on metal on wood. It takes me a second to understand, but I'm on a cot and there's another identical cot stacked on top of it. Above me, slats stare down. Bunks, but where?

The Other who gave me his blood sits on the cot across a short aisle, his sneakers propped up on the bunk I occupy.

Abel pushes his shoe away when it brushes her other hip. It's a damn tight fit in here. Like army barracks. Except I can feel the rumbling beneath me and hear the humming of that fabled exhaust pipe and ever so often, the battering of the wind against whatever structure covers us.

So we're in some kind of moving army barracks. I'm alive. The corpse is alive. The Other who looks fucking stupid and stares at her like she's the sun to his universe isn't trying to kill me, but save my life. A blanket covers me. Beneath it, I'm naked. And Sansan's wonderful drugs are numbing me, but not enough.

"How do you feel?"

I don't want to feel. That's what I'd tell her if I could, but I lack the voice. Instead, I turn my head away and close my eyes and try to push back the sensation of sandpaper sheets rubbing like little razorblades against my too sensitive flesh. I focus on the sensation of air flowing in and out of my nostrils. The smell of a canvas tarpaulin. Grease. Metal. Human sweat.

"Diego, I don't know if you remember me, but my name is Abel. You met me a few weeks ago when you and the members of your gang trapped me and a Heztoichen named Trocker." I'd never fucking forget it. "You saved my life after Jack beat and whipped me. I can only assume that you got at least some of your injuries shortly after that."

She pauses again, as if waiting for me to say something. I don't and I won't.

I feel her shift on the cot beside me. I wish she'd just get the fuck off and go away. Die like she was supposed to.

"We found you on the side of the road five days ago and my friend Mikey gave you his blood to keep you alive. He's one of the Others. So is my husband, Kane, and so are my friends Tasha and Laiya and the Lahve.

"The Lahve isn't with us, but some of his troops are. They're here to protect us as we cross Population. The rest of us are human. There's a long story here that you probably aren't ready to hear now, but I'll give you the bullet points.

"The system of governance for the Others is based on which among them carry light, or glow in their chests, like Kane does and like I do now. These seven Notare have divided up the planet. They each rule a different region and the grey area we humans call Population is what was left to us."

Yes, I know Population. I know it well. My jaw ticks, and so do the muscles in my forearms as I remember years and years of pain and suffering. Not mine, but that which I delivered. So. Much. Pain.

"Through a series of events, I ended up bonding to another Notare when we swapped blood. She killed me and when she was killed in retaliation, her light passed on to me. That makes me one of the seven rulers of the world now, in the Others' eyes.

"I'm taking over her lands and making them a human sanctuary. Heztoichen won't be barred from joining us, but there won't be any more of this cannibalistic shit. There won't be any scavenging, no looting, no robbing, no rape, no killing. There won't be gangs.

"It's going to be a helluva lot of work getting there and it's going to require a lot of manpower and I know it's a lot to ask of you right now, but I'd love it if you stayed with us.

"I don't have a lot of warriors on my team and I could use someone with your skills. It's going to be at least another two months of hard, deep trekking across Population before we get there, and that's only if everything goes well. The plan is actually to try to find people on the road. We want to bring them with us, if they seem…amenable to it."

What a fucking joke. Jack laughs.

I agree with him. What a fucking joke.

Her tone is higher and more severe as she says, "We want to rehabilitate those that can be rehabilitated, both physically and mentally and we want to be able to give everyone we meet the same choice I'm giving you now. I've got Sandra and Ashlyn here as medics, and some of the humans who've spent more time out in Population can act as sort of... mediators. They'll try to help.

"But what I need now are contingencies. It's not going to be easy to convince people and it'll be harder to get gangs to disband and to absorb them. I want people on my team there for when things don't work out. I need warriors to defend us in case they attack and I've seen you in action."

Her voice trickles away as she asks me to give her something so many others have tried to take. That Jack took with love, with psychological fuckery, and with force.

My obedience. My free will.

"Would you consider it?"

"Because we could always just drop you off on the side of the road, like we found you," a hard male voice cracks. The blonde Other. The one with the stupid haircut. Mikey, she called him.

"Mikael," a deeper male voice reprimands. Who the fuck is this now? Fuck if it's that Fake Alien Jack.

You know you miss me with all your bloody soul.

My muscles twitch with an eagerness to smash my fist through Fake Jack's teeth in an attempt to reach the back of his skull. I'm weak though, arms too heavy to lift.

Of course they'd ask me now when I'm at their mercy, because that's what the hungry do when they finally achieve power. They make slaves. They devour.

I clench my teeth together and close my eyes, blocking out the light as I struggle to shut out the other sounds. Whispering nearby, loud talking just a few paces off.

In the seconds that I wonder what they're saying about me, my self-hatred grows. I don't give a fuck. I don't need this woman's protection. I don't need another Jack, even one with tits on her.

"Diego?"

I twist away from the sound of her voice until I feel the stitching on my neck begin to tear. Let it. Who fucking cares?

"Look, you don't have to answer now. I'm just excited to have you here and happy that you're better." I hear her rise to leave and the sound of heavy shoes hitting the ground beside her.

"Just to let you know, Sandra's managed to cut out most of the excess scar tissue. You'll still have some, but it's better than it was." Sandra. The doc's name is Sandra. I hate myself for registering it. For caring.

"I'll get you some food and water. Sandra and Ashlyn have been keeping you on an IV but it'll be good to replenish the old fashioned way, chewing and swallowing and shitting. All that fun stuff."

She whistles, then shouts, "Calvin, would you bring Diego some grub?"

"Sure thing, boss," comes the faraway reply.

I wait for her to leave, but she doesn't. Instead the bitch fucking touches me again, this time my shoulder. I *hate* the feeling of it. I hate being touched. The stress of it brings a cold sweat to my armpits, my hairline and my crotch. It's a contrast to the ferocious and unwanted heat of her right hand on my exposed shoulder. My sternum shudders. I'd have broken her wrist with my own hands if they weren't under the drug-laced spell Sandra put them under.

So instead, I snarl up at her, "D-d-d-don't…fuck-fuck-fucking t-t-touch mmme."

It's been a long time since I've been forced to speak. A long time. Jack and his war dogs knew better than to try. The words come out more mangled than they usually do and I watch the frame of her eyes widen until I can see white on all sides of the iris. She sees me for what I am. Pathetic. And she pities me. And I hate her for it. She looks away and opens her mouth.

"D-d-d-d…" Don't. The word forms perfectly in my mind, repeating itself over and over. But the stutter is like a fucking intruder breaking into my home. I try to push him out the door, but the harder I push, the harder he digs his heels into the carpet. I'm sweating. Fucking convulsing. My face feels hot. My chest feels cold. My palms go clammy. And he's laughing the whole time.

"It's okay," Abel says without giving me a chance to speak. To try.

I'd cut the tongue out of her mouth for it. I've done it before. Jack approved. He held the boy down while I heated the knife, then whittled it in past the kid's teeth.

Jack wouldn't let anybody talk shit about my stutter. He never finished my sentences. He always waited. Patient. Tender. *Because I love you, Diego.* He did. And I worshiped him in return. Let him enslave me. It hurts knowing that he still does.

"Don't," I choke out, the word arriving minutes too late.

Abel nods once, hard, eyebrows knitting together severely over her well-shaped nose. "Calvin'll be over in a second with some food. Just rest up. You've got nothing to worry about while you're here — from any of us," she says, though both of the Others at her back look like they might disagree.

They follow her down the narrow walkway to a bunk bed three over where they whisper and throw uninhibited glances in my direction, judging me, debating their stupid decision to keep me alive and so close to the rest of the innocents.

Of the twenty some beds in the space, most are empty. A few aliens sit near the open entrance of the barracks looking old world stormtroopers, dressed all in black. They look lethal and are watching me like I'm a threat. *Let them come. Let them see what I made you.*

Only two humans sleep within one set of bunks from me. Sandra and, above her, a blonde woman. She doesn't seem to notice me, the blonde woman. The only one who looks over me and sometimes meets my gaze and no matter what, maintains her naive, stupid smile. I hate it. I hate her. I look away.

Coming towards me now is a blonde human man holding a plate and bottle of water. Like all the others *but the stupid, moron blonde chick* his grin fades when he looks at me. Probably because of the scarring, but maybe also because of the twisted expression on my ruined face — a face Jack ruined.

No, I didn't ruin you. You were born ruined.

I turn away from him and close my eyes, sparing him from the burden of having to look at me. Because I know the truth. I'm the most monstrous fucker here, alien or not. It's what Jack made me.

No, Diego. You were born a monster. I merely unlocked the cage and liberated you.

Chapter Three

I don't sleep anymore without the drugs. I've never been able to sleep. I just stare up at the wooden slats above me, waiting for the dimness on the other side of the canvas wall to lighten. And darken. And lighten. And darken again.

The blonde pricks bring me shit to eat — both the man and the woman and I can't decide which one I hate more.

The man, because he always tries to talk to me in this forced, chipper way that I hate, or the woman because she's beautiful. It bothers me in a way I don't fully understand, but that makes my stomach hurt and my chest prick with a foreign pain.

She doesn't speak to me when she brings me dried meat and fruit and nuts. She doesn't smile either. She doesn't really do anything, except meet my gaze directly and hold it and then go away. Like she's used to seeing monsters like me all the time. Like, to her, I could be anyone.

But not like I'm nothing at all. No, that would be easier to take. Because she looks at me like I'm *someone*. I wish I knew who he was.

So lost without me there to guide you, my sweet son.

He's not wrong.

It makes me want to strangle her, but I manage to keep my fists to myself and eat what she offers me. It's strange not having to fight for it — Jack made us eat fresh meat and if we went too many nights without finding anything or anyone to kill, it was up to Jack to decide which two men would fight to the death. The loser became the meal. I didn't mind killing the other dogs, but I didn't like eating them. The taste was off. If I could scavenge a canned vegetable or fruit I did, and I'd kill anyone who tried to take it from me.

Another sleepless night without the drugs has me working harder to sit up and retake control of my fragile limbs. It sucks. Walking around is worse, but after a little while, I manage to stand. I notice the blonde chick watching me with that irritating, unreadable expression as I do.

My legs feel like wooden boards and no matter which way I move, it's like I've got barbed wire wrapped around most of me. The stitching makes it worse, I decide, and I want it out.

Taking an extra second, I sit back down and pick out the threads with my blunt, jagged fingernails.

"You sure you should be doing that?"

The voice is deep and comes as a shock. It's *her* voice. The blonde's. Not the first time I've heard it, but it's the first time I've heard it directed towards me.

She's sitting on the bottom bunk below hers and has some cards laid out on top of an upturned crate. She's playing a game with an older man — also white, but he's all creased lines and tension, glaring between me and the chick like *I* did something wrong, even though I didn't do shit.

I grunt without answering her and watch, a little more strained, as the skin on my leg heals itself up around the fresh pinpricks of blood. The scars however, remain unmoved.

"Sandra will want to take a look at that," she says, like she goddamn owns the place.

I get up and even as the blood rushes to my head in a sudden whoosh, I still manage to make it all the way down to the end of the flatbed, lined in six bunkbeds on either side, a narrow gap of threeish feet between them, to where the canvas covering parts. The back entrance of the truck is fully rolled open on all sides to let in eerie grey light and, for the first time in days, I look out on the rolling world surrounding us.

There are four pickup trucks and two eighteen-wheelers that make up this convoy. Across them, people and Others are laughing and talking. All shapes. All sizes. All species.

There must be at least fifty people — beings — scattered across the trucks alongside boxes and crates and trunks of supplies, food and weapons. Men sit beside just as many women. There's even a few kids scattered among them. One rides now with Abel in the front of a pickup. Abel's driving. Kane sits next to her, the gangly blonde kid between them.

The three of them look like a picture perfect family through the pickup's windshield, laughing like they are. It looks fucking weird. Kane leans over the top of the small blonde's head and kisses the side of Abel's face. He lingers. For a moment, Abel's eyes close and the pickup truck veers, but Kane slides his hand over Abel's and straightens the truck out again.

He pulls back and they look at one another for an extra-long moment and I feel like I'm intruding on something I shouldn't be.

Strangely, it makes my breath come a little harder and my thoughts flash to the blonde on the bunk behind me. I don't know why, but I can't help wonder if she's still watching me.

She's not. Why would she be?

The trucks slow a little while later and I'm still standing at the edge of the truck when Abel's pickup powers down and she approaches.

"Come on, everybody out! You've got to see this."

Curiosity mingles with excitement as the dozen or so folks in this pickup slide by me and follow her out. There's no way I'm going with them, but there's also nowhere for me to go in the tight space between the bunks. Each person has to get by me and I hate it. They come so close. *Kill them. Slit each of their throats.*

My fingers twitch towards a knife in my back pocket that isn't there. Where is it? *You died for it when you gave it to that bitch.* I frown, wondering what happened to it, and I'm still wondering and I'm still frowning when I *feel* a certain blonde woman's presence. She's right in front of me now.

Keep moving, bitch, I think to myself.

But she slows. She fucking slows down, hesitating but only for a split second before she looks up at me, meets my gaze and offers so stupidly, so guilelessly, "Are you coming?"

I grunt, torn upper lip twisting as I snarl down. I expect her to flinch like the blonde man does, but she doesn't move at all. Instead, she *smiles* at me.

My stomach burns, like I'm going to be sick. I'm not sure I've ever felt like this before and I don't understand any of it.

"Of course, you don't have to." She tucks her hair behind her ear and I feel caught up in the gesture. So caught up, I can't stop myself before I look at her face. *Really* look at it, for the very first time.

When I do, I wish I hadn't.

For the next few seconds, I don't breathe. I can't. I'm fucking lost.

I hear waves crashing against rocks. The burst of a thousand symbols. War drums. A gong. A desperate, bloody battle. The squeals an animal makes as it loses to a greater predator somewhere forgotten in the night.

Jack didn't even like women and I know he'd have still found her as fucking gorgeous as I do.

Her beauty is something unfortunate. It makes me want to kill her, just so I don't have to watch as it's taken away. *I will have such fun with her.* My stomach drops. I feel nauseous and the strange urge to run away…and I've *never* run away.

She shouldn't look like this — without scars, without blemishes, without hate. But she does. I don't know how she and I can exist in the same universe. We shouldn't. Or rather, we *should*, but only because we should both be dead.

Blonde hair, flawless creamy skin, dark brown eyes that sweep my face, then widen. I don't know what she sees now when she looks at me, but she swallows and her gaze drifts down to my mouth. Is she looking at my scarring? Probably. But it draws my attention anyway, to her mouth. Her fucking perfect mouth.

She could be yours. You can have her. Just take her out into Population, and show her what the world has become. Jack laughs. Outside, people are laughing.

Inside, does she know just how close to danger she's come?

"Nnnn-no," I tell her.

"Pia." A hard voice draws my attention back to the last body left in the barracks with us. He pushes her forward and she teeters on the edge of the truck before jumping down.

She flips her shoulder-length, light-blonde hair back. "Dad," she admonishes, using a word I don't understand.

"Get, now," he tells her, "I need to have a word with him."

Pia, who's already looking up at me with a weird expression — probably because she must have just realized I'm a defective fuck who can't talk in whole sentences. A worm of boyhood insecurity wriggles inside. I want to slash at it. Slash the expression of her face.

"Diego," she says, and all at once that desire to cut and to burn is cleanly erased. Her accent. Light and like she's not from this part of the US, but maybe some place that lived in perpetual sunlight, grips me. She speaks my name with a dark reverence, like she's a witch about to conjure someone up from the grave. "His name is Diego."

"You know his name, so you think you can trust him?" Her father sneers, like I'm not right fucking here and covered in hidden weapons capable of blowing him and his daughter away.

"Yes. He can be trusted," she says immediately.

"Pia."

"Dad."

"I'm going to have a word with Diego now. Keep moving."

Pia opens her mouth, then shuts it. She looks at me and at the one she calls dad, then some unspoken communication passes between them — a battle that she loses.

"Sorry," she tells me, and I don't understand what she means, or what this is, or the strange tension that lingers in the wake of her looking at me. Why her scent seems to fill my nostrils — like earth and dew and clean sweat and the moment before a battle, something fresh and pure — and makes my thoughts trip over themselves, like clumsy, sprinting feet.

She seems to be waiting for me to react in some way, but I don't.

"Pia," her father says again and she huffs, rolls her eyes, and follows the blonde bouncing child off towards the edge of the road.

I track her with my gaze and my pulse starts to speed just a fraction when the big guy I've heard people call Roderick steps in line beside her. She smiles at him, just like she smiles at me because she smiles at everyone.

Did you think, for a moment, you were special? Oh Diego, you are, but only to me. This is why you should come back to me.

It's a thought that's plagued me for days now.

But I've been held back. Partly out of fear — not of Jack, but of how it would feel killing him — but also because I'm realizing that I *like* the way that I look up and sometimes find her watching me. And I don't like it when the stupid blonde watches other people. Men. Men like Roderick. It makes me want to stay, if for no other reason than to kill him.

"Are you listening to me, Diego?"

My attention snaps to the man in front of me, the one with the creased face and the tanned white skin and the shrewd green gaze that's so different from his daughter's.

I glance down at the man, meet his gaze, watch him size me up as I do the same. White skin that's suffered with age. Or just suffered. He's got a few scars on his face and the backs of his hands. He wears a shabby blue shirt and a green jacket with a black Army Rangers patch on the sleeve.

He's got on dog tags too, like he's ex-military, and says, "I see the way she looks at you, and the way you look at her. You'd do well to keep your eyes to yourself."

He jumps off the back of the truck too quickly for me to rip his arms off, which is what I should have done instead of letting him talk to me this way, but I'm stunned stupid by the first thing he said, more than the threat he leveled my way at the end.

I see the way she looks at you.

Don't read into it. You are nothing *special.*

I know that Jack's right, but he still said it and he claims to be her dad and if he saw something in the way she looked at me that was something more than the way she looks at everybody else, then I want to know what.

But I'm not gonna ask.

But it might be enough to keep me on this truck, that little nagging curiosity that makes me want to find out.

"You coming?"

I jerk as the blonde Other whose unwanted blood courses through my system steps into my line of sight. He looks up at me, one eyebrow cocked.

"There's a waterfall at the end of the river, just a little way into the forest. You wanna join them, you can. I've got watch on the trucks along with Hila, Efrat and Feron. No need to play lookout, if that's what you were doing."

It wasn't, but when I glance back towards the trees, Pia's gone *with Roderick* and I feel stupid for wondering what her father meant and even stupider for not having tortured him for what he said.

Then I feel stupider for caring about any of them at all. I shake my head and Mikey shrugs. "Suit yourself." He pulls a heavy canvas tie and lets the tent flap shut so that I'm swathed in a very familiar darkness.

Returning to my bunk, I lie down onto my left side and pull the scalpel I took from Sandra's medical bag when she was sleeping. I watch it in the non-light, wondering why I care so much to see what the people are doing. Fuck it.

I make a tiny incision in the fabric of tent at about eye-level. It takes my eyes a minute to adjust to the swirling grey-blue darkness. The soul-sucking color of Population. When they do, I see that there's something glittering just beyond the first row of brambles, nestled in among the trees. A little pool has formed at the base of some rocks, water pitter-pattering down over them just behind it.

There's still no sign of the blonde — of Pia — *or* Roderick. That thought makes my legs twitch with a desire to go out there and see if I can see them. Where are they? What are they doing?

He's doing to her what you should be doing. Taking…

I close my eyes against Jack's words and open them again to the sounds of splashing. The little blonde one is plunging into the water in her underwear while Sandra and a dark-haired Other — this one a woman — crouch down to examine some plant or other growing closer to the shoulder of the highway. A few are climbing the rocks up the waterfall and the jarring, jolting sound of laughter fills the world. The whole damn universe.

I can't shut it out, even though I try. And I can't look away. I'm glued to my little creeper peephole and I watch as Abel and her alien Jack freak called Kane strip out of their outer clothes. He wraps his arm around Abel's waist and drags her under the spray of the water. She shrieks out a burst of laughter and they press their ugly faces together while both their chests pulse the color of an old world sunset.

He pulls her feet off of the ground and melds his body to hers. His large, tan hands cup her round, muscular ass and she clutches the back of his neck, pulling him close. She's *moaning* against his mouth. Not breathing hard and in pain, not whimpering, not whining or pleading or begging. Not asking him to kill her, just to end it.

Then they aren't doing it properly, Jack says and I know he's right because the sounds they're making don't belong in this world.

My cock doesn't seem to agree though and as Kane reaches up to cup one of Abel's breasts through the black bra she's got on, I feel a little bit of blood rush to it. Thankfully, the little blonde shouts a disgusted, theatrical "eew!", drawing my attention away from the pair.

The little blonde laughs, tossing fistfuls of water into the air. Mikey has suddenly appeared beside her, but he turns away from Abel and Kane and the rest of them quickly and starts heading back towards the trucks, and me among them, through the woods.

His expression is the most pathetic thing I've ever seen and I only recognize it, because it's an expression I've seen before.

Envy.

He wants his brother's girl.

He wants Kane's wife.

And he's not going to do shit about it.

Fucking coward. *Fucking disgrace.*

I shudder and close my eyes, but the inside of the truck is stuffy and the smell of earth trickles in through the crack I've created in the fabric and tastes like clay and rain, a past fall's forgotten freedom, its lingering peace. It draws my stare again and again and I'm momentarily powerless against it.

A tall tree has strange blooms on it and I notice that, even in the dim light, there are plants and flowers here that have just turned to seed. Their colors are faded, but they're...there. The same color as that blood orange.

It had been a gift from Jack after my fifteenth kill. I'd been fifteen and he'd thought the coincidence was funny. *You were such a good killer back then. And now look at you.* I hear his voice in my head and wince back, away from the peep hole, slip the scalpel under my pillow and cross my left elbow over my eyes. I prefer the darkness.

It's easier for Jack to find me here.

Chapter Four

S andra stares down at my legs with her hands on her hips. The dark-haired Other — a female called Laiya, though I don't know why I bother registering it — lurks over her left shoulder, frowning sternly.

"The point of the stitches wasn't to close the wound, it was to reduce the scarring."

What's the point? I think. I'm already ruined. I don't bother answering though. Instead, I shove another bite of sandwich into my mouth. I've eaten two so far. Never tasted anything quite like it. There's some kind of sliced, salted meat in the middle, tomatoes and lettuce, and there are two pieces of bread on the outsides.

I haven't had bread in years. I'm talking *decades*. It tastes good and is gone too soon. When I look up again, Sandra is rolling her eyes.

"Well, I'll assume you're feeling alright then."

I nod, and that's the only answer she's going to get.

She rolls her eyes a second time. "Fine. Enjoy your BLT."

BLT, I think as she leaves, I wonder what it means.

I stretch my legs out, hating the way the skin stretches in ways that it didn't before. I haven't had a mirror to look at it myself since they scraped me up and threw me together again, and I don't need one to be able to assess the damage. The scarring distorts my expressions — I can feel it every time I open my mouth, chew food, raise my eyebrows.

My left eyebrow lays flat while my right dips and peaks. Passing my fingers over it, I can feel that a notch is missing from the middle, like the blank patch across the back of my scalp. The right side of my upper lip is fucked, making me feel like a fish caught with a hook in its mouth.

The damage done to my body is worse — or at least that's what I tell myself since I can't see my face. My right nipple has been halved, cut right down the center, and three parallel slashes decorate my abdomen from pec to pelvis. My right thigh looks like it's been boiled and flayed then pieced back together again with skin that never belonged to me to begin with. It's all shades of brown, from dark to white. It's disgusting.

Finally reflecting your insides. How does it feel, being able to see what your soul looks like?

"I'm supposed to keep an eye on you."

Mikey frowns down at me and I glare up at him from his position a few feet away, standing on the edge of the road, looking in at me nestled among the trees. We've stopped for one of our thousand daily breaks. How this group manages to cover any ground at all is a goddamn mystery to me.

I wonder if he thinks I'll run.

I considered it earlier. But then I got lost in the sandwich.

And also staring at Pia.

I think he'll elaborate, only to be a little amused when he throws a pair of beat up Nikes onto ground at my feet, size thirteen. I wonder how he knows that the shoes I'm wearing — stolen off a dead man — are small by at least two sizes, but I don't ask and I don't thank him.

Instead, I set the shoes aside, polish off the rest of my sandwich — my B-L-T — and lean back against the tree trunk behind me. Pumped through with Mikey's blood, my muscles burn pleasantly, but the shrunken skin is irritated and irritating.

"You're a real piece of work." Mikael smirks, shakes his head, sighs. "I'm here as a favor to Abel." Of course he is. "She doesn't trust you." She shouldn't.

"Now I don't mind your fucked up sleep schedule, but watching you throughout the day is boring. I'm talking would-rather-take-an-ice-pick-to-the-brain-just-to-feel-something kind of boring. So for the sake of my sanity, take these cards and play."

He's got a crate in his other hand which he turns over between us. He tosses me five cards. I toss them back but he flicks them onto my lap, spraying them every direction.

"I don't need you to fucking talk or tell me all your goddamn secrets. Just check or bet, sweetheart."

I grunt, but reluctantly scoop up the cards and let him lay down the flop. We use dried beans to bet, nickels, bolts, a couple quarters. I'm a better player than he is. Much better. Two hands in and I clean him out.

His face is a burning beet red when he slams his cards down onto the crate and I can't help but grin. A hand later, after I take the rest of the shit I let him borrow, he kicks the crate into the tree, shattering it, and a ragged sound trips on its way out of my throat, but it hits air all the same.

It's laughter.

I laughed.

The thought makes me sweaty, but luckily, when I look up, Mikey's still muttering to himself and picking up cards off the road, not watching me. No one is.

Except Pia.

She's a group away, facing me and when I glance up, knowing exactly where she is, because I've known all day and

I know all through the night, her eyes are on mine. *She* looks away first this time and it makes me all fucking sweaty.

Damn her. I wish I knew why she made me feel this way. Like I could kill for her.

You kill for me. You breathe for me. You die for me. There is no one else.

"You're a dick," Mikey says down to me. Then, "Wanna spar or are you still too fucked up?" He glances me over, making a face when he looks at the bit of scar slashing across my forehead.

Don't care, and nod instead.

Pulling a bit further down the road, we straighten up across the street from one another. Not wanting to get blood on my sweatshirt, I yank it off over my head and toss it to the ground. Mikey does the same. To the right, people — aliens — seated on two pickups watch us, but they don't seem particularly concerned or curious.

"You ready?" Mikey says, flexing his hands and cracking his knuckles. The clouds overhead are thick, but somehow still emanate a sickly light, making everything appear more menacing. And now I'm about to fight. A sense of familiarity washes over me that makes me feel…better, even without Jack.

One edge of my mouth twitches when Jack doesn't respond, and I nod my own response to Mikey. He doesn't hesitate.

He moves fast, lunging left and nailing me in the ass. It sends a ripple down my left leg that could have made me buckle, but doesn't. Instead, it brings him close enough to nail in the ear with my elbow.

Mikey grins when he straightens up and swabs his inner ear with a finger. "Hot damn. I should have known better than to underestimate you after what you did for Abel."

I nod, but absently, because Pia's leaning against the cab of the eighteen-wheeler closest to us. Her arms are crossed over her chest, pulling her tits together and pushing them up.

They're big enough to dive into and I'm distracted at how soft she looks. Edible.

I inhale deeply and I refuse to look again to Pia, even though fighting Mikey suddenly feels more…important. I don't know why, though I desperately wish I did.

"So?" With one edge of his mouth cocked up, he lifts an eyebrow, looking impressed. "Well, come on then."

Mikey wipes the black blood off on the pocket of his pants before forming fists and we grapple over the concrete until the sound of a revving engine forces us to call a truce.

Hard to say who won that one though, when I pass by Pia still standing near the entrance of the truck, it feels like I did.

I've got a stitch blazing across my chest and can barely breathe, but Mikey's limp is so bad he struggles to climb into the truck. I offer him a hand and he takes it, then asks if I'm up for another round tomorrow. Nodding abruptly, the distortion to my upper lip twists and I can feel the blood in my mouth seep out between my teeth.

"Gross," Mikey says, barking out a short laugh as we pass by the bunks to reach mine. "Your ugly mug…" He starts.

I send my fist into his obliques and he buckles around the blow. He nails me in the right leg, right at the epicenter of a scar, and I fall back onto my cot. He's grinning when he straightens out on the next bunk over.

"You're not bad," he says, taking a stray sock to the cut on his cheek, "for a human."

"You're pretty shit for an a-a-a…" The world jams in my mouth, then reluctantly releases, "alien." I wait — simmering, muscles tense, ready to slash into him with my goddamn fingernails and claw out his eyeballs — for him to comment on the fact that I can't put one coherent fucking sentence together.

But he barks out a laugh, and doesn't give me the response I want. The one that will lead me to killing something. "I was going easy on you, ass wipe. Pitying my blood you've got in your system. Tomorrow I won't be afraid to spill so much."

"You guys knock the stupid out of each other yet?" Abel says from a bunk halfway down the row.

"Nah, I think it might have had the opposite effect, actually. We're looking to spar again soon."

Mikey brightens when he looks towards Abel, watching her in a way that makes me feel self-conscious. It's disgusting, the way he follows her around like a beat dog. And I should know. I've been there. *But you were such a good boy. Up until the end.*

Worse, she isn't even his weakness to have.

Kane must be on the other truck. I don't blame him. It must get tiring watching your brother covet what you have. But I don't get him either. Kane should have killed him a long time ago. I killed over canned fruit. Why shouldn't he kill over his glowing-hearted human?

"I'll have to show you how it's done tomorrow."

"You serious?"

"Yeah. I want to give Diego a shot. See if I can take him."

Mikey glances in my direction and crosses his arms over his chest. "You know we don't fight to the death, right?" His dark blonde eyebrow lifts.

I grunt.

"That's not an answer."

I nod, rolling my eyes for emphasis.

"Could I um…" Pia says from where she sits on her own bunk. I know it, even though I'm not looking at her. I'm painfully aware.

"Pia," her dad barks.

"Shush now. You know I need the practice," she says to him before pitching her voice louder. "Abel, if you're going to be training with Diego and Mikey, would you also mind sparring with me, too?

"Maybe next time I can work my way up to Diego." She winks at me and sticks out her tongue. Soft and pink.

I don't know if it's the sight of her face like that, or if it's the fact that she said my name twice and I like the way it sounds in her voice, but I feel it then, once, like a boom. The same thing I felt once before and only once.

Desire.

Back before it all ended, I'd stand outside this lonely, shabby Middle America diner. I'd stand there in the dark, looking in at the low-class families eating in the light wishing I had cookies and some poor, shabby family to share them with. A waitress came out once and offered me one. It's the only time I can remember anyone ever doing anything nice for me.

I went back a few nights later and that's where Jack found me.

He'd asked me what I was looking at, and I told him.

He'd told me to wait, and had waited with me for the diner to empty out. It was cold, but I didn't care. He was so much older than I was, and had this confidence that you can't fake and can't fault. And when only the waitress was left inside, he'd gone in, slit her throat and come back out with a bloody plastic bag full of cookies. We went back to his place and he told me to eat every single one.

I was sick afterwards for two days.

I learned then not to desire, and that when pain and hunger become your only constants, the absence of both feels good enough.

But here on the bunk listening to my name in her voice, watching her tongue and the way pink blood bursts like fireworks in her cheeks — is it my stare that does that? Am I affecting her in any way? — I feel it revisit me like an old friend, that bloodthirsty ghost.

Desire.

I want her bad.

So take her. Make it hurt.

I look away rapidly and concentrate hard on making the heat raging through my torso go fucking down.

It isn't working.

"Sure thing. Lunchtime break tomorrow sound good for y'all?" Abel answers.

Mikey agrees. "Sounds good."

I don't answer.

"It's good for him, too," Mikey grunts. I glare at him, but he just grins in that lopsided way he does. The blood on his forehead is in his hair now. Makes it look a little less stupid. But just a little.

"Good. Then it's settled." She starts to turn away, then hesitates. "Oh and I keep forgetting to give you this."

"Me?"

"No, Diego. I have something that belongs to you."

She reaches into her coat, withdraws a familiar knife and places its hilt in my hand. My fingers curl around three jade beads flush against the sterling silver.

"It's a lucky knife. My uncle always told me that weapons are luckiest in the hands of their true owners. She's yours."

Quieting, she speaks in a voice that's so sincere and so gentle it makes me feel nauseous. "I never said thank you. You didn't have to help me, but I might not be here now if you hadn't."

Mikey's face shimmers in shades of red as she speaks. He looks away, as if he can't hear us or is pretending not to.

"Why did you?"

I turn the blade over in my hands. It's recently been sharpened, but I can still see the small nick in the side where it connected with the Other's femur.

It had been a straggler, lost from a party of Others traveling through Population, and the first alien I'd killed. I'd worn his head as a crown and Jack had never been more proud. *So damn proud of you.*

"I d-d-d-don't know."

She pauses for a moment before she says, "Whatever the reason, thank you. Have you given anymore thought as to whether you'll stay with us for good?"

I just shrug. Staying, going. What difference does it make? Other than the ability to watch Pia and feel my body flush with those foreign emotions that I wish I could incinerate.

"Well, if you're going to stay, then I have one rule. You don't have to be buddy buddy with everybody, but I can't have you hurting anyone either. You send a single person to Sandra, you're out. Understood?"

I lick my twisted upper lip by way of response.

"Good. Mikey can't be on your ass twenty-four seven." She turns to leave, then stops once more. "Well, except for tomorrow. See you tomorrow out on the battlefield."

Chapter Five

"Do you mind if I join you?"

I jerk. Why is she always there when Jack is, disrupting him? I'd just been thinking about Jack. Daydreaming about him and the blood orange and the sixteen year old who'd been my first.

She'd been crying. Then I'd started to cry. Then Jack taught us both the true meaning of pain. *Our first beautiful night together.*

I have a hard time holding her gaze when I look down at her face. Doing so makes my stomach hurt again and my thighs harden. My lower back tingles. Tension threads through my lower abdomen. But thinking about Jack helps keep the heat from making my cock half-harden, as it's had a tendency to do the past day.

Days.

Since I first saw her.

Fuck.

Take her, you sniveling fucking coward.

"Of course. We were waiting for you."

I shift, uncomfortable, as Abel and Mikey turn towards the approaching Pia. She's wearing a tight black tee shirt that's far too low cut and a pair of black pants that are far too small for her.

Behind her, near the start of the trees, both Roderick and her father are looking this way. Her father's glaring at me, but Roderick's watching her hips sway in that intoxicating way that they sway — the sway I've been avoiding looking at, at all costs.

I whistle between my teeth, pulling his attention to me. I shake my head once.

He grins, and swivels the toothpick between his teeth to one corner of his mouth, but the fucker knows what's good for him because he backs away.

Silence.

Then Abel clears her throat into her fist. "Okay then."

I glance at Pia and her face is bright red, but she's watching me with big eyes that look startled. Mesmerized. Like I did something weird that she can't figure out and that I can't explain.

"Pia, you want to knock me around first?"

"I um…I'll just watch the first round? If that's okay."

She'd looked ready to spar a moment ago. Her fists had been clenching in little pulses and I'd caught her stretching before. I wonder what changed.

"Alright, Diego. I guess it's you and me then."

She stretches her neck from side-to-side while a loose ring forms around us. Others and humans stand closer than they did before, watching, but pretending like they aren't.

Her man walks its perimeter with his arms crossed over his chest. He looks me up and down and doesn't need to say anything for me to get the message.

I roll my eyes. Goddamn freaks all freaking out over their queen. Though, I guess for him, it's something more extreme.

My gaze flashes unwillingly to Pia. I can't control it. *You're a fucking disgrace.*

"Diego, you ready?" She's got her fists held out loose in front of her, like she doesn't know what she's doing. Like she *isn't* deadlier than a viper snake.

"Y-y-you aren't ffffooling anyone," I say before I can help it.

Abel pretends she doesn't notice, even though I know she does. They all hear it. Pia hears it. I glance at her, though I feel like a bastard for it. Who gives a fuck what she thinks about me?

"You scared?" She grins.

I don't miss a beat.

I lunge for her, catching her off guard. She tries to slant out of my path, but I anticipate her direction and cut her off. I swing for her face, but she ducks under my arm. I lift my foot to kick, but just as I do, a flash of steel catches my attention, pulling me slightly off balance.

Abel tries to take that chance, but I feel a bubbling panic that isn't mine by right, but that should belong to the rest of the fuckers here — the ones so in love with her.

I should issue some kind of warning, but I know that it'd take me a goddamn eternity to deliver the command and three of the Others *on Abel's fucking team* are already sprinting forward, brandishing blades.

I've got a hunting knife strapped to the inside of my right calf and I free it now. As one of the Others rushes past me, I let her, swivel and stab her in the back.

Withdrawing my blade, one of the Others is closing in on Abel and even though Abel's standing at the ready and Kane is charging forward towards her and Mikey's moving to intercept the third, the Other's got a knife in hand and is close enough to use it.

The Other strikes at the same time that Kane reaches the pair. He wraps himself around Abel and they both fall to the ground at the same time that the hunting knife leaves my fingertips and nails that alien fucker in the back of the throat. He hits the ground with a muted thump — a sound I know well.

Bullets rings with violence and I turn to see Laiya of all creatures unloading into the Other advancing on Mikey.

"Diego!" Pia's voice pulls my attention away from the third alien. Her eyes are wide and she's running towards me and the look on her face makes me fucking scared.

She's *concerned*.

It's that concern, more than anything, that leaves me standing there stupid when the Other I stabbed comes back for its revenge.

She sweeps my legs and is trying to wrap her hands around my neck. Like I haven't been in this position a thousand times before and every time, freed myself. Fucking idiot. She has no idea who she's up against. *Show her who I made you. Show her everything.*

I feel energy rush up my bones as we grapple. She's in the dominant position and has hold of my wrists, but I buck my hips and snowangel my arms downwards, forcing her off balance. She catches herself before she can faceplant and with her arms planted on the asphalt now, all I have to do is lock my fingers around her elbow and wrench down hard. She falls down beside me and as she struggles to reorient, I loop my right ankle over her left foot and lift my hips up. I toss her to the side, off of me, snatch the knife she's still got in her hand and I don't hesitate to jam it down.

I stab her in the center of the chest, knowing that one single cut won't be enough to keep her down forever, but when I go to retract the blade again, it doesn't budge.

The woman is writhing, shrieking now, her face twisted and distorted. She's scratching at the silver hilt protruding from between her breasts, but nothing's happening...

Until it does.

She...she explodes.

I've never seen anything like it, so I'm not sure what I'm looking at, at first. She looks like she's *melting*. The skin around her mouth pulls back and her eyes start to bulge and pop. She releases one keening screech before vomiting all of her insides up.

Red hot nasty pours out of her mouth and eyes in a stream. *It's beautiful. I've never seen anything so beautiful. Well done, son.* I feel a certain pride at the level of destruction I've caused — it'll earn me first rations of meat for a week — and then I remember that they don't do first rations. Everyone just gets the same. Or what they need. Jack's not here to see this. He's not here to be proud of me.

"Diego, oh my lord," comes the sweet voice that's always there to slit Jack's throat when I need him most, only this time, it's accompanied by her hands on me.

She's pulling on my shoulder and arm, trying to get me off of the corpse that's roasting from the inside. I stand and look down at her. She's looking at my chest, and arms and hands.

"You...you're okay, then," she says, half in a whisper. "You fought one of them and didn't even get a scratch?" She looks up at me with awe.

That pride, the one that Jack was supposed to make me feel, sweeps in and blows through me like a goddamn tornado. It's never felt so good before.

I suck in a breath and nod once, showing her my arms wanting to impress her. Want. Desire. What are these words? She takes one of my hands between two of hers and exhales deeply, like she's...no...it can't be relief, can it?

Fuck you for thinking it could be. She's a pretty little thing. You're a beast with more scars than skin and when I catch up to you, Diego, I'll show you just what happens to pretty little things who think they can replace me. I'll remind you where your only allegiance lies. I'll take from you...

"Diego?"

Jack's gone, like he never was, as my gaze recenters on Pia's face.

"You're okay?"

I nod. I am now, I want to tell her, but I don't.

She smiles and gives my hand a little squeeze that's so full of implication it hurts. I feel my jaw harden. Kindness feels sticky to me still and I pull my hand away quickly and turn away from her.

Bodies are crowded around the mutilated Other that I stabbed while Kane and Mikey've formed a protective shield around Abel that they aren't letting anyone cross.

"What the fuck is this?" Kane roars, breaking from Abel's side to advance on one of the Others that Roderick, Gabe, and two male Heztoichen have pinned down to the asphalt on his stomach.

"Did the Lahve send you?"

The male answers in a language only half the group speaks. I watch Mikey's face for a reaction given that he's completely transparent.

A few more hostile words pass between Kane and the male before Mikey turns white as a sheet. "Fuck!" He roars. Abel touches his chest and even though the gesture is small, it's enough to stop him from storming forward. A house cat posing as a lion.

"Don't freak out, Mikey," Abel murmurs, crossing her arms tight over her chest.

He shoves his hands through his long blonde hair. "Don't freak out? She tried to kill you! Do you know what this is? That knife's got carbon dioxide cartridges in the handle. She wanted to inflate your insides like Diego did to that fucker there!"

"And Diego stopped her." Abel cocks her chin in my direction. "That's twice now. Not so bad."

"Not bad at all," Pia whispers too low for the humans around us to hear. But not too low for me too. I shiver all over.

Mikey reaches out for Abel, but she doesn't notice. Her gaze is trained to the Other at Kane's feet. She reaches her husband and slides her hand up the length of his spine. Mikey blanches and looks down at his feet and turns red all at the same time. Coward. He should have killed his brother already. Tried to, at least. *That's my boy.*

"Who is she?" Abel says.

The words rip out of Kane with a vengeance. "The Lahve warned me about a faction of Heztoichen upset with a human Notare that were loyal to Elise. He managed to weed out dissidents and cast them out of Brianna. He branded them with a mark…"

Kane wrenches up on the male's hair, exposing the side of his throat and a series of scars scribbled there. With my Mikey-enhanced eyesight, I see that it looks like tally marks, except the diagonal fifth line is a horizontal one.

"It is the Heztoichen symbol for traitor. I wanted them dead but the Lahve refuses to kill Heztoichen who have committed no crimes."

"Conspiracy *is* a crime."

"Not in Sistylea." Kane's voice is low and full of menace. His eyes are burning with a bloodlust that makes him look, for one instant, like Jack's incarnate.

I take a half step back, away from him and feel my shoulder bump with someone else's. A softer one that sits much lower. I close my eyes and inhale, exhale, and smell cinnamon and sugar. Cookies from the diner. But not filling the bloody bag. Cookies from the diner before the diner was ruined by Jack. I lean into it and inhale a little deeper.

"How long have these wretches been with us?"

"From the beginning. Since we left the Diera," Mikey says.

Kane roars and the sound echoes and reverberates around us.

One of the Others — the male called Feron — says, "We should dispose of the rogues now. They present a threat. We can keep the bodies for later identification."

"You will do nothing!" Kane's voice is startling in its impact. Abel is trying to calm him, but he's barely bottled rage. "I want all of the Heztoichen present to lower their arms until they can be inspected for marks. I want to know how these traitors were able to go undetected among us for so long. I want to know how they managed to join with us in the first place, and I want to know why they chose to wait and why they attacked now…"

"Notare Kane?" A voice that's slightly out of breath picks up and I turn to see a blood-covered Sandra rushing up to the crowd shadowed by Laiya, who's even more blood covered.

"Sandra!" Abel says, "What the hell happened to you?"

"The same thing that happened to you, I believe, only Laiya stopped them."

"*Them?*" Kane looks unstable. I feel my own body shift in between his and Pia's. I glance at Mikey and look to Abel.

Mikey doesn't move in the same direction I do, though.

And then it hits me — I'm stepping in front of Pia to *protect* her.

My gaze happens to lift at that moment and see Pia's father's — Luke's. He's watching me with his head tilted slightly to the side. I don't know what to make of it, and I don't try.

"There were two Heztoichen who attempted to kill me. Laiya stopped them both. She caught them off guard. With their dying breaths, they expressed surprise and contempt that Laiya would side with a human against one of her own."

Laiya reaches down and does something that shocks me. She takes Sandra's hand and the two females lace their fingers together. Almost like they *care* for one another…I blink. Not almost. Would Pia like it if I took her hand like that?

No. She'll run away screaming, then you'll hunt her, then you'll fuck her bloody.

"Why did they try to attack you?" Abel says.

"Because I had just told Laiya a suspicion that I had, one that they overheard."

"What suspicion?"

"Abel — I mean Notare — I think you're pregnant."

Chapter Six

Sandra confirms her suspicion by the time that Kane completes his full on aneurysm.

He makes all the Others — including Laiya — strip down to their birthday gear and has Ashlyn, Sandra, Calvin, and Gabe inspect them one by one.

While the humans do that, he finishes the other two Heztoichen off by announcing that whichever of them can produce a cartridge for their carbon dioxide knife fastest, he'll kill with a regular knife.

They scramble faster than any human would be able to, to fulfill his request. Then when they do, Kane explodes them both along with one other marked Heztoichen discovered by the inspectors. Three were discovered in total, but four managed to break away and disappear into the wilderness before Abel and her people could catch them.

Pity.

I enjoyed watching Kane go ape shit, looking so much like Jack would've if somebody messed with something he'd cla███.

Instead, he'd let Abel talk him down and the second he was more or less settled, he'd done a different kind of claiming...one that forced the group to delay its departure even more and abandon one of the eighteen-wheelers while Kane and Abel made a mess of it.

Mikey made himself scarce, preferring to continue the search for the Others that ran off, while the rest of the humans settled in to wait.

I don't know at what point waiting turned into revelry, but by the time Gabe, Laiya and I finished hacking up the traitors' bodies, there was a massive bonfire built in the center of the road, food and even alcohol was being distributed and people were making *music* out of empty tin cans, upturned crates and somebody even had an instrument from the World Before — a guitar.

Songs were being played and lyrics were being thrown out of throats with abandon. It was a strange sight to see. These people who almost lost their most prized human are fine now. Resilient.

And happy.

Somehow, they're happy.

There is no such thing.

"Hey."

I'm sitting on the back of a pickup truck when Pia disrupts Jack, this time before he can begin. She's got Luke with her this time, and he doesn't look happy to be here.

"My dad has something he wants to say to you."

Luke glares at his daughter, then at me, then at his daughter again. He takes a sip from whatever drink he's drinking and grumbles something unintelligible under his breath.

"Dad, he isn't a Heztoichen. He doesn't have super human hearing. Now say it."

She nudges Luke in the arm and he crosses his arms even tighter, his cup pressed stiffly against his pectoral. "Wasn't sure about you before. Still not sure about you. But…" He waits, hesitating, then spits, "What you did today for Abel was good."

"Well done." She gives him two swift pats on the shoulder, then lifts herself up onto her tip toes to give him a swift kiss on the cheek. It surprises me only because I've never seen anything like that before. Affection that doesn't make you bleed.

"Thanks, daddy," she whispers.

"Wait a second, Pia, I'm not done here."

Pia frowns and she crosses her arms. "You said…"

"I just got a few questions for our new *friend* here." He sneers *friend* like it's the very definition of scum. He'd be right in his assessment.

"Diego, how many've you killed?"

"Oth-thers?"

"Shit." He crosses his arms in a mirrored copy of his daughter's stance. "You killed Others? How many?"

I raise four fingers.

He grunts. "And people?"

I lift a shoulder. Let it fall. How many have I killed? More than the cookies I've had, that's for fucking sure. More than the good nights' sleep I've had. More than the laughs. More than the jokes. But much, much fewer than the number of times others have tried to kill me.

"More than ten?"

I make a sound. It isn't laughter. It's something dark and sadistic. Just like me.

"More 'en fifty?"

I nod.

"A hundred?"

I shrug.

"Jesus Christ," he mutters. Pia's eyes round and the color washes from her face, then rises right back again when I meet her gaze. Good. Now she knows what I am. A killer. Nothing more and nothing less. Why does that suddenly bother me? She *should* know what I am. She *should* fear and hate me.

"Look, it…doesn't matter…" Pia starts, looking away from me in a way that causes cramping in my gut.

Her father cuts her off. "How many you saved?"

The fuck? How many…have I saved? How many? I've taken so many lives I couldn't count them if I wanted to, but how many have I saved? I raise a hand and lift a finger. Just the one.

He snorts. "Yeah that sounds about right. That how you get those scars?"

I nod, surprised that his guess could be so on the mark.

"The one that carved you up — he still alive?"

I nod again, feeling tension thread my muscles. I'd fought my way free of Jack, running but only because he'd let me. He could have hunted me, killed me, laid me out for days. Made it last for months. But he'd let me go to die on my own. Then Abel found me and scraped me off the pavement.

"And the one you saved?"

I nod. "She's qu-qu-queen now."

"Abel?"

I nod. "That ain't a bad record."

"No," Pia says and she sounds breathless, "It isn't."

She's watching me. I can feel the pressure of her gaze on my face, but I don't dare meet it. Because I can already tell she's looking at me like I'm the hero again, and that's too much goddamn pressure when I'm only scum.

He looks between us for a lingering moment then grunts, "Fine. But no funny business."

He stalks off, grumbling under his breath as he walks, and Pia watches him until he reaches the bonfire and plunks down next to the lethal-looking Other called Feron.

I just watch her.

The tension's back in my abdomen and gut as I wait for her to do something. Why's she here? Why's she talking to me? Why'd she bring her father over? I should ask her, but I don't want her to hear me speak any more than she absolutely has to.

"Sorry about him," she says, "he's very protective. I have to keep reminding him that I'm an adult woman." She rolls her eyes and touches the little necklace around her throat. It has a cross on it. The symbol of The God that the mother once spoke of.

"Doesn't seem to make much of a difference."

She smiles some more and I hate this shit — this goddamn fucking waiting. I look for a way to escape, but she says, "Come with me."

She's holding out her hand with expectation. I feel my palms get all clammy as a result.

"I promise I won't hurt you." She speaks with a smile on her face that I don't fucking get. Of course she won't hurt me. I could crush her with one hand around her skinny little neck. Does she not know that?

"I c-c-could hhhhurt you." Why the fuck did I say anything? And why the fuck did I say that?

Her hand stays put, and doesn't relent. "You *could*. But I don't think you will. And even if you tried, I don't go down that easily."

"I could k-kill you."

Her lips pinch together, but her hand hovers without shaking. Not even a little bit. "You haven't seen me fight yet. You don't know what I'm capable of. And I'm always packing."

I know. She keeps a Beretta tucked into the holster on her hips at all times — except for earlier today, when she took it off to spar. Does she know how easy it would be for me to unhook the knife from the hidden sheathe around my belt and take that Beretta from her?

I open my mouth again, but she does something I've killed other men for — she steps into my personal space. She comes so close my knees almost brush her tits and she takes my hand without waiting for my permission.

Her skin is soft.

So damn soft.

Ruin it.

She jerks back from me and I half-hallucinate that Jack spoke to her in my place and told her all the nasty, degrading things I want to do to her. Except *I* don't want to do any of those things. That's all Jack.

"Sorry," she whispers, and Jack disappears.

Because Jack isn't here.

The thought comes and goes just as quickly, but it fills my mouth with saliva and fills my gut with a heat that lingers long after the thought falls away.

"I didn't mean to..." She shakes her head and looks down at her feet. "Nevermind."

She starts to turn from me, and why the fuck can't I watch her retreat this time? I jump down off of the edge of the truck, toss my drink onto the road and grab her by the elbow, spinning her around.

She smiles. "I didn't mean to touch you."

"You c-c-c-can t-t..." The word gets gobbled up by my spit and I have to swallow painfully through it. "Touch me," I blurt, feeling like a goddamn fucking idiot.

The heat in my stomach turns to ice, but only for a moment before she reaches out again and takes my hand and looks into my face and speaks to me like she doesn't notice any of it.

"Good."

She pulls me off the road, away from the bonfire and the sound of so many voices, into the trees. We don't go far, but we're far enough for things to feel dark and sinister, and for the heat in my belly to make me feverish.

Take her.

I could take her here. We're far enough from the road and I'm much faster than she is. I could silence her. *Push her face down into the dirt, wrench her pants to her ankles and...*

"What do you think?"

She points to a small stream and, beside it the two towels that have been laid out. When I don't react at all except to stare, she raises herself up onto her tip toes and breathes into my ear, "You may be a hero and all, but you stink."

She plops down onto her heels and grins at me and without the months and years of preparation I would have needed to survive the moment that follows, she reaches down to the hem of her shirt and whips it off over her head.

I slowly freeze over. She's not wearing a bra. My chest seizes. She's got full fucking tits marred only by perfect little nipples. They're hard, stiffened to points. I can't look away.

I know that my mouth hangs open dumbly, but I can't seem to close it. I can't seem to do anything.

This is a trap. I'm quite sure it is, but I don't seem to be able to get myself out of it either. If I've got to die here, so fucking be it. I guess I'll die here watching her slide out of her too tight pants. Will she take off her panties, too? Please, don't. Fuck me. Please do.

"Diego, you're starting to make me feel self-conscious. Is it…should I not be naked in front of you? At our compound — I mean, at our old compound — it was normal for everyone to bathe naked together."

Normal. What the fuck do I know about normal? This doesn't feel normal, but she would know better than I would.

"But I don't want to make you uncomfortable."

She reaches for her towel and that small action compels me to move. I close half the distance between us, bringing her close enough to touch.

I rip the shirt out of her fingers with one swift tug. She turns to face me. I can't stop looking at her tits and the longer I stare, the harder my cock gets in my sweats. There's no way she doesn't see the tenting on the front of my pants, but what shocks me is that she doesn't react to it. Even as goosebumps prick the tops of her breasts and the skin across her stomach, she doesn't run.

"Are you going to hurt me, Diego?"

Am I going to hurt her, Jack? I wait for his reply, but nothing comes. It's like he can't…break through when she's around, acting as some kind of inhibitor. I wish he could. I need his guidance, his pressure, the knowing of what he'd do to me if I disobeyed, because then I could take her. I would.

But he isn't here right now.

Maybe he isn't even here at all.

I inhale deeply and her skin shivers when I do. I look away from her tits. Can't seem to meet her gaze, either. "What d-d-d-did your dad mean?"

"S-sorry?" She says, tripping over her own words in a way that reminds me way too much of me. "Oh, I know he tried to warn you off, but he's just being protective…"

"N-nnno. He said he sssssaw the way you llllooked at me."

Blood flowers in her chest. It's so strange. My skin doesn't do that and neither did any of Jack's bloodhounds. I was never really good at interpreting body language and this leaves me at even more of a loss.

"Did he?" She sighs and it sounds a little like laughter. It's a sound that makes my whole body feel light enough to lift from the damp leaves beneath my feet. "I um…I guess he thinks that I like you."

I look at her, and tumble deep into the trap of her eyes.

"I do like you."

For a minute, I lose track of time and I retreat through a dense forest of memories I've been trying unsuccessfully to raze to the ground.

Sugar, cinnamon, salt. Those damned cookies so goddamn dry in my mouth. The first woman I took. That sixteen year old. The way it had felt to touch her. She'd been so hot. The way it had felt to touch Jack after. He'd been so brutal. The kills. All of them. Blood-spattered clothing. Chunks of brain flying up around my fist. Mashed bone. Wearing somebody's teeth as a necklace.

Abel.

Seeing her fight and watching her fall. The strange way it had pulled at me. She'd reminded me of the sixteen year old, fighting until the bitter end. I couldn't save the sixteen year old, but some distant part of my brain had malfunctioned, deluding me into thinking that I might be able to save Abel then.

Looking up at Calvin's stupid face while he drops food off on my cot. Watching Pia. Hungering for her, whether I admitted it to myself or not.

Everything that brought me here.

"Should I be afraid, Diego?"

That wasn't what she asked me originally, but she's got a right to this answer too. I nod and lift my hand to her face.

She flinches back, but she still doesn't run. She closes her eyes and holds impossibly still when I touch just the edge of her jaw. I don't know how skin can be so soft. It feels all wrong. And so damn good.

I touch her tentatively along her cheek, then down her throat. I trace the lines of her collar bones, but I don't dare go lower than that.

I exhale a shuddering breath and when I pull my hand back, I rub the foreign, horrible, beautiful sensation off on my pants and turn towards the river.

She's got a bar of soap and a bucket nestled between the towels and I quickly pull my own shirt off and step out of my sweatpants. I hear a slight gasp behind me — likely because she can see the scarring zigzagging its way from my right shoulder to my left hip — but I refuse to turn around until I calm the fuck down.

As I bathe for the first time in days, I realize how fucking filthy I've gotten and good it feels to be clean. I go so far as to kneel in the muddy stream, letting the water come up to my hips.

Pia's watching me as I do with a smile on her face.

At some point, she starts to take off her pants and I have to turn away from the sight. It's too fucking overwhelming.

Most people feel the need to fill silences with chatter. Pia doesn't and I feel strangely calmed by that fact.

When we finish, Pia puts back on her clothes, but offers me clean jeans and a tee shirt and washes the shit that I'd been wearing while I dress. As she works, she hums softly under her breath.

It twists something inside of me, watching her do that.

"Why?" I blurt.

She looks over her shoulder at me as she finishes wringing out my tee shirt. Her hair hangs in damp strands around her face, making her look even more vulnerable.

"Why what?"

"Why d-d-d-do you l-like m-me?"

It's dark now, but I still know instinctively that she's blushing. "You're a fighter. What's not to like?"

The answer comes so easily to her that I snort, reminded that she's clearly got no fucking clue how horrible Population can be. *How beautiful.*

Jack's voice returns softly and I feel comforted by it. His love is something I understand, whereas I feel unseated by Pia's like.

Pia starts humming again…more like singing softly…and then it gets louder and I look at her and realize that she's looking at me and her mouth is open, but she's not speaking now.

Her eyes go wide and my ears perk back. I glance towards the road, but the sound of the song isn't coming from the direction of our camp.

"What in the world…" Pia dumps the things in her arms on the ground and takes a step towards the road, but a flare of panic surges in my stomach that I haven't *ever* felt before.

I shove her to her knees *hard* and she tenses, arms moving up to ward off an attack.

"St-st-stay here," I order, and then I take off without looking back.

I sprint to the road in time to find the camp in full chaos. People are arming themselves. Kane is shouting orders from the back of the eighteen-wheeler while Abel I can only hear shouting from inside of it. Sounds like she's arguing with somebody and when I pass by, I can see Mikey trying to block her exit.

Good boys.

The hum of a familiar energy pulls through my blood as the hum of an unfamiliar tune gets louder and louder. I make my way down the road, relieving that fuck Roderick of his M4 as I go — he curses after me, but doesn't do more than that — until I make my way to the two pickup trucks that flank either side of the road, and the dozen Others and humans arranged in V formation between them. Armed to the teeth.

Luke is among them. "P-P-Pia's in the wwwwoods by the rrrriver," I stammer like a goddamn drunk.

"What's she doing there?"

"Sssafe," I answer. "Make sure she st-st-stays that way."

Luke tilts his head to the side as he assesses me, but only for a split second before he takes off. I take the place in the V between Laiya and Gabe, near its lethal tip, and I wait as the music gets louder and clearer and closer...

Something about being sad? Or maybe something somebody said. Then the chick is lonely...but not anymore? The fuck is goin' on? *"Oh!"* And then much, much louder that music asks a question I've never been asked and that I can't answer.

Do *I* believe in life after love?

Nah.

I don't even believe in life.

By now the source of the music has come into view through the scope fixed to the mount on my — Roderick's — weapon. It's a sturdy thing and I hadn't seen it when I'd raided the weapon's cache. If I had, I'd have stashed it away for myself. He must have had the same idea. Smart man.

A single pickup truck rolls slowly into view, emerging from the darkness and into the light of the fire still burning strong behind us — though to call it a pickup truck does it an injustice.

It's a technical. One of Jack's guys was in the military and taught me everything I know about guns. He'd have called this Ford F-450 mounted with a twin M2HB machine gun, a full technical vehicle.

And damn if I'm not impressed.

It's a beast of a fighting vehicle that looks like it's in stunningly good shape — black paint's faded and there are a couple bullet holes riddling the front cab, but the windshield's still intact and the tires aren't bald and still fitted with deep tread. It's a machine built to strike fear in the hearts of its victims and it *might* have made me a little wary even, if the machine gun were manned and if there wasn't a white flag hanging between the gun's twin barrels.

The music doesn't help either and continues to belt out a roaring screech. A woman with a deep, powerful voice sings a tale of not needing some man anymore. But then finding love after that. Fuck if I know about any of that shit.

I glance to my left and Laiya meets my gaze. The strangest thing happens in that moment — she lifts her shoulder along with one edge of her mouth, and shrugs. Like we're sharing some kind of a secret. A joke, even.

It gives me the chills.

See what happens when you become soft? They think you're one of them.

"*...believe...*" Then the music cuts off all at once.

An arm shoves out of the driver's side window holding another white flag and a voice, from inside the cab shouts, "Don't shoot!"

It's a woman's voice. And when the front doors open, two women step out. Two more women lower themselves down from the raised back seats and one final woman stands up in the cab of the truck. She steps to the left of the machine gun so she can see past it.

They're all holding white flags and have their hands raised in that placating gesture I don't like, and they're *all* strapped to the nines. Kevlar vests cover their chests and the one in the truck's even got a helmet on, titled to one side.

She's the one who says, "Can we talk to the chick leading y'all?"

No one responds, but I can feel the air holding steady as it waits for the other shoe to drop and for this whole road to light up in one act of incalculable violence. *We are so close. Pull the trigger, start the massacre yourself.*

My finger twitches and I flip on the safety.

Coward. Sweat builds on my brow with the desire to do just what Jack says. Give in…

"What do you want with our leader?" The voice comes from behind me and it's fucking Pia's.

I whip around and see her standing with her chest fully fucking exposed and her hands on her hips. Luke stands behind her and I meet his gaze, hoping to communicate that I'm going to fucking skin him. He gives me a sort of exasperated look, like that's got to mean something, the fucker. He had one goddamn job, and that was to keep her protected.

My left foot shoots back while my mind wars with itself — break rank, or leave her defenseless like this? One of the women — the one who'd been driving — takes a step forward.

She's got brown skin a shade darker than Abel's and long, straight hair that shines black in this light. I keep my sight trained on her and watch for any errant movement, but she just takes another step and then another, walking with a confidence that makes no fucking sense. They're outnumbered and outgunned, yet they look at Abel's people like they won't rape, murder, and devour them.

Maybe because they won't.

But we will, won't we, darling?

A muscle in my back twitches and the woman's gaze swings towards me. She narrows her eyes and stops moving. "We come with a warning. We've been trailing your group for the past three weeks now, watching."

How the fuck did they manage that without any of us noticing? I've got a sense for these things — always have — I should have known that an armed group was on our tail. *You should have, but you've gotten soft. You're going to die out here without me alongside all the others. In pain. With nothing. But you know who won't die? Your girl.* My girl. An air-filled balloon swells larger in my throat. *No, she'll live long enough for me to tear her apart. And you? You'll live long enough to watch.*

A shudder wrenches through me and I notice the woman is fully focused on me now. Her fingers do a little dance in the wind, but she doesn't reach for the weapons she's got strapped to the sling around her back. I wonder what they are.

"We were trying to decide what the hell you people are — a community, a gang, a pack of idiots — and how well stocked you were and if you seemed open to trade. That's what we do. How we survive, my sisters and I.

"We were raised by a team of women who were all former navy SEALS. We're good at what we do — tracking, hunting, trading. We don't kill and we never overtake — we don't need to. If a group seems too starved to trade, then we move on. If a group seems too violent, we don't bother.

"You surprised us, though. You weren't trading and you weren't taking either. You were absorbing and trying to help the people you came across. We saw you and what you did for him."

She cocks her head in my direction and I feel heat flare up my spine at the pressure of eyes on the wreckage that is my body, its brutal form.

"You're growing. What for, we aren't sure, but we liked what we saw and we wanted to chance meeting you and your leader to see if we might team up with you."

"Can we talk to her?" One of the others says — a woman with skin as dark as the shadows behind her and long braids tied back into the same low ponytail that the first speaker wears. "The one called Abel."

They were close enough to hear her name distinctly, and I still missed them? *Soft. So soft, my sweet Diego. Come back to me. Let me pull that softness out of you with my hands.*

"You already are." Abel's voice causes heads to turn, including mine. I glance past Pia, still pissed, and see Abel fighting her way free of the barrier Kane and Mikey have presented in front of her.

"Would you...fucking..." She curses again. "I'm the leader of this here outfit and I say move aside," she snarls up at her man.

"Not a chance, Sistana." He calls her the Heztoichen word for *wife* I've heard him use several times before. This time, he speaks the word in a low growl that's half threat.

Abel narrows her gaze and points her finger at his nose, somehow managing to appear tough even though he eclipses her height by two feet. "It's *Notare*." She covers her stomach with her hand in a gesture that distracts me.

It must distract Kane too because he doesn't react quickly enough when she switches under his arm, slips past Mikey like a ghost and makes her way towards the tip of this formation.

As she reaches Laiya and myself and the Other called Hila currently at the formation's tip, her shadows move in behind her, Mikey looking stressed, Kane looking furious.

"Abel," Abel says, stepping right up to the thug with the ponytail like she's got a death wish. She holds out her hand.

The woman smiles in a way that makes her look like a different person altogether, takes her palm and shakes it. "Constanzia. This here's Zala," she says, pointing to the woman with the braids. "Avery." She gestures to a light-skinned woman with curly black hair. "Marine." She points to a blonde holding an M4 that looks about as decked out as the one I'm holding. "And Star." The woman in the truck smiles goofily and waves down at everyone.

"Hi!"

Abel waves back. "We're happy to have you. We can make introductions later. In the meantime, let's sit down and I can tell you a bit about what we're doing here."

She starts to turn, but Constanzia takes her arm. "Sorry, but I don't think we've got time for that.

"We found y'all by accident, actually. We were tracking another group — a community with women, men and kids. They're headed in the same direction y'all are and for a while, we weren't sure if they were trying to find y'all or not. They didn't seem too dangerous.

"Then two days ago, they met up with another group. A bigger gang, this one headed by a bunch of psychos."

"A well-armed group of psychos," the woman called Star says.

Constanzia and the rest of the women nod. "Yeah, and they're closing in. They're *definitely* hunting you. All of them."

My stomach stumbles, trips and falls through the concrete below, diving towards Hell, the place the mother told me I'd go. A group of psychos. Could she mean...

Oh yes, my sweet boy, did you really think I'd ever let you go? His cold laughter makes the sweat along my forehead start to run.

I can't see. I can't feel. All I can sense with my whole being is Pia standing just a few feet away from me and the surety in my gut that she's going to die in violence unless I manage to stay the fuck away from her and forget that she sometimes looks at me in the way that I look at her.

With like.

"How much time do we have?" Abel says.

"If you keep wandering around Population like you've been, searching for survivors..." Is that what we'd been doing? No fucking wonder the scenery hasn't changed at all in the past week and a half. "Then no time. They'll be on you by tomorrow. If you guys move like you've got somewhere to be, then you can probably outrun them. Where are you trying to get to?"

"Place called Brianna."

"Never heard of it."

"Let me fill you in. The rest of you, you heard the woman," Abel shouts. "Let's get our shit together and roll."

Chapter Seven

I don't speak to Pia again. I can't. She comes to me and tells me that she doesn't like that I tried to keep her from coming and helping, but I've got no need to explain myself to the bitch.

That's all she is. A bitch. A nobody. A nothing.

Oh Diego, do you think that matters? I know you covet her little cunt. I'll help you get it. I'll help you pull her insides out through her bellybutton while I watch. And I know you'll do it, because you love me more than you could ever like a fragile little female...

He's wrong. I don't want her body. Maybe I do, but I'm also afraid of what I'd do if I had it. I'd hurt it. *Yes, you would.* So I'm fine to leave her body alone in exchange for what it is I do want from her. Her peace. I like the soothing way she makes me feel. The way she makes Jack shut the fuck up. The way she reminds me that I'm somebody. That I could even be anybody. That I might even, sometimes, on an off day...be good.

He's wrong, but he's also right. At the end of the day, it doesn't matter what I want. He's going to catch up to us and he's going to make me do shit to her that I won't be able to stomach. And then he'll make it hurt worse if I don't — not me, but for her. I'll have to kill her to save her.

I lay awake all night watching her cot.

I gave Roderick back his gun. Why did I do that? Now I've got an inferior AK47, two handguns and three knives stashed on my person. It's not enough. It won't be enough.

I watch her until my eyes get heavy and light outside the canvas turns the whole world a muted sienna.

I watch her until my eyes burn and strain.

"Dude, Pia might be too nice to tell you this but you've got to stop fucking staring." I look up. Mikey's staring down at me, his blonde hair flopping over his forehead.

I grunt and say nothing. He's probably right, but that doesn't make it any easier to look away from her.

"It's time for a break. Come ride with me and the new chicks in their truck."

I hesitate, but at the next break, he pushes me again and I'm too tired to fight. I want to, but Pia's being all shifty and weird and not looking at me but in a way that seems purposeful. I don't like it, but it's what I wanted.

I frown.

I'm still frowning when I climb up onto the truck alongside Constanzia and Star and the engine starts humming. At least from here, I've got a good view of both trucks. If I squint hard enough, I might even just be able to make Pia out in the darkness…

"Wow. You look like shit." Constanzia laughs as I switch my frown to her.

Wind whips her hair back behind her in a flurry, but she meets my gaze and holds it with a confidence I want to tear down.

"He spent all night staring at Pia," Mikey says without prompting.

The fuck? I glare at him but he's smiling too and I feel a little lost. Is he threatening me? Antagonizing me? He wants to fight, doesn't he? Or is he…teasing me? Is this a goddamn joke?

"Pia…which one's that?" Constanzia said.

"Pretty blonde, speaks with kind of a southern accent."

"Hot damn, I did see her. She's gorgeous. You two together?" She's talking to me again.

I hesitate. Kill her or answer her? I shake my head.

She nods and stares after the truck, like she's looking for her. My girl. Mine. I want her. But she's faraway now. Where she should be.

"But you want to be?" She says.

Desperately. I shake my head again.

"Huh. Interesting." It's all she says, even as she watches me with her head slightly tilted. Makes the crossbow anchored to her back look all the more pronounced.

"And I didn't mean your sleep-deprived eyes when I said you looked like shit. I mean, your goddamn scarring. Who the fuck did that to you?"

It's strange, having my scars acknowledged. I can feel Mikey tense beside me, but I don't feel the urge to fight and kill and shred at all. Rather, having my wounds revealed feels strangely liberating.

I stand a little taller, showing her my neck, as if with pride. And then I do the damnable. I speak to her for the first time. "B-b-b-brother."

"Your brother did that to you?"

Brother, father, son, lover, maker, monster. What difference does it make? I nod.

Mikey speaks for me. "He did it saving Abel's life, so don't give him shit for it."

"Give him shit for it? He might look like hell, but that shit's hot. Sorry, but that pretty boy look doesn't fly out here in Population." She gives Mikey a searing look that makes him fidget. Hell, it makes me fidget, even as I try to piece together what she's saying. And then it comes together.

"If he weren't clearly claimed already, I'd take him for myself."

"C-c-c-claimed?"

She cocks her head towards the eighteen-wheeler and when I look up, I see a flash of Pia quickly receding.

Constanzia's grinning at me when I look up. "Claimed, scarface."

I snort.

"You always had that stutter?" Again, shock that she's acknowledging it makes me sit up straighter.

Beside me, Mikey's gone dead quiet, but Constanzia doesn't flinch or break, no matter how hard or menacing I glare at her. On an exhausted exhale, I decide all at once that I like this woman and it has nothing at all to do with the fact that she basically just offered to fuck me and everything to do with the fact that she's a bold motherfucker. Maybe I should fuck her...

The thought makes my testicles shrivel. The fuck? I don't understand it, and then I look back at the eighteen-wheeler where I can see Pia now sitting a little closer playing cards on one of the upturned crates with none other than fucking Roderick.

I squeeze my fists and look back at Constanzia and recognize that I'm fucked.

Because I don't want this woman on offer in front of me. I want the one I'm terrified of.

I nod. "Y-yeah."

Constanzia shrugs again and looks off towards the truck. "Lucky woman. She know it?"

"Kn-know what?"

"That you got it bad." She lights up, bangs twice on the roof of the cab and shouts over the walls of the pickup. "Usher! Hit it!"

A moment later, music wafts out of the speakers mounted on the front of the truck, pulling attention on all sides in our direction. *"Oh nooo, no no no no, no no no no..."*

"What the fuck is happening?" Mikey shouts.

Constanzia responds glibly, "Do you think it's hung around or humped?"

"What?"

I shake my head, no idea what's happening and not interested in finding out.

"Diego, this part's for you!"

The lyrics thrum out words that make my entire stomach clench. It's a dude singing about how he's messed up over a girl. How he's stuck in his house and can't stop thinking about her.

And Constanzia's screeching horribly off key on top of it all, "Diego, do you feel it? Do *you* have it bad? Do you wanna have fun…" She's missing the lyrics, and she doesn't give a fuck. "…with that?" She points directly at Pia in the truck and I lunge across the space, grab her arm and spin her body into me so that her arms are crossed in front of her and I've got her completely immobilized — even if it means her crossbow is smashed against my cheek as her body shakes with laughter.

I glance up to see Pia standing there watching us, frowning. Did she see what Constanzia just did? Does she get why this song's playing? I feel my hackles rise as I release the woman in my grip and bang on the roof of the truck.

"Sh-sh-shut that shhhhit off!"

"Sorry," comes Star's ever-fucking-cheery reply. "No can do. We got a rule — no changing a song halfway through. We have to play to the end."

I can shoot her, but that might get me killed and I'm not about to die for this shit, so I sit there glowering as the song comes to its stupid fucking end.

Constanzia sings off-key the whole time, and the whole time, she's looking at me and laughing. Strange, that I don't want to kill her for it, but that I actually feel a little like laughing. I don't though. Thank The God, I don't.

It's only when the music's finally faded that I get the strength — the stomach — to ask her, "The g-g-group you were trailing. They got a lllleader?"

"Yeah, three of 'em." Three. Jack would never share power and all at once, I exhale a whoosh of relief. "We think they're brothers, but we aren't sure. They look kind of alike and they've got a community of ninety that they're leading. At least, that's the first group."

First group?

"The second group is the real trouble. We've come across them before sometime back and avoid them at all costs. Their leader is a real fucking nutjob. He'd ordinarily have wiped out a group like this, but we think he needs them for their numbers."

Cold wind rushes over my skin like dancing ants, ones that bite and burrow and claw their way through to find flesh, where it's warm. "He got a name?" I say effortlessly, flawlessly. *Like you do everything for me.*

Constanzia gives me a troubled and troubling look then. She licks her lips. "Yeah. Jack."

A buzzer sounds from one of the pickup trucks ahead and the eighteen-wheelers ahead of us screech as they break. Mikey swings his M16 around, Abel's name whispered under his breath. He searches for her as I look for Pia, who's already jumped down off of the truck and is rushing around it to meet the action head-on. I start after her, but Constanzia grabs my arm.

"Lover boy, look alive." She switches her crossbow into her hands, turns, points and shoots.

Chapter Eight

"Thanks for your help, Diego." Abel exhales, massaging a stitch in her side.

In my attempt to find Pia, I accidentally saved the little blonde kid's life when I pulled a knife-wielding maniac off of her.

I shrug, trying to see around her, but Kane's standing at her back as her ever-present shadow, looking out at the humans and Others, enemies and friendlies alike.

The attack was small and pathetic, but one of hers got hurt — pretty boy Calvin — and when she tried to help, Kane held her back, forcing her to watch impotently as forty some-odd humans charged from the tree-line, brandishing sticks and spears and weapons that look like they came from some other millennia.

It was a weak showing. I'm not sure how they thought they'd overtake a convoy of two eighteen-wheelers fully stocked with weapons and Others who know how to use them, but more interesting than watching how they attacked, was watching how Abel and Kane's minions defended.

Among the humans, there are some clear standouts. The ones who've fought before and have spent their fair share of time in Population.

Constanzia and her group were savages. Equipped to work with any weapon on offer. Better yet, they moved as one whole unit, always having each other's backs as they moved in syncopated motion around the pickup truck.

Frustratingly, the man called Roderick also seemed to know what he was doing. A jack-of-all-trades, he seemed just as comfortable shredding bodies with his M16 as he did with the hunting knife strapped into the sling across his back.

Gabe can grapple and was effective on the front line — too confident, he'll definitely die soon but at least he'll take out a few bodies in the meantime.

Ashlyn and Sandra are shit shots, even for medics. They shot from the back of the other truck where they'd be safest, even though the attack was coming from the front. The kid Calvin was equally useless and got taken down by two women with short spears. But the Others…

Damn.

The Others that make up Abel's crew are fucking mean. Whoever this Lahve guy is left behind his prized fighters. They fight with swift efficiency, in tight formations. They rarely ever break line. And if they do, it's only ever in defense of one of the humans who's undoubtedly done something suicidal and stupid.

After shedding the mutinous part of the crew, I'm starting to think that Abel, Kane, their unborn kid, and their entire ragtag band might just fucking make it.

You fucking traitor. Just wait until I catch up to you.

"Hey!" The voice pulls my attention around. It's Constanzia's this time. "This isn't right. We recognize some of these people."

"Recognize them?"

"Yes. They're part of the big group. The community one," Zala pants beside her and I notice that she speaks in an accent I can't place.

"You led us to believe this group wasn't dangerous," Kane snarls.

"And they aren't. Look around. Nobody got seriously hurt. I just don't get why they'd attack…"

But I do…

The group keeps talking, but my neck twitches and my gaze pans past Abel, past the bodies being stacked on the side of the road by Calvin, Gabe, Roderick and the Others, past Sandra and Ashlyn trying to administer medical care to one of the near-dead women — a fucking waste of effort — towards the gloomy tree-line.

Still searching for Pia, I turn Constanzia's words over in my mind and I force myself to do something I haven't done in a while.

I think of Jack. I remember the way his sweat smelled. I feel the blade as he cuts it across my face. I remember showing him my back and letting him cut me there, too. I remember running away. I never run, but I ran from him.

I remember battling him, but beyond that, I remember battling for him. Strategy. Tactics.

This is one of them.

"Thisss is one of them."

My eyes widen. My chest implodes and explodes. Where the fuck is Pia?! I need her nowhere near me. I need her by my side.

"Abel," I bark. "Get back on the truck."

I don't stutter. Not even once. Small bursts of elation blow through me, until Abel looks up at me and says the single word I hate most in the English language.

"What?"

"You-you-you…" I can't get it out. I can't say more.

All at once, all of the Others with us freeze in unison and pivot left. I've always had excellent hearing, but theirs is better. Most of them are already moving by the time I hear it. The rumbling. The rustling. The weak attack explained.

It wasn't an attack at all. *Good boy.* It was a test. *And?* It was a test and a *softening* of the battlefield.

"Abel!" Comes Mikey's shout from three pickups over. He's too far to reach her now.

"Ashlyn!" Abel lurches towards Ashlyn standing far away beside Sandra, completely oblivious. "Kane!" The desperation in his wife's voice must be what motivates him. The only thing, I imagine, that would in that moment.

He takes off after the small blonde one and just before he does, he looks to me as if to ask me to watch her and also with a promise of what he'll do to me if I don't.

Strangely, I find myself...moved by that. *You're not a hero.* I know I'm not a fucking hero, but I'm a killer. Why not fucking kill something?

The only problem with that, is that I can't simultaneously watch Abel and hunt for Pia. The only one I fucking care about.

That's not true, is it? Look at you and what you've become. Soft everywhere. Rebuilding a conscience that I worked so hard to tear out. Tsk, tsk, tsk...

"Ashlyn!" Abel starts to move after her, despite already having sent Kane to do the job, but I grab her by the shoulder of her black jacket and hold her steady.

The Others are moving into formation, but it's clumpy and lopsided as they try to move the bodies of those that have fallen and clear the wounded out of the way. Kane has reached Ashlyn and has sent her and Sandra to separate trucks while he carefully lifts a body from the ground and hurries after Sandra. The Other called Laiya carries another.

Ashlyn reaches us and air whooshes out of Abel's lungs. She pushes Ashlyn behind her. Incidentally, towards me. I step aside and give her space to climb on.

As she passes to my right, I grab her elbow. Fear flushes her face and I let go of her quickly, reach behind a support beam that connects the truck's canvas covering to the flatbed and remove a Glock from where I hid it earlier. I've got weapons stashed all over this eighteen-wheeler.

I hand it to her and her eyebrows arch high over her forehead. She glances at the weapon, then again at me. I cock my head towards the back of the truck and place my hands on the action of my AK, getting ready.

The little girl's eyes get big. Real fuckin big. She darts away towards the safety of shadows at the back of the truck, while I force Abel up onto the bed of the eighteen-wheeler and run towards the nearest pickup.

I jump up into the flatbed alongside a host of supplies — weapons mostly, but also some canned food and medical shit — covered by a tarp. Then I hunker down behind the cab for cover. Up here, I've got height advantage, but it also exposes me.

"You good?" Constanzia says from beside the truck. She's looking up at me even though her body's angled towards her own pickup truck at the back of the convoy.

I nod, confused by the question. Is she worried about me? It's a strange thing to contemplate. "Wh-why?" I grunt.

She rolls her eyes. "Just seeing if you need anything in defense of our fearless leader." Her voice is sarcastic, yes, but I'm too thrown by the way she said *our* to retaliate against it.

I shake my head, but as she turns, I realize, I do need something. "P-P-Pia."

"Pia? You want me to keep tabs?"

"I want you to fffffind her."

Constanzia nods stiffly, then takes off and I'm surprised again that she actually took orders from me. With Jack, only he had wants. Only he had needs. The rest of us were just executioners.

I mount my rifle and flex my ears and wait, only to start a second later at the sensation of the whole truck rumbling. I glance over my shoulder and see Roderick leap up onto the bed lithely. He hunkers down on the other side of the truck and sets the stock of his M16 to his shoulder and lowers his gaze to the sight.

He shrugs. "You heard somethin'. Must be somethin'," he says around the toothpick he's got perpetually fixed in the corner of his mouth. How many of those fucking things does he have? Or is it just the one and he somehow makes it last? I find both thoughts equally disturbing.

He lowers his baseball cap, even though it's far from fuckin sunny. I grunt by way of response and watch as the Others finally get the last of the bodies cleared and move into a careful formation between two pickups — mine and Constanzia's.

Three more pickups sit in front of the eighteen-wheelers and serve an important function — not just for carrying shit, but as getaway vehicles.

They fall into an inverted V pattern behind, reminding me of the errant flock of birds. Just behind them, Sandra's tussling with one of the survivors, but a second jumps over her and breaks for the trees, knocking her to the ground in the process.

Or would have, if Laiya hadn't been there to catch her. Again, I'm reminded that I truly know nothing about people. Or Others.

And then I hear the first bullet.

I turn towards the trees and look up in the direction that someone fired. There. Fucker. I can see a face in the trees. Pale, like bleached sand. I fire. The gun bucks in my grip, but it's a clean kill. My muscles start to sing with electric tension. The gun feels so good in my hand. My thoughts are clear. Free of Jack. I inhale. Exhale. This is easy. Killing's easy. I think then of the way Kane looked at me, and of Abel back at the truck. Of the way I tried to keep Pia in the woods, and she fucking moved. Where is she? Because it's saving lives that's the hard part.

The rumbling in the forest has gotten louder and the number of faces peeking through the trees seems to be doubling with every breath that I take. If the rabid and rapid crunching of feet over dried, dead pine needles is any indication, they've got numbers. But no weapons. It can't be Jack, he wouldn't be this foolish or this desperate. This is some psycho community making its last stand.

"Shit."

Roderick moves from his position to come to my side of the truck. There isn't enough space, and we don't need two rifles shooting from this vantage point. I'm about to tell him as much — or at least shove him back into position — when Mikey breaks rank and moves out in front of the pickup and I realize we could soften the punch their numbers make by setting up an advanced guard to pick a few of them off before funneling them towards the rest of our aliens.

Our. Aliens.

I follow Mikey over the edge of the truck bed and rasp up to Roderick as I do, "C-c-cover Mi-Mike-Mi…"

"Cover the ugly bastard. Got it. Got your back, too. You tryna set up a pick?"

Don't know what the fuck that is, but if Roderick's got half an idea what I'm thinking then he might be more useful than I thought. I nod. "M-move-move 'em towards the Others. G-g-get some guns planted on the back of the truck fini-fini-finish 'em f-f-f-from there."

"Hot damn. It might just be fuckin' worth keepin' your ass alive," Roderick mutters with a big ass grin before he shouts over his shoulder, "Abel, y'all heard that?"

He repeats my command and then Abel repeats it, and then Kane repeats it, too. The sound of my words in their voices does something real weird to my stomach. Makes it pinch in a way I find real fucking uncomfortable like I'm gonna be sick, except, it…it feels good. *How would you know? You don't know the meaning, you illiterate fuck.*

I wince at the violence of the thoughts, grateful when Mikey moves to my side. Shutting Jack out, I step in sync with Mikey around the front of the truck, our legs disrupting the low glare of the fog lights.

"Stay close," Roderick shouts from his position above us. He's got a mount on his M4 now and one elbow planted firmly on the roof of the cab, hat low, right eye pressed to the rear sight while his other arm is tucked in close. "I got nothing. Mikey, you see anything?"

Mikey passes me, leading with the firing end of his weapon. He pauses where the road becomes dirt, brambles snapping up to bite at his boots. His ear is cocked towards the sky and I know he hears the same stomping that I do, and see the same indistinct swishing of bodies through several dense layers of trees, but they're still far away. They were running, and they still sound like they are, so they should be here. What are they waiting for?

"Mikael, anything?" A voice calls to my right. Kane's voice. He's standing between the two eighteen-wheelers, navigating a few Others and humans to guard the convoy from the front.

Mikey turns and opens his mouth but the rumbling from the forest turns to shrieks and war cries, the boom of drums and screams.

Clever fuckers, I think, as the sound of feet crunching through leaves lights up the forest on the *other* side of the street. They're screaming with purpose, trying to cover the sound of a counter invasion, trying to come at us from *both* sides.

I'm shocked — both by their numbers and by the risk they're taking here. Unless this is the biggest gang in Population — bigger than any I've encountered before — then they're sending a lot of people out to die.

Mikey canters back, moving past me towards the trucks. Towards Abel. Not his woman, for sure, but the woman he wishes were his.

"They're coming from both sides of the road. Protect Abel!"

From somewhere deep in the trees, a sudden burst of light. A dozen Molotov cocktails sail through the air.

"Down," Mikey shouts in the same instant that I turn, my bullet piercing one of the bottles aimed for the eighteen-wheeler where Abel is standing.

Flaming bits of glass pierce Mikey's back in twenty different places when he throws himself between the mouth of the eighteen-wheeler and the burning shrapnel plummeting down.

Kane's already in the truck, covering Abel's body with his own. Shielding her with his life. And where's mine?

"Fuck!" Abel curses. "Guys, I'm fine! We need water! Douse that flame!"

I still haven't spotted Pia and I hope to fuck that means she's hiding somewhere — so long as it's not the other barrack. A Molotov cocktail hits its canvas siding, setting the entire structure alight. I feel the urge to run towards it, but bodies are emerging from the woods in numbers I wasn't expecting.

A shotgun goes off.

I duck behind the pickup truck, but not quickly enough to clear it. Buckshot stabs into my shoulder and I glance down, annoyed more than hurt.

"You good, bro?" Roderick shouts.

"Y-y-yeah," I grunt. I feel the urge to ask him if he's fine too, but I'd rather get shot again than voice it.

I look up. Ashlyn's watching me from beneath the lower bunk in the open entrance of the barracks — the one that currently isn't lit like a roman-candle. She shows me the Glock I gave her and I feel the corner of my mouth twitch. I nod to her once, but she's already leveling her gun at a point slightly to my left, panic smeared all across her pale face. An urgency grips me — one that doesn't want to watch her shoot anything. She shouldn't have to do that. I don't want her to.

Because I'm not like Jack.

You are *me!*

"Water!" Abel is still yelling.

Three of the Others move out of formation, rushing back towards the barracks while I switch out from behind the pickup and gun my way forward.

I meet a man with orange hair and four other men behind him. Shots taken in quick succession make my shoulders ache with the recoil, but it feels good, hearing the sound of their bodies hitting dirt and asphalt.

A guy closing in on my left goes down and I give Roderick a grunt to thank him. The Others are decimating anybody that we funnel their way, but I can still hear Abel cursing and I can smell smoke on the wind.

Roderick hollers a warning and I swivel to the right and pull the trigger and the approaching duo only to feel the gun jerk in my hands. Clip jam. Fanfuckingtastic.

Tugging the gun strap over my head, I flip the butt of my gun around and wield it like a baseball bat. Wait…wait… wait…then release.

I'm battle drunk instantly.

One single swipe. Two distinct cracks. I turn and nail the incoming attacker. It's a woman this time and when she hits the ground, she screams, still alive. She's older, but that doesn't matter. *You know what to do.*

My skin sizzles with an energy that needs release. Jack's right. I'm glad he's back, that he's here with me as I stand over the wretch with the broken jaw, eyelids uselessly fluttering.

She moans as her legs bend in unnatural shapes and I kick them apart, reaching for my belt, the action as automatic as breathing. *You know what to do.* I do know what to do. What I'm supposed to do now. What Jack taught me. *Take your prize any way that you can.*

I hear Jack's voice in my ears, sense his hands on my hips as he urges me forward and feel the ground on my knees as I submit, knowing what would happen if I didn't.

A hazy fever grips me. I prepare for it — the moment I black out — because even though I took those women, I can't remember a single one of them after the sixteen-year-old. *You don't need to remember the things you destroyed, Diego. They were weak. Prove you aren't. Prove it to me. Diego, do it now!*

"Diego."

Is the voice real?

I blink and look up, uncertain as a thick cloud of grey smoke rolls across the pickup truck, then the street, making its way into the trees. As it clears, I see Pia's face among them, but only for a moment before it disappears.

Is she there? Was that really her? If it was, why's she running *towards* the enemy? They might not be Jack's jackals, but they could still hurt her. She can't defend herself. Not like I can.

I lunge after her, but trip over the woman's legs, scissoring on the ground.

Furious, I switch around, lift my gun and prepare to slam the butt down between her eyes. *Watch the flesh cave. Watch flecks of bone spear her brain. Watch her eyes bulge from her skull as she blinks up at you. You've done it before. Then you take. Just like I taught you.*

She lifts one hand while the other clutches her jaw. Her palm is filthy, black creased around every line. So many lines. No lifelines. None of them are long.

"Don't," she cries through a slack, broken mouth. I think of Pia disappearing into the woods, and the expression she'd worn — if she'd even been real at all. Eyebrows together, her mouth turned down...she'd been upset in some way, and she's running now.

Jack might not be here, but I can feel him. He's on the hunt. *I'll catch up to you and when I do, I'll let you keep her. But she'll be stuffed.*

I shudder. Not fucking happening.

I jump over the woman's body and race towards the edge of the road, only to be blocked by two men wielding a weapon I know well, only because I've made so many of them — bone spears.

I don't know the names of bones, but I know which ones are the best to use. The smaller shin bone is good for a dagger while the longer, thicker one can be given an edge so that it works like a machete.

The thigh bone however, is the true prize since it's tougher than the others, bigger and heavier. Perfect for bone spears and these men wield two of them and with experience. They attack almost perfectly in sync with one another, like one soldier fighting alongside a mirror.

It's disorienting at first, until I realize that the one on the left favors his right leg and the one on the right lets his calm slip whenever I engage the one on the left. *Good. Use their weaknesses against them.*

I spin and kick, aiming for the wounded leg. I connect with my heel and when he goes down, his weapon clatters noisily over the concrete. The one on the right lunges for me, breaking the perfect formation they've created. I anticipate the move and bring my gun up to parry, whacking his stick out of the way.

The one on the ground is slow to get up, so I'm on him before he can stand. I knock the butt of my gun against his forehead, and his head clatters on the ground like spilled marbles.

Disoriented, he thrusts his spear towards me unevenly, but I grab it by the handle and with one clean pull, rip it away from him and place the pointed end to his neck.

On one knee, lording over the fallen man, I square my shoulders towards the attacker still standing. I fully expose my chest as I blink back the sting of smoke — it's getting thicker now, and smells like burning hair, burning canvas.

I meet his gaze — not the one below me but the other one standing wearing an expression I've seen before. Pure desolation. *It's beautiful.*

It's horrible. It's wasting my fucking time because there's something that I want and he's slowing me down because I've got all these fucking feelings now. The feeling that I shouldn't kill him. That I should be chasing her. That I should be giving in to whatever orders Jack relays through my skull. That I should be screaming loud enough to raze him out.

"Please," his lips mumble. They're full, like mine, but his hair is slick and black. Jack would have liked him. He would have liked them both.

The guy on the ground has white, sun-chapped skin, brown hair, brown eyes and brown stubble on his face. He's wheezing beneath me, dabbing at the fresh splash of blood winding across his forehead, dripping into his hair.

"Please, just…let him go." The man tosses his spear aside and holds up both hands.

People are always doing this around me and I never know what the fuck they think it means. Never got to ask either. People who hold up their hands, palms out like that without weapons in them always die by my weapons, fists, feet and teeth.

He kicks the spear over and I loop the strap of the busted AK47 around my neck before grabbing the second bone spear. Now what?

Kill them. I should kill them. I know I should kill them.

But I didn't kill the other woman. She's still lying on the ground a few feet behind us, closer to the pickup truck where Roderick's still hunkered down and firing.

He glances my way and I meet his gaze and he looks a little surprised. I'm surprised. They should be dead by now. *Kill them!* But I can't stop picturing the way Pia had called my name, then ran away from me.

She looked so…disappointed.

I told her I wasn't a hero. I told her that.

The only thing I forgot to tell her is that she belongs to me. *And you belong to me.*

Fuck off. Fuck this. I can't fucking think straight.

I growl through gritted teeth, haul the bastard below me off the ground by the hair and keep the spear pointed at his neck. I drag him away from the trees towards the woman still on the ground. The other follows, as predicted, face twisting in and out of pain, even though there's nothing the matter with him.

Except there is.

He's lost the same thing I have, and we're the only things standing in each other's paths to getting it back.

"Where are you taking him?" The dark-haired guy shouts as I shove my captive up onto the pickup beside Roderick.

I don't answer. I just point at the concrete and he gets down on his knees. I point again, this time at the woman. "H-h-help her."

She's got tears on her face and her hands around her jaw are shaking. I'm surprised and a little impressed she's still conscious.

"I'm not a doctor," he blabbers. "He is though. He's valuable. Don't hurt him."

"Then *you* hhhhhelp." I don't care which of them helps, just so long as they do it.

The man on the truck stares at me agape. Roderick seems to be struggling to focus, too.

He curses and I turn around towards the eighteen-wheeler to see Abel emerging from behind it carrying Gabe's full weight. Kane appears from fucking nowhere, leaping over the tops of a human's head to arrive at her side. He takes Gabe's weight from her while simultaneously shielding her back with his body.

Dangling there, Gabe looks like he's been stabbed a couple times. He's also got a gash between his temples — a jagged, yet relatively straight line, almost like those fuckers tried to scalp him. From where I stand, I can't tell if he's conscious.

"Sandra," Abel shouts. Sandra and Laiya appear out of the smoky haze of the far truck and when Laiya moves forward to help Kane with the body, I cast a glance around and see that the crowd has thinned.

There's a pair of humans battling it out with one of the Others, and on the other side of the road, an injured Calvin and one of the Others have already moved on to the next step as they try to reason with — *indoctrinate* — a handful of survivors. Less than a handful. Looks like about six from where I'm standing.

Meanwhile, I can hear the sounds of people shouting — Mikey louder than most — as they deal with the burning wreckage. Judging by smoke's thick pall that's starting to boast a tangible presence against my skin, they aren't winning.

And I'm still standing here like a fucking idiot, worried about these fucking pansies that aren't doing anything but acting as blockers, preventing me from getting to where the fuck I'm going.

"A-A-Abel," I bark. "P-P-P…" Nothing. Pia. I can't even say her name. I don't deserve to. But Abel's already sweeping the space and jamming puzzle pieces together to form some kind of shape.

"Are you…you're from the group…you attacked us?" She asks the two men I'm threatening, while ignoring the fact that I've just grunted a mangled "Pia" out under my breath.

The one on his knees beside the woman doesn't say anything until Roderick points the barrel of his M4 between his eyes. "You fuckin' answer when our queen talks to you."

"Cut it with that shit, Roderick."

Roderick grunts while Abel rolls her eyes and approaches the man. Roderick offers her cover, making it clear to anyone that the guy is one insult, one wrong move away from losing half his head. The top half.

Might be the only reason Kane's okay hanging back a hair. But he's watching. From his position kneeling at Sandra's side, he's watching his woman's every move as she comes towards the pickup, and me by consequence.

"You were with the attackers?"

"Yes." The word practically explodes out of the guy. "It was my idea to attack with the rest of the group. Don't hurt him. Don't hurt Matt."

"Matt." She nods, crossing her arms over her chest, making her bloody tee shirt bunch and gape, revealing gold. "And you are?"

"Mo. Please. Just let Matt…"

Abel cuts him off and glances at the woman. "Who's this?"

"I…I don't know her. That…guy just told me to help her."

"Diego." Abel holds up both hands and the guy shuts the fuck up. But she doesn't look at him. She looks at me. "You didn't kill them?" *Because you're a coward. Completely worthless.*

I don't have fucking time for her surprise. I don't have time for Jack either, no matter how correct he is. Pia's getting away. Every step I wait is a mile between us. She could be fucking anywhere by now.

I glance up at Roderick to see he's looking straight at me. "P-P-Pia ran." His jaw clenches. "Hhhhold this side."

"You got it, brother." Brother. "Bring her back."

Brother. He called me brother.

Jack never even did that.

I turn from the group at the sound of my name shouted in Abel's voice. Ignoring it, I plunge into the trees. It takes me a little while to be able to decipher what it is I'm looking at.

Tracks wind all across the ground, trampled leaves and broken moss and little ruined bushes evidence of the invasion. But with some concentration, and a painful amount of time, I veer away from the carnage, following a set of tracks slightly different from the others.

Because they're heading in the wrong direction.

Clever girl tried to avoid the attack by veering away from the convoy at a hard angle. She seems to be running in a straight line, but at a point, she loses her way… Where is she going?

I'm deep in the trees now, too far to see the road or smell the smoke on the wind. The disrupted leaves have settled somewhat and a fierce panic grips me. Did she start walking? Did she double back on her tracks to throw me off? Did she try to hide? Did I already pass her or…

A slight shuffle pulls my attention to a copse of trees up ahead. A curtain of Spanish moss is draped between two gnarled pines, but behind it, I can sense movement.

I reach for my gun until I remember it's broken, then take my bone spear in two hands. I maneuver through the trees, light on my feet, careful to step in patches of soil, avoiding the leaves, which crunch.

The gaunt, half-dead trees start to grow closer together, branches and low boughs cracking and snapping when I punch my way through them.

"Dad?" Comes the voice and I feel the tension tightening my fist to stone, release.

I trudge forward, through the ivy and see her sitting there amidst the leaves. I want to fucking hit her. I want to hit her badly. My fists tighten around the bone spear and I see her gaze flick to my hands back to my face. The muscles in her jaw tick.

She says, "Are you going to hurt me, Diego?"

Yes. Because that's what love looks like. *You know it does. Love is pain.* I nod.

She lifts her Beretta. "Like you hurt Cleo?"

Cleo? My steps falter, but only for the one step. I start towards her faster, even as she clicks off the safety, chambers her next round and pumps the action.

"Do not make me shoot you."

She won't. Even I know that. She's too good with a soft little center.

Backing up quickly now, she speaks faster and faster. "Diego, I know you think I'm worthless." Is that what she thinks? How? "That I'm not a fighter like Constanzia and Abel. But I won't leave without my dad. They dragged him off into the woods while the others stayed behind to distract y'all.

"They tried to get me too, but I ran. My dad told me to. And I'm not running anymore.

"I need someone to believe I can do this. That I'm not a worthless princess worth saving." She firms her stance. Exhales on a breath. "I thought that someone could be you. I guess I was wrong."

She pulls the trigger.

She fucking pulls the goddamn trigger.

I don't expect it, so I'm still standing there like a fucking moron, staring down at my chest and the blood seeping into my grey tee shirt from the fresh round she pumped into my right shoulder alongside the buckshot my skin hasn't closed over yet. I can smell blood and burnt skin in my nostrils.

And I revel in it.

She takes off at a sprint, pumping her arms. Rage rushes over me. *Yes, there's my boy. I knew you were not lost to me.*

I don't bother pushing Jack out, because I can't. The rage is denser than the smoke was, too hard to breathe through.

She wants to run? Let her. Because I like the fucking chase.

The leaves crunch, crunch, crunch ahead of me and I sprint after her, noticing the slight stagger to her step. Her right hand clutches her right thigh as she runs and I feel a momentary chill surge up against the battle fever that's taken hold. Is she injured? How? Who the fuck did it to her and where are they so I can fucking skin them?

But the thoughts are gone when I realize she's picking up speed, increasing the distance between us. Hot damn she's fast. I've got their blood in my system, but I have to concentrate to close the widening gap between our bodies.

I didn't think she'd be so fast. I don't know why, because I don't know a fucking thing about her except that she's calm to my storm.

Not right now though. Right now, she's a storm meeting mine head on.

I sprint with everything I've got, slowly narrowing the divide between us. As I run, it occurs to me that I've got no fucking clue what to do with her when I catch her. It's clear she needs to be punished. *Yes, she does. You'll need to make her bleed, son. Show her what obedience looks like. Show her what defiance tastes like. Make her beg for mercy.*

I ignore Jack, begging me to skin and burn and flay. I'll keep it quick, I think, then I shake my head as I picture Abel's expression as she looked at me when I let those two guys live and asked them to help the woman with the broken jaw. Cleo. How does Pia know who she is?

My mind flashes to the woman with the broken jaw. I picture her face and the way she looked up at me with fear and revulsion.

She looked at me like I was Jack.

And that was all me.

Because Jack wasn't there.

And he's still not here.

Pia's not afraid of him. She doesn't even know him. As I tackle her from behind, taking her down to the leaves, she screams because she's afraid of me.

She should be. No. No.

I need to tell her that, but I need her calm and right now she's scrambling over the leaves, pulling ahead and reaching, reaching, reaching for the bone spear I dropped. She grabs it, turns and swings with a strength I underestimated her for, gouging a line across my chest from shoulder to shoulder.

I'm shocked and shock's got me moving slower than I should be considering she's clearly planning on gutting me when she shoves the bone spear towards my stomach. I lurch backwards, falling onto my ass. She slashes and only misses me when I grab her ankle and wrench her body towards me. She squeals as her torso jerks back, the bone spear coming down onto the soft ground as she uses both hands to keep herself sitting upright.

I swivel my knees beneath me and rise up over her, cock one fist back and let it fly. My knuckles meet her cheek and she collapses back, a red stain at the corner of her mouth that hadn't been there before.

I'm shocked at the sight of it. Shocked in a way I shouldn't be. That I don't like. I've hit, I've stabbed, I've flayed, I've butchered, I've killed dozens — maybe hundreds — of men and women. I don't fucking discriminate.

But I'm so stalled by the sight of the blood on her face that I don't react when I should when she lifts her knee to her chest and kicks.

There go my fucking testicles.

Pain radiates through the tops of my thighs and I collapse forward onto my hands. It's luck that my hand lands on her shin.

I wrench back, sending her smaller body scattering among the leaves and she screams in frustration. She kicks, meeting my chin and injured cheek and I snarl out an indistinct sound while inside, I rumble with obscenities.

She tries to kick me again, but I block her sneaker with my forearm. With my other hand, I grab her just above the knee, wrench down once, *hard* and pull her body beneath me. She stabs for me with her bone spear, but I've got it in my sights. I catch it inches from my nose, and I'm stronger than she is, so when I push it back towards her, she has to whip her head to the side to keep from being impaled by it.

I slam my hand down onto her wrist, keeping it and the bone spear anchored. She struggles, jerking against my arms while her legs futilely kick, but I gain the dominant position over her in less than a breath. I straddle her hips while her free hand reaches for anything she can. She finds the rip in my tee shirt around the bullet wounds and pulls, shredding the fabric so that it exposes my chest and abdomen, leaving only the cotton collar dangling uselessly around my neck.

Her fingers are so damn soft as they trace the lines of my pecs. I'm stalled by the sensation. It reminds me too much of being with her by the river, when she'd touched my body and let me touch hers and everything had been so soft and delicate. She'd been sure. I hadn't been.

I'm not sure now either, and I let her keep touching me, hating how good it feels and loving how good it feels. I don't stop her fingers from traveling freely over my skin...finding the buckshot holes, and then stabbing into them.

I roar as pain explodes behind my eyelids. At the same time, my whole body lifts with the movement of her hips. She bucks them while her arms snowangel down. As my face careens towards the dirt above her head, I have to let go of her wrists in order to catch myself.

Anticipating me, she loops her hands together around my right elbow, breaking my arm down, while her feet trap my right foot. When she bridges and pivots her hips, I'm on my back with no idea how I got there.

And then I remember — that's my move. Was she watching me, even then? Or does she know how to free herself from the submissive position, too?

She's straddling my hips. I'm looking up at her face, past the eclipse of her chest. I didn't need Jack to introduce her to Population, did I? I already have.

She's got blood at the right corner of her mouth, just a little watery red smear from the edge of her beautiful fucking mouth to her round, puckered chin. Deep pink and flushed, full lower lip equal to the upper. But the lower is swelling bad now and so is the right side of her face. Her cheek's got my fist imprinted onto it in bright red shades.

I reach for her, forgetting momentarily that we're locked in a fight to the death. She jerks back and then refocuses her gaze on my chin. Her fist is swift to follow. She tags me hard enough to distract me, but I think she might hurt herself even worse because her face twists when she pulls her hand back and flexes it carefully.

Shit. What the fuck am I doing here? It's like her punch knocked something loose in my brain. *You're punishing her for disobeying.* Fuck off, I tell him. His hideousness has no place in her presence. *And what about yours?* You're not here. You're not real. *I am a part of you.* You aren't. Not anymore.

He doesn't answer me, and I feel surprise open up some strange door in my chest. Cobwebs and debris flutter in and out of the hollow space left behind. And do I dare? I peek inside…and see an almost insignificantly small heart sitting there beating.

I'm a human. I'm not Jack's human, no matter the terrible shit he's done to me. I'm not Abel's human, no matter the wonderful shit she wants me to do for her. I'm not anyone's. I'm just me, staring up at the beauty above me.

And she's just her.

I growl and lurch up as her fist pulls back a second time. I don't want her to hurt herself on my ugly fucking face. It isn't worth it.

She jolts when she realizes that the entire weight of her body can't keep me down. I sit up when she tries to push me back, moving through the barrier of her arms like I'm swimming through clear water. Before she kills one or both of us, I need to get her under control, so I do it the only way I know how.

I grab a fistful of her hair and yank her head back, exposing her throat. The desire to hurt her is entirely gone. Poof. A flame chewing through the smallest slip of dry paper. It's instead been replaced by the urge to lick her. Taste her. Swallow her whole.

Breath jerks in and out of her lungs and her lips part, looking even softer than the rest of her. I smear the blood off of them with my thumb and she flinches. Maybe in pain. Maybe I'm touching her too hard. But my hands know only pain and how to cause it.

Marshaling my touch into something more…stable, I lean in towards her chest, drag my nose across the tops of her breasts. Smell her clean sweat. Something earthy and divine. It rattles my self control. I bite.

I squeeze a mouthful of her tit between my teeth, wanting and wishing I could reach her nipple through her bra. I wanna see it. Want to lick it.

But what does she want?

The thought crashes down, hard and fast and with all the strength of a Molotov cocktail, swallowed. I rip back from her and she whimpers in a way that frightens me at first, but only because it doesn't sound like she's in pain. No, it sounds like she's making a sound like the one Abel made that one time I was watching when I wasn't supposed to.

Under the waterfall's spray, she'd been laughing. Kane had been kissing her with everything he had. And she'd been looking up at him in the same way.

But fake Jack is a looker. Real Jack was too. And pretty things like this blonde can't want ugly, scarred things like me. Whatever sounds I hear, I know better than to read into them. I'm not killing her now, or stabbing or beating her. But I'm still attacking her. A threadbare pair of jeans away from rape. My cock is screaming against the fabric, damn near rubbing itself raw as she shifts above me, her thighs straddling my hips. And what the fuck fabric are her pants made out of? They're thin, practically painted on her skin. I want to touch…

I swallow hard, heat breaking out across my face.

What am I? Am I the bastard Jack created to cause harm? Or am I the bastard who threw his knife in the soil, every intention of making sure that Abel lived?

I pull back from her skin and lick the place I bit, hoping to provide a little relief.

She sucks in a deep breath. A deep, deep breath. And then she moans. It's just a light sound fluttering out of her.

Almost too soft to be noticed. But it's enough to draw my attention up to her face.

Her neck tilted back to a point of pain, she's entirely immobile in the cage of my arms. But her arms are free... she's not trying to escape, at least not as hard as she was before. I don't want to release her hair in case she's just biding her time. I don't want to move from this position. The heat between her thighs pressed right over my cock through two layers of fabric. I'm no virgin, but if she wriggles any more I might bust without her having to do anything.

My treacherous free hand skims her spine, finding the buckle on her bra...and then moving past it. I exhale a strained, pained breath. Where is Jack when I fucking need him? Because I want her. *Fuck*, how I want to take her. But in his absence, I don't think I can.

I slide my palm over her ass and wrench her closer. A hiss escapes my lips as her crotch comes down hot and hard over mine and the thin material of her black shirt scratches my chest. I mash our chests together, wanting to be close, wanting to be closer.

"Did you hurt that woman, Diego?" She says, warm breath fluttering near my temple.

The air releases from my lungs and my shoulders deflate slightly. I look away from her face and shake my head. No, I didn't hurt that woman and I'm not going to hurt her. Dammit.

Her breasts press up against me with each breath she takes. "Then don't stop."

I don't hear her right. Because it sounded like she said not to stop mauling her. I retreat, loosening my hand in her hair and pulling back enough to be able to look down into her face. Her eyes widen as they meet my gaze. She licks her lips, tasting her own blood on them. My fingers curl in the hair at the nape of her neck as I watch her tongue, all shiny and pink. I want to gobble it up. Swallow it whole. If only pretty little things could make those high, breathy sounds for monsters like me.

"Don't stop," she repeats.

I blink once, but that's all the invitation I need. I know I won't get another chance, so I lean in and press my fucked up lips to the skin of her throat, feeling the blood pulse through her veins. I lick her up to her ear, nibbling on her jaw hard enough to cause her to jolt, before sucking on her earlobe.

The sound again. This time there's no mistaking it. She *moans*. It's a whimpered gasp ending in a low, throaty sound. Almost like the sound Abel made for Kane, but it can't be. Because pretty little things don't make sounds like that for monsters like me.

She pushes me, using her entire weight to shove me back. Finally, a reaction that feels more normal until...suddenly... things get weird.

She shoves my torso back into the dirt and leaves and instead of slugging me good or scrambling off of me and running for her life, she braces both of her palms on my chest and...dear fucking Population...she grinds her hot snatch down onto my hard cock through my jeans.

An embarrassing choking sound comes out of my mouth, but she doesn't seem disgusted by it. Instead, she meets my gaze and her lips quirk, just a little. The bloodied edge. It makes me wince, but I don't pull back. Can't pull back. Not when her fingers are deftly undoing the button on my pants and then tearing through the zipper.

She wrenches them open and I don't have boxers on, so there's nothing to keep my cock from springing towards her delightedly. It bounces against her pants-covered pussy, staining the black material with a glistening globule of precum, working like a goddamn slingshot. I growl out a sound that might have been a curse if I could talk right, but her lips just quirk a little higher and her eyes, as she looks down at my length, widen.

And then her hands...she...her fingers cradle my cock before I can stop her. And I should stop her. Because either she's about to cut it off — which she'd be within her right to do at this moment — and I'm the sucker who's about to let her, or something else is going to happen that I can't even imagine and don't have the words for.

I curl up, but instead of pushing her away, I grab hold of her thighs and ass and squeeze. A deep rumbling is coming out of my mouth now in a steady stream as I watch her touch me *willingly*. But how willing can this be? Maybe she's just trying to get away? Thinks that she has to do this in order to get away from me. I probably should ask her, but I don't do that either. I just watch her fingers circle my cock and stroke.

I'm breathing hard, and holding her even harder, fingers sure to leave bruises in her skin underneath those damn pants. I want them off. Like she's reading my mind, she starts to lift up onto her knees and shimmy those black tights down her hips, but I...can't. I just...can't.

When Jack went into the diner to kill that waitress — one of the few people who was ever halfway decent to me in the World Before — it ruined those cookies. It ruined everything.

I'm not going to have the second time I've desired in my entire life ruined, like it was in that moment.

I snatch her right wrist and she starts, blinking quickly. Her gaze meets mine and her blonde shoulder-length hair looks so light against it. "You don't want..." she says, but she doesn't finish.

She swallows and I watch color flare in splotches across her chest and tits. There's a bite mark where I took her into my mouth and fuck if that doesn't throw me. I want to plant bite marks all over her, just as bad as one of the aliens. I want everyone to know she's *mine*. Even though she'll never be.

I shake my head once, no. It's the hardest thing I've ever done in my life.

My cock weeps precum over her fingers in rebellion. She looks down at the glisten of cum on her hand and then sweeps her gaze up to me again. I can't read her expression. I could never read expressions. But then it doesn't matter. Because she starts to move.

With her black pants still on, she lowers herself down the length of my cock, teasing the shit out of me. The material is so thin and so soft, I can tell she doesn't have anything on underneath. I can feel the folds of her pussy parting for my cock, like her pussy is speaking to it privately and they've come to some kind of agreement.

A groan chokes in my throat and my hands start to shake. To fucking shake. I've never had shaky hands. Men with shaky hands can't pull triggers, can't make decisions, don't deserve to live. My hands are steel, and even though my spirit is filthy, my resolve is clean.

Until now.

Is she gonna chop my cock off? Fuck it, let her. Because it'll have been worth these few seconds.

I try to keep myself curled up so I can watch, but my abdominals have started to shake with the effort. Hot breath squeezes out of my mouth between my clenched teeth. I feel like I'm fucking hallucinating as she moves up and down and up and down, her pussy hugging my cock as she picks up speed.

Fluttery breaths float out of her mouth and I swear if I could, I'd snatch them all out of the air just so I could keep them forever. Her cheeks turn pink in a way mine don't and that I always found off-putting. Now I find it fucking ravaging. Because she's pink like that for *me*.

Her tits bounce high above my head and her belly muscles clench with each move that she makes. She starts to grind down harder, her moans becoming deeper. Meanwhile, I can barely catch my breath.

My cock is wedged against my stomach and she's grinding down onto it like she's trying to wink it out of existence. Which, given how this fucking feels, is just fine with me. If this is what death is like, I don't need to recover from it.

She slows down as her eyelids flutter and I swear I've never seen anything so beautiful as when she loses her rhythm and uses one hand to catch herself on my chest. She lowers down, dropping so that her chest is mashed against my chest while her hips keep pumping, humping. Me.

What the fuck is going on? I don't know but I don't have an ounce of protest left in my body. I'm holding the back of her head, fingers tangled in her blonde hair. I want to kiss her but the new shape of my mouth doesn't allow for it...but I want to kiss her.

And this is all just a hallucination anyway, right?

I revolve over her body and she huffs out a breath as she lands hard on her spine, but she doesn't whimper. She doesn't scream. She doesn't try to fight me. She just wraps her legs around my hips, forcing me as close as possible without actually joining my body with hers and plunging cock-first into her.

I look at her mouth, wanting her to know what I want and wanting her to let me have it. She licks her lips — is that the invitation? — then she lifts her head up and whimpers — *that's* the invitation.

I crush her mouth with mine and devour the taste of her gluttonously. She tastes like rain and like fire and like something sweeter than those diner cookies but just dark enough for me to be able to overcome it. I shudder as the past scrapes its bloody claws down my back, and then shudders itself...and then...just breaks apart.

Does she know I've never kissed a woman before? I feel clumsy. Clumsier because of my lip as I bite her lower lip between my teeth and try to touch her tongue with mine. I want to taste every inch of her mouth. She opens for me though, and lets me take what I want to take.

Our hot breath mixes together and I'm panting hard and so is she as a wave of dizziness assaults me. I want to be inside of her, but not yet. Not when she tastes so good and I don't know what this is. Why is she here? Where did she come from? Why did she handle my cock? What does she want, if not to destroy me?

Where Jack failed, I know this bitch will succeed. Jack tried to take from me, but right now, I'd give her anything she wants. Everything.

The thought terrifies me enough that a desperate surge of resistance crops up between my shoulder blades, begging my arms to move and for my hands to form around her throat and to squeeze the life out of her.

But if I did that, I'd have to let her go and right now I'm enjoying mounting her enough to risk the magic she's slowly weaving over my body. The one I know I'll *never* escape from.

My hips hammer against her in the only way they know how, but her thighs squeeze me hard, as if in some silent communication I don't understand. I slow, wanting to read her face so I can learn. Our eyes meet and lock.

"A little faster," she says in a gasp against my throat, "but not so hard. Please." She swallows and I can't fucking believe it. She's telling me how she wants me on top of her. This has never happened to me.

Too stupid and stunned to do anything but obey her, I start to pump my hips against hers in slow, even thrusts. "Oh there. Yes. Just like that."

Her lips quiver. Her eyelids flutter. Her fingers digging into my back and the nape of my neck, pulling me closer and I grunt as pressure in my abdomen builds.

My stomach tenses. I blink many times. And then I feel it. Her smaller body begins to shudder beneath mine. She's got her feet planted in the soil around my knees and is shoving her hips up to catch my thrusts. She starts bucking slightly, body jolting as her face twists.

For a moment it looks like she's in pain, but when I try to pull back, she shouts, "No!" And then she releases a high-pitched moan, grinding a figure-eight shape with her pussy over my erection.

"I'm coming," she gasps. "Kiss me."

I crush my mouth to hers without question and she loops one arm around the back of my neck to keep us joined. Her lips cradle my lips and her tongue is so fucking soft, even as she screams into my mouth.

Screams as she comes for me. As she comes in a way I never even knew was possible for a woman.

I lose it. I lose my goddamn mind.

My hips go fucking wild. I grind hard against her — hard enough to see pain twist with the pleasure already contorting her features. I press against her heat so hard my cock starts to sing with its own special brand of agony. One built by her, just for me.

She reaches up over my scalp, feeling the new growth of my hair there, and pinching it. It makes me wish there were more of it for her to pull, but hair is a waste of time, a luxury in Population I can't afford.

I suck in her flavor, swallow all of her breaths. I coil one hand in her hair while my other snakes down her body to lift her hips up.

Her tits flatten against my chest. I want to release all of my weight onto her, crushing her, but more than that, I want her to be all right.

"Diego!" She screams my own goddamn name against my lips and in the darkness between our faces, nothing has ever felt so intimate.

And it's that feeling of being joined to her that does it for me, more than the rug burn I've most definitely got on my dick. I've never been…close to anyone before. Never touched the tip of my nose to the tip of their nose. Never had a woman hold me.

It feels good.

Good enough to die for. And I would die for this moment, if my life is what it would cost me. Because I've come in women's bodies before. But it was their lives or mine. It was threats, it was pain, it hurt them and it hurt me.

But this is something else. A word I know exists in the English language, but that I've never used, never witnessed and definitely never fucking experienced.

Pleasure.

When she blinks her brown eyes up at me, I feel pleasure anchor me, even as the water level rises up over my head.

Drowning. Coming. I groan out something unintelligible. I come all over her, drenching her stomach, her stupid black pants, her pussy through their barrier, the outside of my jeans, my abdomen. I come harder than I've ever come in my life — for the first time in my life, because I wanted it.

Semen shoots out of the tip of my dick, so high it hits the front of her tee shirt. She's fucking soaked. I grind my teeth and dig my knees into the earth beneath me and I hold her against my body as tightly as I can.

I broke our kiss somewhere in the middle of the storm, and before the finale comes crashing down onto me like a brick to the pate, I find it again and I open my mouth to her open mouth and I invade her.

I pull on her hair and cup her breast, fighting my way through the fabric until something pops and tears. I pinch her nipple and I reach around to her ass and slide my fingers down her pants so that I can cup her bare skin.

Without panties on, all I grab is raw, hot flesh. So soft. So fucking smooth. I'm going to lave my tongue over every inch of her. That's a motherfucking promise.

But only if that's what she wants, too.

I touch her asshole, that little tight, puckered gem. I touch down lower, finding a pool of wetness where my cock should be. I slip a finger inside of her. She cries out. My voice cracks and my fever breaks. Sweat slicks my body and I glance down at her hers to see my bite mark first, and then her satisfied expression right before it fades.

"Diego, I…" I shouldn't have done any of this. This is a mistake. I know that. Don't I fucking know it. A pretty little thing like her could do a fuck lot better than a ruined little shit like me. Her eyes get cloudy. Leaves crunch to my right.

She whispers, "I'm sorry."

I'm so lost in the smell and touch and feel of her body that I don't hear the footsteps until the cool brush of metal crosses my temple and an anxious, angry voice says, "What the fuck is going on here?"

I rear back, but where the voice shakes, the gun to my head does not. I rear up just enough to block Pia from view. Don't want them looking at her. Don't want them hurting her. If I've got to die for this indulgence, that's fucking fine by me, but I won't have her coming with me.

I meet her gaze, hoping to communicate all that and more. Her eyes widen and gloss. Her lips tighten. She sucks in a swift breath and the expression fades just as quickly as it came. Her gaze swivels past me and hardens and all at once, she's a stranger.

The irony is that the cruel way she smiles is something more familiar to me. Finally, she looks like she was made for Population.

"Finally! I was wondering when you folks would catch up with me. Now can you stop standing there and get this big guy off of me?" Her voice is haughty and hard where before it was breathless and *mine*.

Hands land on my back and I snarl, resisting when they start to lift me up off of her. Two hands become four become six. Shit. Three. I can take three of them. But then I hear the murmuring of soft voices in the distance.

Fear again pierces her expression before it quickly fades. She barks, "What is going on? How many idiots does it take to move one guy?"

"Just shoot him," a male voice says.

"Don't shoot him. Don't you think there's a reason I didn't?" Does anybody else notice the way her voice catches?

What the fuck is going on?

Some more grumbling until finally the hands win out and I'm hefted back upright and onto my feet. I don't react instantly, waiting and watching to see what they'll do next. I *will* fight my way free of this, leaving bodies in my wake, but timing is everything and right now the bitch on the ground has given me a few moments to calculate. Odds. It's all about odds.

I'm pulled away from her and each step I take fucking hurts. My now limp cock flops around on my thighs and when one of the men sees it, he curses.

"Did he rape you?"

"I'm fine, Ken."

"Did. he. rape. you?" He repeats.

She breathes out of the corner of her mouth, sending a tuft of her hair fluttering. "Tried, the animal. But he never managed to get my pants down."

Surprise. I've raped a lot of women. But to be accused of this now…it's no less than I deserve…but it still hurts.

Several of the bodies around me whisper curses and when I scan the crowd, I see that it's near ten people now, all armed. Three I could've killed, no problem, but ten is where things get a little tricky.

The man who'd spoken — a dark-haired guy with a flat fucking face who stands a little taller than the two men flanking him…*Ken* — grits his teeth and looks at me like I'm every bit the monster I know I am and raises a semi-automatic — a nicer weapon than any that the others attacked with — to my nose.

He spits, a good solid wad landing on my stomach. Blends in nicely with the cum still caked there. "Give me one reason I shouldn't end this guy, Pia."

"Because he's part of their inner circle. We can trade for him. Weapons. They're well-armed."

She doesn't meet my gaze even though I'm staring at her hard. She the leader of this pack? And more importantly, was everything that happened between us fake? She…I thought she…came or something. Can a woman fake that?

Cold sweat breaks out on the back of my neck and a certain numbness settles over my skin. Whatever. It felt good for me so… I try. It doesn't work. It felt good for me because I thought it felt good for her. I hallucinate cookies and my stomach revolts. Did I just rape her? I thought… *That a pretty little thing like her could want an ugly fuck like you?* Fuck!

I growl as someone starts looping rope around my wrists. The bitch turns her back on me and it has no effect. I still want her. Does she own me now? Is she worse than Jack?

The guy with the gun breaks my concentration when he steps in close to my face. "The minute the Dixie brothers are done fucking you up, I'm going to enjoy being the one to plant that final bullet in your skull."

They get the rope secure and Ken slams the butt of his gun into my stomach. I use the opportunity to buckle and pull my jeans up.

I shove my cum-crusted dick away and rise to my full height. She still won't look at me. But I don't look away. I watch the back of her head as the heaven-woman called Pia leads me and my captors away.

Chapter Nine

C aves. Clever.
Jack-like cleverness. It makes me uneasy.
They lead me through the woods for a while until we get to a rocky patch that leads down. Down. Down.

Eventually, I start to see the holes. They lead me to one of them and force my body through. It's a hard incline, damn near vertical, and though the space can barely fit my shoulders, I find myself half-falling half-crawling down even further until I start to hear the sound of water.

My feet come out of the end of the tunnel and I smell rich minerals and rain. A second later, my feet slap down into a shallow puddle and hands are on my body, on the rope, pulling me relentlessly forward.

We wind through a series of tunnels. Some look more manmade than others. Orange electric torches hang recessed into the rough, brown and green and purple walls. The colors aren't familiar to me, and seem even more vibrant than the dull world above us.

The tunnel finally spits us out into a cave packed with bodies. Thirty, forty? Maybe more. Could be less. Hard to count with the bodies jammed in next to so many trunks. Opened and closed, I can see food — even what looks like *fruit* though that seems unimaginable — packed alongside the hilts of swords. No guns though. The only guns in this place are worn around the necks of half a dozen soldiers, plus Pia and her Beretta.

Rock walls squeeze in tight even though they dome high above us, creating a towering impression. A single skylight lets in Population's grey hue, along with water. It drips down in a steady, sparse current, forming a small pool of water about six feet across in the center of the room where three of the gun-toting men stand watching us.

"Pia!"

Three men approach as a unit and I tense as they converge on Pia at the head of this pack. Whispers light up across the room.

Pia stands strong and I'm reminded again that I don't know her yet.

Yet.

"I know what y'all are thinking, but I didn't run. Luke ran and you know better than anyone why I couldn't abandon him."

Two of the men slow, but the third one doesn't. I know he's going to hit her — not the big one, but the shorter one who's got a fresh face, greener than the others. The one who looks least like he's capable of violence.

Actually, he looks a lot like Calvin except for the wild gleam in his glowing brown eyes. They're remarkably similar to Pia's eyes, especially when they narrow.

I can't stop it from happening, I know that. I know that my best option is to stay completely still and to reveal nothing, but I still flinch at the sound of knuckles meeting her cheek in the same place I laid into her before. Her head whips to the side and she spits blood that I feel to my bones.

I growl and Ken me shoves me in the back. His naturally narrowed eyes narrow further. Fuck. His gaze switches from me to Pia and back again.

"Don't know what your game is here, you ugly fuck, but you keep your eyes to yourself and I might just let you keep them. Lock him up," he says to the others holding me and I lose sight of Pia when they lead me to a series of cages right of the pool. Metal and rusted, they look like they'd a been used to store some pretty big animals. Now, just one is occupied. My gut tenses.

"Dad!" Pia's voice is a screech. "What the fuck did you do?"

As they toss me into the second cage, Pia arrives at the first. She drops to her knees and reaches inside the bars to grab the back of Luke's coat. She tries to haul him towards her, but he groans.

"Let go, baby girl. I'm alright," he growls, but he isn't. He isn't at all.

He's a crumpled smear on the stone floor, bloody hands cupping his abdomen. I feel...something at the sight of him. Maybe it's just Pia's grief echoing through me, but she's gotten into my head, stolen my attention. I want it back but I'm worried about what I'll have to do to her to get it.

Worry. I've never felt that emotion before. At least not outside of spending time in the hole with Jack. And that was hardly something to worry about. That was inevitable.

The bigger of the guys steps up to her and grabs her by the back of the jacket and hauls her away from the bars. "Rico, you little shit. She's your sister. Don't be nasty. Don't disgrace your mother."

"You don't get to speak about her. You know why we're doing this."

"I know you listened to the wrong woman, let her get under your skin and make you crazy. You know as well as I do that the ritual won't fucking work!" His voice hitches, twisting in and out of pain.

The smaller guy who hit Pia smacks the bars with the barrel of his gun. They clang loudly. "It will. We'll show you."

"How?" He laughs and I like the man more than I did before. He's a Population-born maniac. One who's insane and reckless.

He peels his hands away from his stomach and I can see a jagged wound zigzagging across his gut. He's one wrong move from losing his intestines.

"Just tell me how I'm supposed to complete the ritual like this." He laughs. He laughs until tears weep down his cheeks. He pulls himself up to sitting on the bars and grimaces. He's breathing hard through his teeth. He doesn't have a lot of time. He needs that good alien shit.

"Oh my god, what did you do, Rico?"

All three men turn, the lighter-haired one moving in a way that's more manic and psycho than the other two. Rico still seems to be their leader though, because when he holds up his hand, the other two quiet. But Pia's question clearly caught him off guard. His mouth opens but his eyes slide sideways to his crazy brother, the one who looks like the embodiment of youth.

Pia catches on. "*Clay?* Clay, what is wrong with you? That's your father!"

"He's weak! And you're just a lazy bitch!" Clay surges towards her and I'm grateful that the tall blonde Rico manages to catch him this time, hauling him back. Doesn't change the color of Pia's face though. Bright red, but darkening on the left side.

Don't try to give him the credit. You know that work is all you, you savage beauty.

"Just get on your back and finish the fucking ritual! We want her back!"

"You can't have her back," comes the growl from the cage beside this one. "She's dead!"

"You bastard!" Clay tries to attack the bars, but Pia shoves out of the grip of the other brother with the darker blonde hair. He caves easily and I can see in his shifty posture that he's uncertain.

Maybe, about everything.

She shoves him in the arm. "We can't do anything without Luke. Why hasn't Matt taken a look at him?"

"Matt's gone," the dark-haired one says vacantly, in a tone I recognize. He's completely given up.

"What'd you say, Adam?"

Rico answers in his place. "Matt's gone. He went with the others. He didn't come back."

"You sent our medic." Pia speaks bluntly, stunned and derisive. It makes the corner of my mouth twitch. It's a tone I've heard before. Abel uses it. Usually when she's talking to Mikey.

"You sent our *only* medic. *How* could you send our only medic?"

"We needed the numbers. That was the agreement."

"Agreement…with that crazy guy? You teamed up with them? I…" Her mouth keeps working, but nothing comes out until she blurts, like word vomit, "We didn't have enough information to overtake them. I saw their trucks, their ammo, their weapons. They have *Others* with them. *Others*. Why would you send so many? Why would you send Matt? I'm assuming you sent Mo too?"

When Rico nods, Pia staggers. "If you want to bring mom back, then you needed Matt. I don't know what you were thinking. You're dangerously near to being every bit as stupid as dad says you are."

He punches her, this time in the stomach. I try to stay grounded, but I don't. My body lurches. My whole body lurches, like it's not under my control. I don't move much, but I move enough to rattle the bars and draw their attention.

The three men — the brothers — *Pia's* brothers? — turn towards me.

"Ken says you think we should keep him alive. I don't see why." He cocks his head towards the guy standing just off to the side, smirking at me. Fucking Ken.

He would have made a nice addition to Jack's team. He's just as bloodthirsty. I'd appreciate him for it on any other day when it wasn't a potential danger to Pia.

It takes a while for Pia to answer. She gathers her breath one little sip at a time. It hurts my lungs watching her recover.

I don't understand why.

She showed me heaven. Then dragged me out by the crotch and slammed the door.

When she speaks next, her voice is a whole octave higher. "To get info…on the trucks," she wheezes. "I think he's one of the leaders." Wrong. "He was out front, giving orders." Wrong. I haven't known her to be a liar. Why would she say that?

"We should kill him. If he escapes, he knows how to get back. He'll bring the Others," Clay says.

"How could he escape the cages? No one escapes."

"Not unless he has help," Rico simmers. He edges into Pia's personal space so that they're nearly chest-to-chest. He seems to be implying something, but I don't get it.

"Why would I help him?" She asks, and it's a good fucking question.

"You're helping him now."

It's a good fucking answer. And it hits me like a swift kick to the asshole. She *is* helping me. But she's their leader. Or at least, their sister. And they're hurting her. I'm not made for thinking like this.

My head starts to hurt and I grit my teeth together, making it hurt worse. Thinking is Jack's domain.

"No, I…I'm not," but unlike mine, her stutter gives her away.

The three brothers share a telepathic stare, then decide that I should be dragged out by my entrails and strung up, but

I'm not too pissed about it. I'm still thinking about the way Pia fucked up for *me*.

Knowing that makes the door to my heart room shudder, wilt and cave in the corners. I guess it wasn't much of a fortress, was it? More like a rotted thing. It's not guarding anything of value…not until I breathe life into it.

Terrified, I feel it inflating. *Worthless,* he whispers. No — it's not worth much, sure, but if Pia's willing to lie for it, then it must be worth *something*.

"Rico, you're not thinking clearly. None of you are thinking at all." She steps between her brothers and the cage as they take a step towards me. She holds up both hands and this time, I understand she wants them to stay where they are. And she's putting her body between mine and theirs.

No one in my entire life has ever done that for me.

No one.

The door to the heart room stands rotting before me. I kick a foot through it, breaking it down for good.

"Adam," she finally shouts and the dark-haired one winces. "You know you don't think like they do. They might be our brothers, but they're fucking insane. We can't bring mom back to life. You know that."

Well, this story just got more interesting. Pia was right. I don't know shit about her, but I do know one thing. I'm going to get out of here and I'm sure as fuck taking Pia with me away from these lunatics.

Luke can come too, if he manages to keep his intestines in his stomach.

I glance over at Pia's father and see him tense up — I know he'd defend his daughter if he could — but he's fading. He's trying to stay strong now, but it isn't working.

His face is pale, drained of all color. His jowls are slack. His lips are ashen. He's got dark blue bruises around both of his eyes and his eyelids are slightly swollen. He's dying. He needs Other blood.

I've got Other blood.

But I'm about to be strung up.

Rico comes around to the cage door and pulls out a big, rusted key, but the moment he touches it to the lock, a shrill voice echoes through the cave, surprising in its familiarity.

"Stop! Don't do this! He saved our lives. He had every opportunity to kill us, but he didn't," the voice pants and two men burst into the clearing, running straight into the water puddle.

What were their names again?

"Matt!" Pia shouts. She jolts forward, but Rico holds her back from reaching them. "Mo! You're okay."

"Yeah," Mo says, breathing hard. His gaze meets mine through the cage bars and is intense in a way that leads me to believe he's trying to tell me something. Got no fucking clue what, though. "Thanks to him."

And then a second voice, one that could only be Matt's says, "It's true. He had every chance to kill me and Mo, but he didn't. Instead, he let us go and asked us to help Cleo, even after she attacked him. He's a good man."

What?

Look at what they've done to you, my precious little killer.

I'm a good man?

I want to laugh, but I can't do that anymore than I can break through the cage surrounding me.

A voice that doesn't belong to any of those speaking lights up the other side of the room. A woman with dark hair clings to the shoulders of a small boy child. She's looking at Pia and Matt and Mo and me as if we are a promise of something she hasn't seen in a while. Maybe hope?

"You confronted the convoy with the Others and they let you go?"

"Yes," Matt huffs, "Yes and we were wrong. They didn't kidnap Pia and Luke with the intention of hurting them or trading them. They wanted them to join with their community. They want us all to join with their community."

Mo continues when Matt runs out of breath. Did they run here? And if so, what for? Are they here for Pia?

"Their leader isn't an Other, either. It's a human woman. She's married to one of them and is recognized by their government as a leader herself. Because of that, she's been given a safe territory down south near Georgia."

Matt shouts, "We are welcome. All of us!"

Murmuring on all sides of the room picks up, growing louder and louder as Matt blathers on about Abel and her glowing chest and Kane and their union. He even tells them a bunch of shit about the Lahve and the seven regions and what they're called in Otherspeak.

He talks and talks and talks and as he does, tension builds and builds and builds. "We should go," I hear one voice say, louder than the others. Some murmur assent. Some reject the idea in a panic.

The brothers meanwhile take on the same hue Pia does when strong emotion comes over her. Like bright red kettles set to burst. Matt needs to stop talking. He *really* needs to stop talking. Mo is trying to tell him, and so is Pia now, but the talking in the room is too loud and Matt doesn't see the danger until it's standing toe-to-toe with him.

"Come with us now. We'll show you the way!"

"The fuck you will!" A ravenous roar accompanies the sight of a boot catching Matt in the ribs. He flies back, splashing down into the puddle hard

"You think you can come in here and tell us that we should just abandon everything we've worked for and fold into some maniac's community? We're going to take back our community and we already have all the help — human and alien — that we need!"

"Matt!" There's more splashing as Mo storms forward, then the sound of a small fight when Clay and Rico react.

Pia. "Don't! He's our only medic! It's a miracle we got him back."

"But Mo isn't."

"You think Matt is going to do anything for us if you hurt Mo?" Clay spits.

"I won't." Matt answers.

"You don't have a choice."

"Enough!" Rico roars. "Throw Matt and Mo into the cage with Pa. Matt, keep him alive long enough for the rest to get back. Ken, block the exits. No one comes in and no one goes out.

"If people want to join that traitorous bitch and her bandits, then they can leave here as part of the sacrifice."

Motion. Movement. As Matt and Mo are dragged into the cell with Luke, they keep arguing and pleading with Rico and I'm shocked that even sometimes, they beg for *me*.

"Let him go," Mo grunts, hands on the bars as Matt hunkers down beside Luke. "He's not a part of this."

"He is now."

"Well, if he is, then are you going to let me into his cell to treat him? He's injured, too — shot by the looks of it."

"He needs to die."

Huh. They might both be right.

Chapter Ten

"How am I supposed to treat him without medical supplies?"

"We gave you everything you need."

"You gave me a needle and thread — not medical thread or a surgical needle, mind you, but the kind Doris uses to darn socks with. I can't work with this!"

Matt's shouting like a banshee now and it's starting to give me one hell of a fucking headache. Makes it too hard to survey and assess my options for getting out of here.

Our options.

Because as shitty as it is, I don't think I'm gonna be able to get Pia to leave this place without Luke or the rest of this sorry lot. So really, that means focusing on doing what I do best — slaughtering the brothers.

And Ken.

I'd really like to kill Ken.

Just for fun.

"Shh," I rasp as Matt opens his mouth to start shouting again. The two men look over at me, but I keep my face forward. Don't want them to think we're conspiring or anything.

"A-a-ask me to c-c-come over."

"Ask you…" Matt starts, then clicks. "Diego, can you come over here and hold this?" He pitches his voice loud, almost theatrical, but the brother Rico just sneers and turns his back on us.

The three brothers are running damage control now. With Matt's announcement, a few folks wanted to brave Ken and the other goons placed around at two cave entrances to make it to Abel on the surface. They killed two people — a man and a woman — and that sparked greater outrage. Pia's been doing a good job of keeping fucking quiet, but she's pretty immobile, with one asshole on her back at all times. Nowhere for her to run.

I grunt and edge over to the side of my cage that abuts theirs and shove both my arms through. "Llllie d-d-down," I tell Luke.

He looks skeptical, but I don't give a shit because he obeys. "What's your plan here, Diego?" Mo grits.

"Cut my wwwwwrist. Not a lot of Mi-Mi-Mikey's b-b-b-b-blood, but should be enough to clean out inf-infection."

Matt's eyes widen. "You have…"

"Shh," Mo barks. "Don't say that shit loud." He meets my gaze as he pulls a small switchblade out of his back pocket. Pretty fucking stupid of those fucks not to search him.

"Thank you, Diego."

I'm surprised to hear him say my name until Matt says, "We owe you. That's twice now."

Mo makes the incision and mutters, "We don't owe anyone anything. This is Population, Matt."

I feel myself smile at his words. At least one of the two of them's got some sense.

And then Matt has to go and ruin it. "If everyone thought like that, then there wouldn't be any point to living."

"Do I get a say in this, boys?" Luke grumbles.

Both men answer, "No." I shake my head and feel my mangled lip tilt up a little bit more.

I tilt my wrist to Luke's lips while Mo works on blocking the action from view and while he drinks a few shuddering, sulfuric sips at a time, Matt starts taking the flimsy needle and heavy black thread to Luke's stomach.

As he works, Matt keeps talking. He prattles on about things I already know, presumably for Luke's benefit more than mine, but who knows. He says that he wants to join the group and I can't help thinking that he only talked to Abel for five damn minutes and now he worships the ground beneath her obnoxiously large shadow. How'd she indoctrinate him so quickly?

I realize I ask the question out loud when Matt laughs. "She didn't have to. We were indoctrinated by you."

Something ugly shifts in my stomach. Like the face of a cliff, falling off in chunks. It's big and it's most of me, and without it, I worry there won't be anything left to hold onto.

"She was going to come back for you herself, but her husband refused to let her. The blonde Other — I think Michael?"

"M-M-Mikey," I stutter.

"Mikey, yes, he offered, but we realized they'd be much less likely to kill us and if we returned, we'd have an excuse." Well, that was stupid.

I shake my head and am about to say as much when the very first word jams in my throat. I can't speak past it and the sensation comes over me faster than it does usually, harder too. I can't breathe and I feel my lungs strain to the point of bursting.

"Hey, relax man," Mo offers and a cruel laugh whips out of my mouth that I'm grateful for. The breaths come on its heels and I suck them in greedily before snatching my wrist back and massaging the broken skin.

I feel woozy and I can't decide if it's from a lack of air or blood. Either way, once I calm down, I'll crack Mo's nose and make him forget all about ever coming to my rescue ever again, because I don't need anyone talking down to me like that. I'll show him. I'll show…

"Mohammad, do you realize how ignorant you sound? Stuttering is not a physiological disorder. That would be like me telling you to relax as a solution to your snoring," Matt balks and even in the darkness I can see the shape of Mohammad's eyes widening.

His teeth glint in the light. "I told you not to call me that."

"I only do it when you're naughty. Are you going to behave and let Diego finish his sentences like a civilized adult, *Mo*?"

Mo glances from Matt to me to Luke and back again and there's a faint dawning in the black pools of his gaze. He mouths a curse. Rubs his face. "I'm sorry. I'm an ass. Go ahead, Diego. I mean, whenever you're ready."

The big empty space around my heart suddenly squeezes together, the walls bending in, the roof caving. Everything just…tightens. Everything just…releases. I let go.

I let go.

I let go because nobody has ever said anything like that to me. Jack killed a few guys who made fun of my stutter, but that only served to further distance me from the other men. I didn't want them to die. And I've never even admitted that to myself.

I let go because nobody ever made me feel normal before. Not until this.

"I…" I lick my lips as a thick wad of something totally alien gets caught in my throat. Got nothing to do with stuttering this time. This has everything to do with something equally as useless. Emotion. I'm feeling emotion. Two times in one day it's hit me. And it hurts.

I cough to get the fucking useless, dangerous thing out and I say in one rush, "How many of them are th-there?" I wipe the blood on my wrist off on my pants and I only stutter once.

Mo does some kind of tally on his fingers. "Before today, there were ninety of us." Ninety. Fuck. That's a lot. Jack's band at most was only ever thirty. Jack said more than that was a liability. I think what he meant was a community.

"But the Dixie brothers sent forty-five out this morning."

"Forty-five?" Luke's body bucks up off the ground and Matt hisses.

"Hold him down."

I do as I'm told and press Luke's shoulders into the stone as he struggles and twitches. "Forty-five? They sent out half our fucking community?" Luke seethes.

Mo whispers, "It might have been more. Since you left, they've been going crazy, Luke. They killed four people the night you two took off. Alabama and her family tried to take off, too, but Rico had Ken shoot them all, execution style."

Luke closes his eyes and keeps them closed. His lips are pursed and I can feel hate and anger and something more profound waft from his skin like a stench.

"I should have shot that woman when I had the chance."

"Wwwwoman?"

When Luke doesn't respond, Mo answers for him. "Luke and his wife Moira were our leaders until she died four months ago. Luke was military in how he kept things safe and organized and in control, but Moira, she was a mom to everybody. Safe, comforting, and resilient above all else. She's like Pia in that way." That I can see clearly.

"She glowed every bit as much as your Abel, even if she didn't have the whole chest thing going for her, but she got got like all good things get got in Population," Mo says. "Wasn't even people that took her."

"She died from dysentery, if you can believe it. Largely eradicated from the US, it took two weeks to kill her. Likely came from drinking bad water. We ran out of medicine and I...I couldn't save her. Maybe if I could have, then we wouldn't be in this mess."

"Hey, I was on the raid that came back empty handed. Maybe if we'd had the right supplies, you could have."

"Enough," Luke grunts, breaking his silence. "You both did as much as any of us. More. Moira died and that's what happened. Everybody's bound to die at some point but we…I didn't expect…my sons…" His voice falls away. His eyes are still closed. Whatever he's seeing behind closed lids, it's pain.

Slowly, Matt continues, "Luke took over with support from Pia and the brothers. Things were going okay for a while, until we came across another community. They were much smaller and tried to steal supplies from us — this was back when we were in Washington State area, not that I have any real idea of where we are now," he amends quickly.

"We killed them," Mo interjects.

Matt winces. "We had to."

I don't need their explanations. Like Luke said, everybody's gotta die in Population. I nod and Matt exhales, like he thinks I might judge him. Like *I* might judge *him*. It's a laughing thought, but I don't laugh about it. If only they could see my history painted in brushstrokes of all the bodies I've buried. So many shades of brown and red.

"We didn't kill everyone. A few of them gave up and agreed to join with us. One of them was a woman…she got in good with the brothers. *All* of the brothers. She convinced them that there was a way to bring their mom back through some kind of ritual sacrifice."

"Claimed she was a witch." I give Matt a blank stare. He shakes head. "I wish it wasn't true, but it is."

"It is," Luke sighs. "She wanted me and Pia to be the sacrifice in a ritual, so we ran. We were on the road for almost two weeks before Abel found us. We were out of food and struggling to scavenge and stay ahead of my sons. When they offered to let us join, we did.

"We should have told y'all that we had a tail from the beginning. That was our mistake. We thought we'd be able to outrun them. Didn't realize that it was Abel's mission to pick up every goddamn straggler Population had to offer and by the time we realized that my sons were on our trail, it was too late."

"C-C-Constanzia," I say.

"Yeah. She and Star and the rest of the SEAL team. Pia and I snuck out and tried to find the group to reason with them — not about stopping the ritual, but at least about not attacking. We thought if they saw us, they'd be satisfied and go and we thought that they'd understand that there was no way they could possibly win, but I guess..." He doesn't bother finishing his sentence.

"Well, we're here to get you out. All of you," Matt says.

I scoff. "You got a p-p-plan?"

Matt huffs. His face squinches as he ties off one last stitch, rocks back onto his heels and glances at Luke's face. "I think, with Diego's help, you might just survive this."

Luke makes a sound like a horse and grumbles something that might have been a thanks had I had that supersonic hearing Pia once spoke of.

Matt switches his gaze to me then. "You next and yes, we do have a plan..."

"I'm fine.

"You aren't, but you will be when we get that buckshot out."

There's no pressure in Matt's kind blue gaze. There's nothing there but the most horrible respect and appreciation. He looks at me like I'm a goddamn hero. And I know the only reason he's still alive in Population is because he's got a skill you can't give up and somebody who loves him enough to stand up for him. And lay down his life for him, if he must.

I grumble just like Luke did but press myself closer to the bars and as I do, Matt whispers, "The plan is to..."

"Hey," Pia barks, her voice loud and mangled and weird. Maybe I've just never heard her shout.

She's standing near the bars, her hands balled into fists. Her brothers are watching not too far off.

"Are you happy?" She's talking to me, but I've got no fucking clue what she's talking about. "My brothers are pissed because of this. They want Matt to perform an exam proving you didn't rape me in front of everyone."

The fuck? I growl. That isn't fucking happening. Don't care if she hates me. Don't care what she thinks happened between us. It meant something to me and I'm not having her spread open like a goddamn BLT sandwich because of something I didn't even do to her.

"Tell them you didn't rape me," she orders, her words incriminating enough to make goosebumps rush up the backs of my arms.

This woman hates me and I'm the fucking freak who read more into it. Who wanted more. Who's still stuck in the woods with his pants around his ass, still hallucinating.

"I d-d-d-didn't," I say, speaking even though every word is a tweezer pulling off my fingernails.

"Louder!" She bangs on the bars with her hand, then spits on the ground at my feet.

"I didn't," I growl, no louder than the first time, but full of menace and threat. I feel like hitting something — not her, no, never her, never again. Maybe, I rather feel like having someone hit me. What happened to stringing me up and stringing me out? That sounds better than the weight of another word slamming into me.

"Pia!" Luke shouts. "What has gotten into you?"

She doesn't answer him. She doesn't look away from me. Instead, she spits again one more time before turning back to her brothers, who receive her more amicably than they had before.

She's still arguing with them when Matt says gently, "Come here, Diego. Let me get that buckshot out before your skin closes over the pellets. And is this…" He's prodding at my shoulder now. "Is this a bullet wound?"

I nod. "P-P-Pia shot me."

"She shot you?" Luke hisses.

I grin miserably. Yeah Luke, now that I think about it, it surprises me too. Though I guess it shouldn't. I had every intention of hurting her. Or at least, that's what my inner Jack wanted me to do.

Luke kicks the bars between us and the motion draws my attention down to the rocky floor and her spit. I bite my fucking teeth together and force myself to stare straight at it so as not to give into the base desire that seems to have overtaken me. The one shouting that I look for her.

And I keep staring, eyes squinting up as I start to make out something *strange*. Something that doesn't look like rock. "You said you have a plan." Distracted as I am, the words come out easily, all at once.

My fingers poke at the spit foam on the rock floor. From its foamy center, I pull out a piece of metal with one squiggly end, and then a second piece of metal, shaped like an L. Together, the perfect lock pick.

"We've got a plan," Mo says and when I meet his gaze, I see he's looking at me and what I'm holding.

Matt, bringing his partner's switchblade to my shoulder to start rooting around in there, grins. "Looks like we aren't the only ones."

And then this horrible feeling that had hold of my heart room earlier presses down on it again. Squeeze squeeze squeeze. Exhale. Choke. Pleasure collides with want and I feel it grip me again, not for the first time...

But for the second.

I want Pia. Not just her body, but her. I want the peace that she brings and the hate, I want her bullets in my shoulder, I want her fire, her fight, her deception and her kindness. She's a human of contradictions. A puzzle where no two pieces fit together.

I want her even if it's only because she's only the second person in my entire life to show me something good, lying back in the leaves, her body towering over mine demanding something of me that I've lost before in a fight.

But I'm not gonna let anything ruin it this time. Not like that night, standing out there in the cold clutching a bloody plastic bag filled with cookies.

I should have killed Jack that night. I should have saved the waitress.

I curl my fingers around the lock pick, knowing that I won't make that mistake again.

"Ffffinish," I order Matt, "then tell me the p-p-pplan."

"Can't tell you. We'll have to show you," Mo whispers, coming closer. He opens his jacket and the lining's covered in weapons that clatter against one another in a way I should have taken note of before, but didn't.

"You ready?" He asks me.

I nod, then look to Luke, who stares agog for a moment before his face softens. "They might be rat bastards, but they're still my sons." Son means nothing. "They're still Pia's brothers." Pia means everything. "Try not to kill them."

I frown, but make a concession I've never made before. I'll try to keep the bad guys alive for the good guys.

Fuck. Does that make me one of the good guys, too?

"We should try to take as many of these people here with us."

I snarl in the face of Matt's irritating fucking optimism. "C-c-can't move ffffear."

"He's right. And we can't risk it. They've been brainwashed by the Dixies."

Mo looks out at the cave, and I can see him counting under his breath. Matt pulls Pia's bullet out of my shoulder while Luke grabs hold of the bars and struggles to pull himself up to sitting. He's got color again, but he's still slow. Not enough of Mikey's blood to tackle the full scope of the damage.

"Abel said she'd wait for us. They're putting the burned bunks back together now with some tarps. There's plenty of space. No reason for us not to try to take them all…"

"Matt, let's just focus on getting out of here first."

"A-a-a-alive."

Mo grimaces. "Alive.

"What are we waiting for?" Luke grimaces, sliding back down the bars as his strength gives up. That gives me an idea. "Let's go now. What do you say, Diego?"

Why the fuck is he asking me? I think, until it occurs to me that this is what people do who are working in a *team*. Team. These people are my team. They came for me, and even though it would be easier just to slit their throats on the way out and sacrifice them for me, I'm not going to do that.

Because Jack isn't here.

Because Jack is dead to me.

Discomfort lays its cold hands over my bones and I have to swallow before I speak. "An-any of 'em got Oth-Other blood in their systems?"

All three men shake their heads.

I nod. "G-good. Then L-Luke, lllllie down."

"What? Why?"

"Th-th-they need you alive ffffor their r-ritual, r-right?"

"Yeah," Luke huffs miserably before his face lights up. He slides onto his back on the stone and, from his position below me, looking up through the bars, he grins. "You know kid, you might just be smarter than you look."

I huff out a sigh that sounds too much like laughter and when I look up, Mo, Matt and Luke are smiling too.

"Try to fake a seizure," Mo says, moving to the other side of the cage, attempting to look like he's settled in casually.

"How helpful is that? There are multiple kinds of seizures. Do you mean a grand mal seizure?"

Mo runs his hands through his hair and heaves, "Just jerk around for a minute. This isn't an exact science."

"I got it," Luke hisses under his breath. "Shut up and get ready."

He lies down and starts to twitch on the ground. It doesn't look convincing at all, but I'm not really sure what I'm looking for and luckily, Matt plays his own part like a natural. Who knew all these nice kids would make such conniving liars?

"Adam! Clay! He's seizing! Pia, Rico, do something!"

Rushing feet splash through water before four bodies arrive at the cages. Pia's fear is real, I can see that as she comes around the cage. She tries to kneel down, but Clay holds her back while the other two brothers rush forward.

I clutch the lock pick in my hand while Clay hisses, "Let him die. He was always going to."

He starts to turn, but Pia grabs him by the shoulder of his army green jacket. "Clay, please."

"Please," he spits. "You're so pathetic"

I'll give her credit, Pia doesn't back down, not even when he wrenches his arm from her grip, cocks it back, and swings for her stomach. Oh yeah. That arm is mine.

Pia staggers back, struggling to catch her breath. I say Clay's name and it comes out clearly, without hitch.

That seems to surprise Clay, because he pivots towards me and hunkers down to watch me a little more closely while his brothers swing their guns around at Matt and Mo in the cage. He comes close enough that I can see the small brown freckles covering the bridge of his nose, and the half-healed scar running along his jawline.

"I'm going to k-kill you," I whisper low he can't hear it.

"What'd you say, freak?"

"I-I-I-I'm going to rrrrrip y-your arms off."

He still can't hear me and takes half a step closer. He's forgotten about the gun hanging around his neck even though his hands are resting on it.

The stock of his M4 clacks against the rusted bars as he presses himself against them. I'm sitting about two feet in from the bars myself, so he's about close enough to touch.

"Shut the fuck up," he growls, the mania of Population a rare gleam in his dark brown eyes. The same eyes Pia's got.

"I'll let you live, but-but-but you'll be b-b-broken af-af-af-afterwards."

He must have heard me that time, because his face twists and his hands flex, remembering the M4 in them. And that's my cue. I take quick stock of my body, cataloguing what hurts too bad to move through. Quick canvas from scalp to soles reveals that the answer is nothing.

I reach through the vertical bars in front of me, pushing my arms to the limit, even as they feel like they're dislocating and make contact with the warm heat of a human body.

I see his eyes. Bright brown and cracked wide open. Nothing like Pia's eyes at all, actually, because behind his forced machismo, there's nothing inside.

My fingers curl into his jacket and I can feel him trying to swing his weapon around and point it at me. I let him, waiting until he's got the muzzle awkwardly pressed between the bars, then I grab it by the hand-guard and wrench it forward, the shooter along with it.

He bangs into the bars with thunder. The top rail of the cage clips his chin, sending his head whipping back. I do it again, this time using my hand on his yoke to angle him lower and slam his forehead against the bars. There's shouting around us now, some of it Pia's. She's telling me not to kill him, which annoys me, because I already know that.

I slam her brother forward three more times, until his eyes slide shut and I'm sure I've concussed him — but not killed him. Neither she nor Luke will get more than that from me. Not when it could mean her life. Meanwhile, behind me Matt, Mo and Luke have each got handguns and they're using them to back Adam and Rico out of their cage and into the cave, hands up in that way that I'm starting to really fucking like.

As Clay's body slinks to the floor, I loop the sling over his neck, thread the gun through the bars and take Pia's pick to the lock. I free it at the same time that movement pulls my attention left.

Checking quickly that the safety of the gun in my hands is off, I bring my hand to the stock and lower my gaze to the sight.

"No! Please!" Pia's got her hands on her brother's coat and is dragging him away from me.

But I don't give a shit about him. He's not a threat. Not like the fucker closing in behind her. "Pia, mmmmove!"

Her eyes widen, but she listens to me enough to throw her body to the ground over her brother and wrap her arms around her head. Her blonde hair cascades over the floor as I shoot in the space where her body had just been.

A guy with a machete drops to the ground, his body landing on top of Pia's. She jumps and that makes me jump. My ears ring. In the cave, shooting a semiautomatic rifle is fucking *loud,* which is why I don't immediately register Mo's voice behind me, shouting, "Diego! Come on!"

I turn and see the door to my cage hanging open. Mo offers me his hand. I stare at it for a beat too long before taking it and letting him help me out and up onto my feet.

"Pia!" Matt shouts, "Help me!"

I don't realize it, but she's standing next to me. Close enough to touch with my gun if I swivel to the left. Her gaze flicks to me once uncertainly before firming again with renewed purpose.

She ducks into the cell and grabs her father by his right arm, while Matt drags him out by his left. He struggles to get his feet under him, and I see now that it looks like he got beat badly before getting cut up. His army jacket hangs in tatters around his shoulders and he walks with a slight limp. Shit. He needs more blood than I can give him.

But he still tries to walk and something about that trying makes my jaw ache. "Y'all should leave me," he grumbles, "I'll just slow you down." He's right, but I won't do that.

"You're out of your goddamn mind if you think I'm leaving you here." She blushes abruptly, then looks straight at me like I don't curse or think in curses all day. "Pardon my French."

I snort out laughter so suddenly, it draws eyes. Even Rico and Adam are glaring my way. "You won't get away with this," Rico snarls as Mo slowly relieves him of his weapons. "They're coming. They'll come for their guns. They'll come for you and if you leave now, we won't be able to protect you."

I hate the threat. I don't want to hear it. I swing my weapon up at Rico while Mo turns to ward off Ken and the other goons incoming.

"She'll be ffffine," I whisper.

Rico's face caves and I fight the desire to plug a round in his skull. He's a liability, because no matter who *they* are, I know for sure he won't just let us go.

Kill him, Jack tries, such a feeble attempt.

"Diego, let's go," Pia says. I feel her palm in the center of my back. It's so warm, it's like it has a pulse of its own.

I back slowly away from Rico, who's looking far too dangerous sitting against one cavern wall, empty-handed. He doesn't trust us with his sister's life and trust isn't my forte. That's Abel's job.

Mine is loaded in the magazine of the gun slung around my neck. It feels too light to make it out of this.

"W-w-we need wwweapons," I order.

"Y'all go. I've got Rico and Adam," Pia shouts.

Mo nods up ahead of me, swiveling right. "I've got Ken and Josue."

"And I've got Luke."

"Fuck," Luke grunts.

I don't waste the opportunity given to me and stagger out in front of the group, careful as I swing the barrel of my gun around at the dozens of faces pressing in on us. Some are taking the opportunity to flee, some are cowering, most are whispering, but in here they might as well be shouting.

I clear a path to the bucket of weapons on the other side of the puddle on the floor find another magazine for the M4 and load it in my back pocket. Then I take a machete and shove it through my side belt loop for good measure.

"Wait...where's Clay?" Matt says.

I sweep the space, looking first towards Matt, and then towards the screams that take up near the entrance we came through. Bodies drop on the ground and I roar, "Pia! To mmmme!"

Pia stalls as Clay comes into view, but only for the first second. Luke grabs her by her jacket sleeve as Matt and Mo begin to hustle towards me across the cavern.

At the same time, a bloody and crazed Clay comes into view. How the fuck is he up and moving? Unless, he has Other blood, which they said he didn't...a feeling of unease stirs my stomach, making it roil at the same time that he brandishes the machine gun he's carrying — a model I've never seen before, but it looks fucking lethal.

"Adam! Rico! Ken! Josue! Kill the fuckers!" He open fires. The screams grow deafening. If there hadn't been other people in the cave with us, my bet is that half our group would have died right then, myself among them. But the fresh-faced fuck just unloads on the people between us. Women and men. A kid. They drop to the stone and I feel an ache in my chest.

The screams get louder, people calling other people's names. Hope before the mourning wail.

"D-d-d..." When I need my vocabulary, it's fucking elusive and for once, I'm grateful for the people around me who finish my sentences.

This time, it's Pia. "Everybody get down! Emery, Sylvia, Casper, get down!"

They aren't listening and even though my group has all hunkered down beside the huge metal tins holding the weapons stores, the Adam fuck unloads again. The sound of two more bodies hitting rock makes Pia shriek, "No!"

The sound of her suffering feels like a wound in itself. Heat rises in my face as I glance over at her. She's kneeling on the ground beside me, looking out between two crates with tears in her eyes.

I switch my focus to Mo. "M-Mo. Now," I order.

Mo looks up at me, stars in his eyes before I snap his name a second time.

He stars digging rabidly through his inside jacket pocket, finally withdrawing a small black cylinder. He pulls the pin and launches it into the center of the cave because the idiot Dixie fucks were too stupid to search him. Guns were too big to carry in, so Abel sent the lovers in with something else.

Pockets full of fucking grenades.

A sibilant hiss is followed by new shouts, these ones in panic. Mo and Matt start unloading smoke grenades, at least a dozen of them, enough to fill the entire cave, but only for a hot minute.

I tear off a bit of my tee shirt and wrap it around my nose and mouth and before I wait for the others to rally, I dive out into the chaos.

The bodies are bumbling and fumbling, and the Clay fuck, in his panic, is still firing even though Rico is telling him to stop. The one called Adam is just silent.

I don't know how many rounds Clay's got because I don't know how many guns he's got on him, how many magazines or clips, and within them, how many bullets or where he scavenged any of this shit. This is far too high-tech for the group that attacked our convoy with machetes and hatchets. What's going on? What's not coming together right?

And why the fuck do I keep saying we?

I shove people to the ground and out of my way and make my way around the outside edge of the cave as the entire thing fills with smoke.

"Clay…" I hear Ken's voice say, "where are they?"

"By the guns! Get them! Kill them all!"

"No! Don't touch Luke or Pia! That's a goddamn order. Clay, stand down."

Clay fires again.

Pounding feet are accompanied by a few distant wails. The slashing of a weapon leads me to believe that somebody else has joined the fray and that they don't have a gun, but some sort of blade. Another mangled cry. Another tortured moan of somebody losing somebody and screaming their name.

There are too many people in here, and frightened animals are the most dangerous. Clay will kill everyone in here in order to cull us out, and with the smoke, I don't know how fast I can drop him. Or how many people will die before I do.

I need to get these people out of here. I need to save the lives that I told Matt weren't worth saving. But how?

And then the clear ring of Pia's voice shatters the silence as she practically sings, "If you want to live out from under the rule of my psychotic brothers, then you need to come with us. You can't stay here…"

The sound of gunfire exploding through the cave picks up, this time just a few meters in front of me. I can see the sweep of the barrel disrupting the gas as it searches for its next target. Presumably, me.

I let the M4 fall against my chest and free the machete tucked into my belt loop, carefully stepping over bodies as I advance towards the weapon and the one carrying it.

As I walk, the mist thickens in time with the fizzle of a second canister of smoke being released. I hear the sounds of a fight behind me and shudder, worried. Fucking *worried*. It's a crazy thing, but I don't turn back from them. Can't when Clay is a fucking nightmare ahead of me. He's close now. I can hear his frantic steps.

My next step draws a soft, pained grunt from a body under my heel. It's a woman and I recognize her. More like, I recognize the fact that she's got a kid and is shielding his body with her life.

I kneel, then bend down low, low, low. So close that my lips are pressed to her ear through her hair. "T-t-take your sssson, fffind the surface. Wait for us there. The c-c-c-c-ommunity is rrrrr-rrrr....real. There, no one will hhhhurt you again."

I get up, unsure of whether or not she understood my garbled words or their Matt-brand of optimism, or if she does, if she even trusts it, but I've got other worries when Clay shouts, "Where are you? Show your ugly face, you scarred fuck!"

Ah. He must be talking to me then.

And luckily, despite the echo, his loud voice has completely given him away. I sprint forward, moving fast as I lock on the sight of a shifting body through the clearing smoke. He's got his gun out, one hand on it like he thinks he's fucking invincible. Or he's trying to lose it, because there's no way the recoil isn't killing him.

He fires and the fucking thing swings wildly in his hand, like a goddamn power hose. So I do the only reasonable thing to do in that moment — short of killing him. I swing my machete, and relieve him of it.

The gun, and the hand that belongs to it.

He screeches as he falls and as he falls, I wrap his body to my chest and wait, wait, wait...

It only takes another few seconds before the smoke fades enough to see through.

There are about a dozen people standing, all of whom are armed. Which annoys me. Mo and Matt were sent here because they knew shit, but evidently, not enough.

I've got my arm snaked around Clay's throat, but he's falling down in my grasp, fading with the blood loss. I can feel the stump of his hand melting into my jeans and dripping down my leg. I give him a jerk, causing him to grunt, which pulls the attention of a few heads my way.

"D-d-drop your weapons."

Somehow Ken is the closest kid to me and he's glaring at me like he'd like nothing more than to pull my stomach out through my ribs. He's holding his gun, but he must have run out of ammo because he's also got one of my bone spears.

And well, I'm feeling just a little sentimental.

"T-t-t-toss it-it over," I tell him.

He flinches, but doesn't.

"You want him to l-l-live? He doesn't have-have long." I shake Clay's floppy arm.

Clay screams.

"Ken," a woman says. She's got dark skin and little gold beads in her hair. "Do what he says. We'll go after them when the others come back."

"He's planning on taking Pia," Ken growls, but the woman cuts in bluntly.

"It's either lose Pia for now, or lose Clay forever. Rico, Adam, am I right?" She looks towards the brothers with their hands up, standing near the far exit. Looks like they were trying to keep people in.

Rico shakes his head slowly, looking fucking murderous. Ken repeats the gesture, but it's clear that he isn't sure. Eventually, after too many moments, he tosses his bone spear over and takes the sling from around his neck. He drops it on the stone ground in front of him and kicks it in my direction.

I'm not stupid enough to lower Clay's limp body yet and keep him pinned to my chest as I awkwardly edge forward, close enough to be able to snatch up the bone spear that was just discarded and shove it through my jeans' right pocket. Got no belt for it, so punching a hole through the pocket will have to do.

"P-P-Pia, go," I say, cocking my head towards the exit without looking at her.

I keep my gaze trained on the others around the room who slowly discard their weapons at the Dixie brothers' command. Slowly, I feel the distinct presence of a few people shuffling past me towards the tunnel and I know that I should slowly be following them out as I go, but I can't help think of Matt. Optimistic little shit.

I open my mouth and speak as quickly and cleanly as I can, using words I've never used before. "C-c-community I'm with is headed by a g-g-g-g-good…good woman." Good. Whatever the fuck that is. "Scraped-scraped me up off the ground when I was only scars."

And pain and bloodlust and anger. And Jack. But right now, standing here speaking, I feel far from him, too.

"She-she's got plans for humans to have a safe territory. She's work…" My voice cuts out. It takes a moment to rebuild it. "…working with the Others. They-they-they help her. One of them is in lllllllove with her." Two of them, but I guess that shit ain't relevant here.

"St-st-stay here and survive in ffffear. C-c-c-c-come now and live."

I lick my lips, hating how my face is all hot and shit and how I'm all fucking embarrassed. *Embarrassed.* As if that were an emotion Jack ever experienced. Embarrassment means killing whoever made you feel like this. I've done it before, but that was back before.

Some people called the time before the Others came the World Before, and after, the World After. But for me there has only ever been the grey hellscape that lives within and around me. Until now.

Until this weird fucking group of freaks attacked a woman with a glowing chest and I just happened to be the one self-appointed to chase down a different woman who took me to heaven, then accused me of rape.

Maybe Life Before and Life After are better terms for me. Because at the end of the day, in my world, the aliens' arrival changed absolutely nothing.

"Bethany," comes a hard voice just behind me, so close my skin prickles. "Come on. Grab your daughter and your husband. Morgan and Gracie, Lou and Rebus, Chuck...all of you. And everyone that's injured. You can't stay here. My brothers cannot replace Moira. They tortured Luke. They threatened me with stuff I can't even repeat. You need to come now while we still have Diego to show us the way and protect us." Protect them. Is that what I was doing? "Before the others come back."

A long, pregnant pause. Pregnant. I always wondered how the hell a thing could be pregnant, but in this moment, tense as hell, I feel it. As if the universe could split right down the middle and give birth to chaos.

We could all die — every single one of us in this cave — if somebody makes the wrong move, says the wrong thing, blinks...

And then I hear movement, a slight shuffling, sniffling, whimpering, tears, and when I dare spare a tenth of a second to switch my gaze across the cavern floor, I see the woman I whispered to earlier ambling to her feet. She's watching me. She has a little boy linked to her arm.

"Jack and I are coming."

Ice spears my gut and for a moment that pregnant universe damn near shits itself because my still hands suddenly develop twitchy fingers. I'll blow everybody in here to pieces — including me — if Jack's face appears. Where is he? Where is he!

But as the woman starts shuffling slowly forward, weaving around the bodies on the ground separating her from Matt and Mo, who are reaching forward to guide her away, I look between her and the boy. Jack. He's a pale-skinned, dark-haired little thing. Not Jack. Not capable of the kind of hell he reaps. At least, not yet…maybe he will be… maybe he never will be…

The woman and the small not-gonna-fucking-call-him-Jack-ever-never-ever kid getting up has a ripple effect. Bodies are on the move and a lot of them are injured.

"St-st-stay low," I order just as a man clutching his blood-spattered leg steps directly in the path of my gun, severing the hold barrel mouth has on Ken. Oh Ken, Ken, Ken. Why aren't you dead yet? It's a mystery, even to me.

Instead of dropping his ass, I wait for the sounds of shuffling to recede into the distance while those that remain look between one another, unsure.

Staying, going, they're all unsure.

"Diego, we're ready," Mo says to me, tapping me twice on the left shoulder.

"Th-th-they have any we-weapons?"

"Not that we know of."

I don't like that answer, but I guess I'll have to take it. "You-you follow us, I'll g-g-g-gut all of you. D-don't care what P-Pia thinks." It's not true, at least that last part, but the first part is. If they threaten me or Pia or anyone in *our* fucking community, I'll stretch their skin and use it as a fucking umbrella.

I start to edge back towards Mo slowly — very slowly — while he swipes the weapons Ken and the other little boys playing soldier tossed onto the floor.

Ken calls after me. "You're going to get them killed up there."

As I lope after Mo down the tunnels, I know that he's right. The others haven't realized it yet and I don't want them to realize it, but I'm not the hero Pia sees when she looks at me when I'm giving stupid little speeches, or beating the shit out of Others. I'm not, but I'll lie to her and pretend.

How long can I keep that up? Probably not long, but I'm going to keep pretending anyway until Population cuts my throat and shits me out on the side of the road and this time, there won't be any fucking Abels around to jam me back together and breathe life back into my withered soul.

Chapter Eleven

There's no time to regroup, get numbers, secure provisions. Those that ran took the shirts on their backs with them and that's fucking it.

They follow Mo and Matt as the two men tear a path through the sparse woods, which only gets sparser the further we go. Means less cover. I've never felt so exposed. Maybe it's because I see less, the flash of fear in people's faces — a fear I know and like and am comfortable with — and more, their strange and putrid *adoration*.

They're all giving me that goddamn hero look and pretending is fucking miserable. How long has it been? Ten minutes. Get it the fuck together, Diego.

Pia is trying to fix her jammed Beretta as she runs. It's slowing her down and soon we're nearly running side-by-side at the back of the pack.

She doesn't notice me until I reach over and swipe the gun from her grip. I shove her in the center of the back, urging her to pick up her goddamn pace as I open the action, see the jammed round, and reach into my pocket.

Her mouth is all twisted in a pouty frown until she sees what I'm holding. Then her cheeks get all fucking red. I don't get it. But she's running faster now while I whittle the lock pick around the edge of the bullet and pry it free.

I rack the slide a couple times, make sure the magazine is loaded all the way in, then hand the gun back to her. As I pick up speed myself, I press her forward, urging her a little faster again.

She ducks under a low tree branch and a few low-lying twigs scratch her hands and cheeks as she tries to block them. I push ahead of her, breaking through the next boughs with my shoulders first. Don't give a shit if they get torn up. They already are. And besides, it's worth it. Because when I glance at her over my shoulder, she smiles just a little bit. Just enough to crush me.

"Shit." The sound comes from ahead of us. Matt, I think. "They're gone."

"Mmmove," I grunt as I press my way between the bodies. There are more than I thought there were — not that I got a good count down in the cave. Running, I thought we might have been a dozen — twenty at most. Out here in the daylight — the greylight — I can see clearly now that we're almost thirty.

A few men, mostly women, and four children limp and laugh and weep and sprint towards the road. I double take at the smallest one — just a little lump of skin in a white woman's freckled arms. It's a goddamn baby. I trip over my own two feet at the sight of it. I've *never* seen a baby before.

Pushing through my shock, as well as all the bodies in my way, I reach the front of the crowd and the murmuring becomes clearer. The panic.

On the road, there are only scorch marks and a few darker stains — definitely human blood — where two eighteen-wheelers once stood. Where they should still be.

I clench my front teeth together and have trouble controlling my temper. It's never been a volatile thing, but it is now. I want to see Abel. Want her to be right here. Want to reach out and grab her. We never did have that fight. I brought her back from the dead and this is how she repays me?

Or is her debt already paid from when she brought *me* back?

My temper claws up the back of my neck and consumes my ears. Doesn't matter that I'm shirtless or that the grey weather has never been less friendly, I'm fucking pissed. I'm going to unload. How dare she leave. How dare she...

"Diego?" Comes the small voice from behind me.

I turn and see Pia and watch her big wet eyes get even bigger as she blinks up at me. She looks afraid. Downright terrified. It's not an expression I've seen her wear before and I don't like it. Pisses me off worse.

I angle my shoulders towards her and she flinches. I want to tell her not to panic, not to worry, that she's gonna be fucking fine, but I don't do any of those things.

I just glare down at her and all I feel is hate. Because I can't protect Pia and Matt and Mo — not without protecting the rest of these sad fucks — and I can't do any of that without supplies and shelter and weapons and medical gear.

She reaches up to her chest and touches the small golden cross nestled just at the V of her throat. She does this absently, a nervous gesture.

"I..." She clears her throat, then lowers her pitch. She angles herself away from the group slightly, leading, but only because I follow her. "I'm so sorry I didn't tell you about my brothers before and I'm so sorry I got you involved in all of this. With us. I'm sorry. It was wrong. I know that."

She shakes her head, looking away from me. Looking damn near shaky. She keeps biting her bottom lip. Her perfect bottom lip. The one she let me taste once. The memory of that makes the anger I feel easier to bear. I can breathe through it.

"My parents raised me better than that. My mom did anyways. Dad would probably say that I did what I had to."

She smirks but there's no humor in it. Her gaze drifts past me to her father, a few feet away, speaking with Matt and Mo and a few of the others. Likely debating a plan. But I see them watching Pia — no, watching me. They expect me to lead them. To tell them it's all gonna be peachy keen and hunky dory. To have some kind of idea about what the fuck to do next.

They can go to hell. That's what I'm condemned to. If they follow me, at least they should know where they're headed. And that they're headed there fast.

I don't know if she's waiting for me to answer, but she's just standing there looking more and more agitated. She lifts her fingers to her mouth and starts biting on her thumb nail. I can't stand that shit and take hold of her wrist.

She stares at the contact between us for longer than a beat. When she speaks next, her voice is thicker than it was. Her eyelashes are long and dark blonde. When she blinks their fragile tips touch her high cheeks.

"What happened between us in the forest…"

"Shouldn't hhhhave."

She makes a face, then it softens. "You have every right to be pissed off at me, but I have to ask you at least for now to take us with you. I know that Abel wouldn't have abandoned all of us like this, so either she's really hurt or they'll be waiting for us down the road."

She starts to bounce on her toes and glances over her shoulder. Nervous. She must know how critical these moments are and how desperately we need the distance.

"Diego, I'm really willing to do *anything* for you to consider leading everyone here, including finishing what we started in the forest."

My gut hardens and I can't believe fucking believe it — that she would say this to me here now. That was one of the best moments — no — that was the *best* moment of my fucking life and here she is reducing it to a trade.

I'm not going to let her get off that easily.

"Say it. T-t-tell me what you'll g-g-give me t-to show you the wwwway."

Her face lights up a brilliant scarlet, but her voice is level as she says, "I've only been with two other men in my life and I'm confident that I'm clean. I'll give you...me."

"Jesus fucking Christ, Pia!" Her father shouts so loud it makes me jump.

I drop her hand like it's poison, but I don't step away. My anger. Goddamn that fucking anger. Without touching her, I lean in close enough I can smell her hair. She smells like those caves and their minerals, so decadent.

Bringing her under the awning of my heat, we stand so close that her breasts brush against my chest, but she doesn't back away.

Her father grabs my arm above the elbow and growls something inaudible, but I switch free of his grip and hold up my hand in that placating way.

He quiets. I'm a little surprised that he does, but he must trust me in ways that I don't with his daughter.

I continue to lean in and whisper against her hair, feeling its satin texture against the satiny scars winding across my face. "I'll take you to A-Abel and wwwhen we c-c-catch up with her, you don't make that t-t-t-t..." I take a deep breath, then push until the rest of the words come tumbling out, "...trade to me or to anybody. You d-d-do, and I'll k-kill him."

She sucks in a breath, face turning a bright and shiny red. I want to grab her and force her to look at me and also to shake some sense into her, but I can't touch her again. Not now. Not with *this* hanging between us.

"Pia," I bark when she doesn't answer me, and I feel like a fucking god when I don't stutter her name. "W-we understood?"

She winces like I've just hit her and I remember that I've already done that. Why I expect anything more than to be treated like an asshole is a riddle I'm damn sure not smart enough to solve. So I take it and step back, well aware that that heaven she took me to is a memory I'll have to immortalize, because there's no going back.

Pia bites her bottom lip and the intense color in her face holds.

"You answer the man, Pia," her father barks.

"Yes," she snaps, hard, "Yes, I understood. I understand." She looks at me and shoves her Beretta into the back of her pants. "I just…I know I shouldn't have put all this on you. To ask you to take us with you. It's a lot, and I'd do anything for these people."

"I know." I nod. These people. Is scum like me included? She said she liked me once, but that was long ago. "B-b-but you d-d-don't have to."

I start to turn away from her, but she grabs my hand, rubs her thumb across the scar that halves it and gives it a slight squeeze. I don't know what it means.

And then she says to me two words that cut deep. Only because it's the first time I've heard them that they were directed at me. "Thank you, Diego."

I stare into her eyes. Deep, deep, deep into her eyes. How is it that, just by looking at her, I can feel so *big* and so small at the same time?

A slight grunt to my right pulls my attention around to her father. He's giving me a look I don't like because it makes me hot around the collar — or would have, had I been wearing one. I let go of his daughter, step away from her and keep my hands to myself. He gives me a slight nod and I understand without knowing how, that that was his intention.

"Lllllet me see…it," I tell him, half as a distraction, half because I need to know.

He hesitates. "I'm fine thanks to you. We need to get moving."

"Nnnnot enough blood. I n-n-need to see what I'm working with." I take a deep breath. After my fucking speech, talking this much is fucking tiring.

He grimaces. Matt, just behind him, says, "It's not infected, but it's not healing all the way, either. Makes me worried that there's worse going on inside that I couldn't see."

I nod. Sounds about right. "C-c-can you run?"

"Do I have a choice?"

I shake my head.

Luke grunts. "You know what, Diego? I'll regret saying this in about five minutes, but you might be alright."

"R-r-ready?"

"Where are we going?"

"B-B-Brianna."

"Brianna?"

"You mean to Georgia?" Pia says, aghast. Her words cause a stir among the riff raff. One I'm going to have to quell and quick, if I expect this group to get anywhere.

I nod. "G-g-get your shit. We-we need to move."

Luke stares at me for another drawn out moment, then hacks out a laugh. "Goddamn, this guy's fucking crazy. You know what? We just might make it."

"I'm with you, Diego," Matt says.

"Me too."

Slowly, their certainty *in me* spreads, and even the ones who look ready to bolt, gather their stuff.

"I'm ready, too. Lead the way, Diego," Pia says and the door around my heart room dissolves. Even the walls cave a little.

It's the way she says my name. Diego. The sound of my name in her voice fills me with a surge of possessiveness. I want her. Not just because it's the heat of the moment. Not just because she wants something from me. I want her for real this time. Forever.

"Diego?" I jerk up, then freeze when I notice she's come closer to me by about a foot.

"F-follow me. St-stay close."

Pia nods feverishly and turns, stooping down to her father to collect his other side. I wave her off and take her place, acting as his other crutch. As we make our way back into the woods, sticking close to the road, but not close enough to be seen from it, Luke complains that he can walk himself the entire time. Even as he leans on me. The other members of the group talk among one another in panic and excitement and fear.

But it's strange because even though we've got no supplies, no water, no food, and few weapons, I feel, for the first time in a long time, something more than just the will not to die.

I feel a strange desire to live.

Chapter Twelve

They're tired.

They're weak. That's what Jack would say, anyway. Fuck it — that's what *I* think. They want to stop for food and water before night even hits. Not happening.

I push them harder for a few more hours down the mountain until the grey blackens around us, becoming a black so thick, we can't even see our hands in front of our faces without light. We shouldn't use light either but it seems there's no arguing that.

Two sorry sacks brought flashlights with them. Somebody else brought a solar lamp. Clever. Especially now that we have no trees for cover. We're sitting fucking torchlights.

Finally, the sound of the baby crying is what drives me to make that final, damning call. It blazes like a goddamn siren and I recognize quickly why there are no babies out in Population.

With a baby, it doesn't really matter how much light we use. Might as well grab flares and set them off. Might as well build a screen in neon and announce our presence.

Free women and human flesh for the taking!

I push them a little ways more, the crying baby lighting our route, until we come upon a house. It's one of a few farmhouses we've crossed, now that we've descended the mountain.

I could hear groans and complaints as we passed other houses — one woman even started crying, something about a blister or a cut on her foot. I laughed at that. Fuck her and fuck her foot. She can cut it off for all I care. I've been itching for a new bone spear anyways.

Those houses were too open, too exposed. This one's big with a lot of rooms and a lot of exits and a lot of smaller sheds and coops and other barns surrounding it. If we're invaded, there's at least places to run to. To hide in. Most of us'll die, that's a given, but some might make it. At least somebody's gotta tell Abel I tried.

We barricade the major entrances, then hunker down in the living room. Some scavenging produces a few cans of beans and corn that somebody manages to whip up into something that actually tastes…passable. I choke down what I can, then head upstairs to claim the closest bedroom to the road.

Not too worried about trespassers that attack on foot, but if they're coming by car, I wanna know.

"Hey, you uh…in the mood for company?"

I twitch, startled by the sound of her voice even though I heard floorboards creaking and knew that somebody was walking towards me. Don't know why I didn't think it'd be her. Don't know why I thought it'd be anybody else.

I glance away from the window towards the doorway. She's holding a candle in one hand, a pile of material in the other. She lifts them when she catches me watching.

"A towel and a change of clothes. I found them in one of the other bedrooms. This place is massive. Must be seven bedrooms at least."

She tries a smile. I find it disarming. My dick finds it disarming and tries to stand up straight. I will it back, remembering that I've still got cum crusted on my jeans and that she offered herself to me in a trade and that she never wanted me in the woods in the first place. I'm fucking disgusting.

"You know there's water. It's cold, but the tank's still got something in it. Must be from that reservoir we passed. You should shower off before any of the others think to do it. You deserve it."

I hesitate. On the one hand, I don't want to move away from the window, in case I hear something out there hunting for us in the dark. On the other hand, I can barely stand the smell emanating from my body.

Pia takes another step into the room and closes the door behind her. My heart starts to beat harder, faster. What the fuck is she doing? What the fuck is she thinking? I suddenly feel the urge to run, but I'm a caged beast locked in here with no exits.

I move to the only other door in the room and fling it open. A bathroom. It's so damn neat and tidy and covered in a layer of dust so thick I wonder who the fuck used to live here and if anyone's even bothered trying to live here since the last folks moved out. I wonder where they are now if they didn't come back to this spot to claim it.

Hell, I might've claimed it if I were intent on breaking clear of Abel's gang and seeing the rest of this sad thing called life out.

But I'm too stupid for that.

My hands move to the button of my jeans and I can sense that Pia's still there, in the bedroom, watching me. "Last chance to lllllook away, P-Pia."

"Do you want me to?"

"D-d-d-don't fucking care."

"I never told you this, but you curse an awful lot. You could use other vocabulary."

Vocabulary? Fuck that. I drop my jeans and feel the disgusting crust of crap flake off around me. I step into the tub and flip on the water, grimacing as the pipes scream.

An icy, lackluster stream spills onto my chest first and I brace against the sensation as I take a dust-scented bar of soap from the wall mount and rub it angrily across my chest.

I'm just realizing this is the first time I've bathed properly with my new skin. The first time I've taken the time to actually touch it. Feel it.

Feels disgusting and is only made worse by the fact that Pia is watching.

My dick wants to come out to play at her attentiveness, but the discomfort of the icy spray plus the discomfort of touching my own flesh puts a stop to that right quick.

I bow my head under the water, letting my fingers touch the grooves carved across the back of my head. The water runs through them like rivers through canyons. Slick and smooth, around my fuzzy hair it makes no sense. I take the soap to that too.

"There's shampoo," she says to me. As if I cared. I look up and she's in the doorway, holding her stupid fucking candle.

Its light is the brightest thing in here, but she can still see enough of me in the faint light coming in from the windows if she wants to. And it looks like she wants to. I don't understand why when she said the things she said to me and used me in the way she used me. I'm just a thing to her, a means to an end, a mission. She said she liked me once, but I know that's a lie. But if that's a lie, then why is she watching me like that?

Her gaze is on my chest and when I look at her, it tips back up and holds.

She licks her lips. My cock responds, despite the conditions. And when she sets her candle down on the sink and starts to slip out of her clothes, I hold my breath.

"Pia," I bellow, half-growl, half-plea. "The fuck are you doing?"

She's got her jacket off and is pulling her shirt off over her head. She doesn't have a bra on under it. Her tits come into full view and they are fucking divine. Just as perfect as I remember them. The light from the candle casts a soft glow over her skin, making it look like she's stepping out of some world where only good things exist.

She freezes and I almost go blind. My jaw is slack, mouth dry with want. I want her to continue. Why the fuck did she stop? And then she has the balls to say to me, "What was going on with you and Constanzia?"

"Wh-what?"

Pia's arms cross over her chest, hiding it from me. "I... saw you two together. You don't talk to people...ever, but you talked to her right away. I kind of thought maybe you were into her."

"You sssss-sssseen the way I look? H-h-heard the way I t-t-talk?"

"Yes," she says, and her pitch carries absolutely no cadence. If anything, she sounds a little confused as to what the fuck I'm talking about.

I power off the water. I'm probably not anywhere near clean enough, but I'm done with this. Don't want to stand here and have this conversation with her.

Only I do.

I really do.

"I'm done. Not gonna lllllive out your lllllllittle...fucking fantasy of fu-fu-fu-fucking with the fffff-ffff-fffreak." Takes me a goddamn eternity to get that one out and my frustration level is through the goddamn roof. I want to hit her. Bite her. Take her for everything she's offering.

She blocks my path with her naked tits. If she doesn't move out of my goddamn way, it's gonna end in pain. Mine. Not hers. Never hers...

"That's not what I see."

She sounds so naive. So fucking stupid. "Then let-let-let me paint you a p-picture. I've rrrraped more w-w-w-women than I can-can count. I've k-k-killed at least ten times that nnnumber."

"That's not what I see," she says, but her voice has lost some of its conviction.

I latch onto that uncertainty and wring its bloody neck. "I hhhhurt people. That's all I'll ever b-b-be good for."

She inhales deep and a strange rage crosses her features. Her shoulders roll back. Her nostrils flare. "Then why haven't you hurt me? I *shot* you, and you said you would but you didn't."

"I sh-sh-should have," I snarl, slamming my hand into the wall behind her head and leaning down so that we're nearly lip-to-lip.

"Why did you hurt other people before? Rape them and kill them?"

I scoff and pull back, taking the towel from the pile she set on the bed and wrapping it around my hips. "Y-y-you d-d-don't need to know."

"So there *was* a reason." She's still here. Why is she still here?

"P-p-p-put your fffffucking shirt on."

Her lips twist, and I know she doesn't like it when I curse, which only makes me want to do it more. "If you don't want...*this* then that's fine. I'm not trying to force you. And the first time...I..." She chokes. I thought that was my line.

I can't help it, I look back at her. "Wwwwwhat?"

"I feel like I forced you, back there in the woods. I'm sorry."

She thinks *she* forced *me*? Oh, the irony. The sad fucking irony. "So you're make-making up ffffor it now?" I make a heavy sound, whole body weighted down by it. I must be tired. Need sleep. Even though I'm afraid of it. Jack lives there.

Pia tosses her arms out and sweeps one hand back through her hair. The strands fall back around her face, a few of them clinging to her chin and cheek, looking like slivers of silver. Don't like when she does that. Nope. Don't like it at all. My restraint is already threadbare and when she shows emotion like that, she looks fucking edible. She's *mine*. Why not take her? Who gives a fuck why she's offering?

"Why are you so determined to believe that I don't want you? Maybe I should paint *you* a picture. I had to run away from my brothers with my dad out of fear of what they'd do to us. On the way, we had to scavenge and fight and hunt, but when we got overtaken by a rolling community, they were good to us. And when they took you in, you took your injuries in stride and kept going. Kept fighting. Kept living.

"You breathe life."

Her hands come to cover her heart. She cups them, like I can see life right there in the palm of her hands. Then she lets them fall and she's half-naked again and I don't know what's more powerful — all of her words magnified, or that simple offering.

"Why wouldn't I want to be with a guy like that?" She steps back from me and heads towards the door, becoming less distinct. I can't have that. I want to see her clearly. I want to see everything.

"I got...overwhelmed in the woods. There was a lot going on and a lot of emotion to process. I used you in a sense to help myself get through it, and later, I treated you badly in front of my brothers, but I only did that to protect you. I'm sorry for it and if that's why you're rejecting me, then fine. But I don't want to hear any of this sh..."

She catches herself, licks her lips, takes a breath and repeats, "I don't want to hear any of this crap about your past or what you've done. We've all done horrible things. It's only the horrible who survive this world.

"I just want to know if you even...want this? I *like* you, Diego. I already told you that. I just don't want to throw myself at you if you don't like me or women or are into somebody else."

I just stare at her. This is the most she's ever said to me in one go and she's shirtless and she's basically asking me the same thing she asked me once before.

To fuck her.

I'd been sure of her then, but she'd confused me afterward and here she is attempting to offer an explanation. It's all so unclear and I'm not a cerebral kind of guy. I'm more tactile. I need something to grab hold of.

She pulls the tee shirt from the stack of clothes she brought for me and, turning, starts to put it on. She heads for the door and my feet are moving before I have a chance to stop them, faster, faster now, until she's pressed right up against the door, my body behind caging hers against it.

"That's mmmmine," I say against her hair. So damn soft. I tilt my face against it, let it whisper over my cheeks and nose.

Her outstretched hand, the one braced against the doorframe, tenses. "You told me to put a shirt on," she says, half in gasp.

"D-d-d-didn't say you could have mine." I pull the shirt slowly out from between her fingers and toss it behind me onto the bed.

I clench and flex my right hand, careful that she can't see the gesture. I don't need her to be afraid. Because I already am. I'm petrified.

I skim her stomach with my palm. I can feel how she clenches her abs and I'm shocked when she drops forward onto her elbow. She bows her head and her breath deepens. Is this a good reaction, or a bad reaction? I'm fucked that I don't know. But how could I? I've never seen it.

I wait for her to tell me to stop and when she doesn't, I count my way up her ribs, memorizing their shape as I trace them one by one. By the time the back of my hand skims the underside of her weighted breast, my cock is rock hard and poking at her ass through her jeans, wishing they were the black pants she had on before, but they aren't. She smells different. Clean.

The towel slips off of my hips and I let it, and when it slaps against the floor, she jumps at the sound it makes. I grab her tit and press myself further against her. I grab her hard.

In her ear, I whisper, "I don't know how to be-be gentle." I push her hair out of the way with my nose and lips, then bite down on the space where her shoulder meets her neck. I lick the bite marks, missing the way she tasted, like it's something I got used to even though I only sampled her once.

"And I d-d-don't d-d-do once." I reach my other hand around her to meet the first and take each of her breasts in my palms. I spend a long time just feeling them, trying to decide which one is more perfect than the other. They both are, is my conclusion.

Her voice is higher, more strained when she answers. But don't think I can't hear her hesitation. She's got to know what she's in for if we go through with this. If *she* goes through with this.

"You hardly know me. How can you be sure you'll want me more than once?"

I lean into her even more, moving my hands down now to the waist of her jeans. I find the button there and pop it open, then drag the zipper down.

"You remind me of someone," I say against her neck. I taste my way up and down her skin, taking her earlobe and sucking it between my teeth.

She releases a little gasp that has my left knee buckling. I spin her around and press her shoulders against the door with force, in an effort to distract her. She blinks up at me. She blinks a lot. She seems to be struggling to get her bearings. Like she's a little lost.

"An old flame?" Her lips turn down at the corners and I don't like it. I also don't understand it.

I shake my head and lower my mouth to the collar of her throat. "A wait-wait-waitress. I was ssssix."

"You were six and you wanted to fuck a waitress?"

"No. I wanted to ssssave her." I pull back and can't help the foreign expression that moves over my face, infecting my intensity and twisting it into something lighter, something sacrosanct. "And I th-th-thought you don't cu-cu-curse."

Her brown eyes blink and then she smiles at me, a little surprised. Does she know that this is my first joke?

Pia shoves my chest and I let her, backing up until the edge of the bed meets the backs of my knees. She pushes me again and I plop down onto it and watch Pia step back from me.

Confused as to what she's doing, it takes my mind a second to process when she reaches up to her hips and slowly — so goddamn slowly — lowers her jeans over her ass. My mouth goes dry. Dear heaven fuck. What did I do right to deserve this?

She doesn't have on any panties. Just a blonde bush and her willingness are my only barriers.

She watches my reaction and I wonder what she sees, because at first, she looks away, and when she looks back quickly, she grins and bites her bottom lip.

"Move back on the bed," she commands.

I don't do orders unless they're Jack's, but with her I do exactly as I'm told. She stalks towards me like a predator and I have to divert all my energy into keeping my shit together when she touches me. She places her perfect fucking palm on the mess of skin and scar tissue that is my right leg. I flinch and she grows less sure. She should be uncertain. She's on dangerous ground.

"I want to touch you," she says, voice a whisper. Her tits are near my face, but she's not offering that now. She wants to touch me.

I press myself up near the pillows, welding my back to the large wooden headboard. I grab onto it instead of grabbing onto her and nod, just once. That's the only confirmation from me she'll get.

I watch her hand, her pale fingers, stroke their way up my inner thigh in a way I don't like because it reminds me too much of something else. I grab her wrist as she reaches for my cock. She jolts, meets my gaze. I shake my head once.

Her eyes widen. "With my mouth?"

My cock wilts as Jack makes an unexpected reappearance. No. Fuck no.

How can he be here? I thought I killed him.

You know I'm never really dead.

I jerk as a tidal wave of memories punches down on my head, then buries me. There's no recovering from them. From him. From this. Fuck this. Fuck him. Fuck me. *I have, Diego, and I know that you can't have forgotten all of our special little moments.*

"Hey." Fingers touch my cheek.

They're soft and delicate — not rough and callused — as they trace the lines of my scars. I didn't have those scars back when Jack was around.

Death liberated me from him, but it took its pound of flesh. Nothing comes free in Population.

I blink to clear my eyes and when I look up, I see a face that isn't Jack's staring down at me. Her dark blonde eyebrows are drawn together, but even then and even with the harsh shadows the candlelight casts over her, she looks soft. Too soft for anything in Population to ever be.

I swallow hard and something shifts in her gaze. She takes my hand from the headboard — damn near pries it off of there — and places it on her right tit. She moves my thumb over her nipple and her breathing gets a little more frantic.

"Yes, Diego. Just like that. You can twist it…and you can touch me anywhere you want."

Anywhere I want. With permission.

I shake my head, confused but trying. The first time this all happened so fast, there was no time for thinking. This time everything is harder and I don't want it to be.

I grab Pia by the waist and by the back of the neck and drag her onto her stomach across my lap. I'm left staring at her perfect ass and while I like the shape of it, I don't like that I can't see her face. I never wanted to see their faces before, but I do now.

I roll her onto her back and push her halfway down the dusty, quilt-covered mattress, spreading her out like a feast. I hold her knees apart with my hands and stare up at her while she looks down the length of her body at me.

I wish it were light out so I could see. I want to see everything. I want to taste…I know it's probably a weird thing to do — I've never done it — but she said I could do anything I wanted and I'm about to test the limits of that offer. It's easier touching than being touched, for me. Being touched is too startling and vulnerable.

I grab her ankles and lower myself down into a crouch between her legs. "I want to ffff-fffeast," I groan against her calf and start to slowly work my mouth up her body, tasting every salty inch. Every sweet curve. She tastes like candy. A better meal than I deserve.

"Yes." Her eyelids get heavy. She's holding onto the blanket with one hand while the other massages her own tits. The sight of her touching herself stirs something deep in my gut and I find my cock reanimating.

Heat fires through me, igniting my bones. I lean in closer to her, closer, tasting my way up her inner thigh until I reach a haven of dark blonde curls. I run my fingers through them and she shudders. I like that. It seems like a good sign, but the fuck would I know? I've never done this before. I wonder if it shows. I feel like a goddamn idiot and for a moment, I'm uncertain whether or not I should keep going.

"Don't stop, Diego," she whispers, reading my mind, "keep going. Please." Her fingers touch the back of my head and the scar winding across it. And hot damn, the little firecracker starts to push me, urging me to come closer to her.

I pull up on the skin, revealing more of her to me. I won't fucking lie, I'm a little startled. I've never taken the time to look at all the bits and pieces before and there are more of them that I thought. Pink, glistening folds hide a core that looks way too damn narrow to stick a dick inside.

You never had that problem with the others.

"Diego?" Her voice brings me back, but strangles when I slide a finger through her wet center.

I wrench my hand back. "F-f-fuck. Did I hurt you?"

"What?" She asks, breathless. I hope not in pain. Please, don't let it be pain.

"Y-y-you h-h-hurt?" Hurting her already would crucify me.

"No," she says, and her laughter pulls the nails out of my hands. "For someone who claims not to know how to be gentle, you're not doing so bad at it." I know she's mocking me and that I should kill her for it, but how can I with her hands stroking my head so gentle like that?

I huff, "Don't know what I'm lllll-llll…" I inhale, exhale against her wet heat and I don't know that I've ever minded taking a break before finishing my sentence so much, "Looking at."

"You've never…" she starts, then she seems to remember the shit I told her. I see her swallow, the little muscles working in her thin neck. She having doubts yet? "What you're doing now feels amazing. You could…try with your mouth."

With my mouth? The thought brings heat to my stomach that makes my dick press hard into the mattress underneath me — and it's not just the thought of doing that to her, it's the thought that she's *asking* me to.

I firm, feeling resolve slide through my bones. I'm back in the forest where everything was easier. Where Jack tried to speak to me and I told him no.

Without warning, I lick a long line up through her wet folds, tasting her everywhere, all the way down to her asshole and back up again to her full pink lips.

"Oh…oh god. Yes, Diego. I…I'll orgasm if you move up a little higher to my clit."

Orgasm? I don't even really understand what she means. I just remember what happened before when she shook and shivered and I came all over her. If I can get that reaction from her again, I'll die a happy man.

Nah. I'll die a man. Period.

She starts to move her hand down her body to show me, but I don't want her to stop touching me yet. And I also don't want her to show me. I want to find it for myself.

I spear her heat with my tongue and her head falls back. She releases her weight onto the mattress and continues to trace little patterns across my scalp.

I like the way she tastes. It's not a taste I can describe in food terms, but in feelings. Licking her insides makes me feel like a different person. The kind of person worth trusting. She trusts me.

It hits me like a brick.

She trusts me to let me do this to her. Otherwise, how could she? Here she is splayed open before me, completely at my mercy to do whatever I want with. It makes me want to be a person worth trusting. It makes me want to hold her trust like a precious little egg and never break it.

A moan bubbles out of me before I slant my mouth over her pussy, kissing it like it's gonna kiss me back.

"Oh my go…sh, Diego," she stutters, "I've never…oh flip…oh…shoot…a little…higher…please…"

"Shh," I snap back, "You'll g-g-get wh-wh-wh-what I g-g-g-ive you." But I still move higher, following the movement of her twisting, arching body.

There's a bit of folded skin at the top of her core, above the opening that's so hot and tight and weeping. I spread her folds apart with my thumbs and her whole body tenses.

There's a little glistening nub of a thing nestled there, like some rare and precious gem. I can feel the tension threading through her and decide that this must be her clit. It looks so fragile. Very carefully, I lick it.

"Augh," the mangled sound comes out of her throat. Her back arches up off of the mattress. I have to hold her hips down now with some force.

"Th-th-this your clit?" I whisper against that hot, pink skin.

She nods feverishly and when she looks down at me, her eyes are completely glazed. She looks confused for a moment, then she nods and smiles just a little with one corner of her mouth.

"You have no idea how good that feels."

I hold her gaze while I taste her a second time. She struggles to maintain the connection, and when I suck that little nub into my mouth, she loses it.

Thrashing, pulling, pushing. I don't let her go. I lick and suck and am shocked when I feel a surge of wetness against my chin.

I pull back enough to look down at her pussy and for a moment, I panic. What is all the wetness coming from? Did she piss on me? Doesn't smell like piss. Doesn't smell like anything. And it's thick and viscous. I slide one finger through it, then inch it further inside of her.

"Oh…oh! Diego, yes. Please. Please…Do you feel how wet I am for you?"

Wet for me? This wetness is for me?

"More…" she breathes. "Please." She's begging me. I'm used to hearing people beg me for things, but it's usually for their lives, or not to do whatever it is I'm about to do to them. Not this. Never like this.

The trembling walls around my heart shudder apart as I bury my face between her thighs. I suckle her little clit and pump first one, then a second finger in and out of her wetness. *My* wetness. It's mine.

Then those walls come down, leaving that blackened pumping organ so exposed. Her thighs clench around my ears in a parody of a wrestling hold. I fight against it, hold her down, pinning her, and when shudders wrack her body and she starts to mewl and whimper and bite back high-pitched screams, I press even harder.

"Diego...oh please..." She bites down on her own wrist and a sudden violent spasm twists her legs. She bucks and then all at once, releases.

"Oh my god," she says on a laugh. She tries to get away from me, but I hold her and keep licking while a fresh surge of wetness coats the bottom half of my face. I bathe in it.

"Oh Diego, please," she says, pitching her voice as a whisper. I don't know what good that'll do. Everyone in the house already heard her. And *I* did that. As I relax my hold on her just a little bit, I can't help the grin that spreads across my twisted lips. The pleasure...it's everything in this moment.

"It's so sensitive, please, you have to stop."

But I don't want to. I keep going, licking and biting and sucking until I wring two more orgasms out of her. By the time I'm finished, she's a slack, disheveled mess on the bed. So easy to move. Pliable. I drag her towards me and she struggles to sit up. I hold her down and shake my head.

"What?" She says.

"You d-d-d-don't nnnneed to d-d-do..."

"I want you, Diego." Her gaze sweeps my body, settling on my cock. "But we don't have to do anything *you* don't want."

But what if I don't know what I want? I mean, I want her. I *want* her. My cock is singing about it at the top of his goddamn lungs. I reach down and grab it, wrangling it like a snake, while precum beats at the slitted tip.

She licks her lips while looking at it and I just wish...I wish so fucking badly I could just let her...but I'm...scared. It reminds me of him too much. And I don't want him to be here right now. I want him gone, forever. Cut out of my memories like infection from a wound.

And if I loom over her and plunge into her heat, how can I do that without thinking of all the women who came before her, the ones who damned me and cursed me? They had every right to for what I did to them. Things I can't undo and can't unsee and can't unfeel. I deserve to have the skin skinned right off of me.

Like Jack did once already.

"Diego, are you with me?" She says.

I meet her gaze, unsure.

Just as uncertainly, she edges forward, coming towards me until I'm sitting up and leaning back with my legs out in front of me with her palms on my shoulders. She sits up too, straddles my legs with her legs and lowers herself down on my lap.

I don't move. I don't dare move. Not with her wet, wet pussy pressing against my cock, just like it was before, only this time, there's no material separating us. Every bone in my body locks together and every muscle steels and twists until I'm one screaming knot of tension.

"What if I'm on top?" She says breaking the sound our mingled breaths create, like water on a rocky shore.

What if she's on top?

No memories, no sounds of resistance come to me. If I wasn't holding my breath before, I am now. The look of relief that crosses her expression throws me.

She really does want me, want this…I want to ask her why, how, what the fuck is going on, but I don't want any of the answers. I just want this, right now. Just once, I want it to be perfect and good.

And then I want it again forever.

Her skin feels damp and hot in my hands. Her rock hard nipples are at my eye level as she lifts herself up once again and then takes my cock in her fingers. I close my eyes, hating the memories, hating their bloody origins, but I breathe through my nose and force myself to keep breathing.

Her scent isn't like his. Her scent is her own. Rich and fragrant, like the earth, like stones. She's grounding me even as she lifts me up to a place of transcendence...and comes down slowly. So slowly time unravels like a string, and wraps around my neck. It tightens...and tightens.

And then I feel it, the pressure of her pussy's entrance on the head of my cock, and then the shaft, swallowing it up. I have to see.

My gaze snaps to the connection of our bodies and a crude groan bellows out of my mouth. She huffs out a little laugh, one so light it's almost like she was trying to contain it.

"You l-l-llllaughing at me?"

She sucks in a breath as she lowers herself down a little further. "Only a little." And then she seats herself entirely. We moan, just like we're joined together — as one.

Oh Jesus heaven fuckballs. I swear my eyes roll back into my skull and I hallucinate lifetimes passing. When I come down, she's still sitting where she was looking at me with surprise painted across her pretty face. She smiles and I smile back with my tortured mouth, even though it feels weird and alien.

I want to ask her what happens next — I've never been in this position before — but before I get the mutilated words out, she starts to move. Her hips spin dizzying shapes and her core clenches tight around my cock managing to be even *tighter* than it looked as she dances to a beat I don't know, but am beginning to.

I start to move myself before I ask her if I should, and when her voice hitches in that way that it did before when I was eating her out, I know I'm onto something. I hope.

Sitting, I manage to piston my hips up in time with her movement until soon it feels like we're joined in a ritual we've done a thousand times before, in other lifetimes. She says I don't know her, but I know her enough for this.

"Diego, I'm going to…"

"Yeah," I bark out.

I been there. Been here, riding on the curve of that wave for the past however many minutes we've been locked together. I was about to come before I entered her. How I'm still here, holding out is a mystery. Maybe because I'm doing it for her. Because I want it to be good, even though I don't understand the definition.

And then I'm moving before I can think, rolling over so that I'm on top of her and she's underneath me. A moan escapes her and I fight through eclipse of memories that linger there. No, I don't fight, I cut through them. She cuts through me. Her gaze is hooked on mine and refuses to let go. Brown. Dark brown. In this light, they're black. Don't know how eyes so dark can be so expressive or so cruel. Because this is a torture. She's cleaving into me, body and soul.

I heave out a breath and shake my head as my hips slap against hers in the quiet, lonely dark. "C-c-c-can't hold…"

"Me either," she breathes, reading my thoughts. "Don't forget to pull out."

Pull out? What the fuck's she talking about?

"Don't want to get…get pregnant…" Pregnant. Shit. I didn't even think of it. Because every woman I've been with before her died right after. I clench my eyes shut, hips suddenly breaking rhythm. I feel fingers on my face. Small, softer fingers. Not hard, damaged ones.

"Diego, stay with me," she says, she commands, she pleads.

I open my eyes and dive into the deep, and then I feel it. Holy fucking god. Maybe He is real after all. Because nothing made in nature should feel like this. What possible reason could there be for the sudden violent clenching of her walls around my shaft as she milks me for everything I'm worth? How am I supposed to survive this? Do I even deserve to?

Probably not, but I'm here all the same. I was a fucking idiot to think that she was the vulnerable one in this.

"Diego," she whispers, biting back a louder cry. Red flares in her cheeks.

I manage to pull my hips back just in time for a river of cum to explode out of me and onto her pussy. I can't see for a second, can't move. Everything freezes. I don't think I've come so hard before. Orgasmed. That's the word she used. I'm definitely sure I haven't done that before. All those other times were so quick, so desperate, so depressing. Her or me. Her or me. There was no us. No together. No this.

I hang my head over Pia's shoulder, burying it in the bedding. I focus on the scent of her hair and her sweat, instead of the mildew. I try to calm the pounding of my heart, because it's got only a little to do with my orgasm at this stage, and mostly to do with the strange, shattered world I thought I knew as well as the scars swimming across the back of my hand.

Turns out, I know nothing.

It's not supposed to be like this.

I let my hips sink into the cradle of her hips. The stickiness between us slides like oil. Pia is breathing hard, her chest rising and falling beneath the cage of mine. I comb my fingers through her hair, trace the softness at her hairline.

"For someone who says they don't do gentle, you do gentle like a damn professional." Her fingers cup my shoulders and smooth down my back. She smiles. She's always smiling.

I lean in and kiss her mouth. I wonder if she can taste herself on me.

"For sssssssomeone who s-s-s-says they don't cuss, you cuss like a damn pro-pro-professional."

She laughs hard and from the chest. I can feel it and it has its own life force. I don't want to let it go, not even as she pats my ribs and tells me I'm crushing her to death. I roll off her and pull her into me. She tells me she's cold, so I somehow maneuver her and myself under the blanket without breaking contact between her ass and my dick. It's almost fully hard again by the time we settle, her body cocooned in mine, where it should always be. Where she'll be safest.

"G-g-gonna ffffuck you again," I tell her, lining my cock up with the heat between her legs, finding where it's wettest. Then I remember — permission. It feels just as good as that climactic finale. Maybe, even better.

Pia exhales, voice light as a sigh as her ass shimmies further back into my cock, "I thought you'd never ask."

Chapter Thirteen

I wake up disoriented and confused.

"Diego," comes the whisper, "It's dawn. I think we should keep moving."

Keep moving. Where am I? Who is we?

I crack my eyes open, careful not to give any indication that I'm awake as I take in this fresh world and prepare to kill my aggressor, then make my escape.

"Diego?"

Shit. Whoever it is, is right here. Right on me now. Close enough to kill me if I don't kill them first. My left hand snakes out to snatch whatever it can. A throat, if I'm lucky. A tight scream is followed by the light flapping of fingers on my shoulder. She swats me.

My eyes open and I'm greeted by the sight of a woman's face. She's got blonde hair and brown eyes and pink lips that pucker when she scowls. My hand is on her shoulder, my thumb just above her clavicle. There's a mark there and the funny thing is that I can remember making it because I sucked on her neck when I was fucking her and when she was fucking me. Willingly. And now we're in the bed together.

The God is real.

I let go of her immediately and watch as color rolls from her cheeks down her neck. She looks unsure. "Did you not expect me to sleep in the bed with you after?"

After. Holy hell. She let me enter her willingly and now she's talking about an after. There's never been an after before. A sudden surge of fire and lust shoots up the backs of my thighs. I think she mentioned something about getting on the road, but there's time for moving and there's some things worth waiting for. Dying for, if I have to.

I roll on top of her body and she lets out another chirp when I press her down into the mattress. "What are you…"

I bite down onto that spot on her neck that's already got my signature on it while my hands spread her legs apart and tilt her hips up.

"Can-can I?" I say — my last hesitation.

The confusion and momentary flicker of fear on Pia's face morphs into something else quickly — a smile. "We should really get moving…"

"That a nnno?"

"No." Blonde hair sticks to her cheek. Very carefully, I slide one finger around her hairline, pulling them free so I can see every inch of her perfect face in the morning light. She's even more beautiful than she is in my dreams.

"That a yes?"

Pia smiles. "Yes, but we really should…"

I slide home in one clean movement and she screams, "Diego!"

I hold for just a second — but only the one — while sweat breaks out on my hairline and heat rips down my sternum.

The heart room is gone. Jack is silenced. The sins are still here, but they're fading and that's all I could ever hope for. I look down at her face and feel emotion well up in me so strong, it pulses with its own pain.

"Wwwwe've got time," I say.

Two hours later and we're on the road. At least I think it's about two hours, judging by the light. It's stronger than it should be, but that's my fault and I feel nothing but satisfaction because of it.

The grey rumbles and roils overhead, like an ocean storm, but beneath it, the people around me are all chattering like nothing's amiss. Like this is all just normal. People are laughing, some kids are running around in circles, playing some game I've been trying to figure out for the past half an hour but can't.

Pia's in the back of the group talking to her dad, propped up by another man who isn't Matt, while I lead the charge through the grasses — the *tall* grasses. The farmhouse was surrounded by trampled grass, so it wasn't so noticeable, but out here, in the thick of the farmlands where there aren't any houses near us, the grasses have gotten taller, stalks standing as high as my goddamn chest.

The kids are running around blind, no concern at all for what might be living in this shit. I'm using my bone spear to measure out my next steps, careful to stab hard in case anything's lying in wait, ready to spring.

"You angry about something or are you always like this?" Comes a voice to my right. It's Mo. Not a shock. The others all still look at me like I'm either The God or his cosmic counterpart.

I shrug and glance over my shoulder *again*, making Mo laugh, "Yeah, you should be happier. We could all hear how happy you were last night. I'm sure Luke was just thrilled."

"H-h-h-he's pissed at her b-b-b-because of me?" I glance back again and this time Luke notices and Luke meets my glare. Don't like her being in trouble. Don't like it at all.

I start to slow, but Mo grabs my arm and pushes me forward, forcing me to keep pace. "Doubt *pissed* is the right word. I just don't imagine a father likes hearing his daughter get some is all. But Pia's a grown woman. She makes her own choices."

A sudden thought creeps over me and I scan the crowd of people we're with. "She-she-she make a lot of her own choices?"

Mo laughs. He tries to cover his mouth with his hand and nearly chokes on his own tongue. I elbow him in the gut and, when he collapses forward, loop an arm around his shoulder to disguise the way he crumples and together, we keep walking side-by-side.

Mo curses a few times in between rattling breaths. "You're a psychopath."

"Yeah."

"So I'm not answering that question."

I squeeze his shoulders a little harder. "She mmmmake other choices with the mmmmen *here*?"

"No. Not that it's any of your business what she did before you." Mo shrugs me off, finally finding his breath and his footing. He rolls out his arms and looks over his shoulder, waving dismissively at someone.

I'd bet my left nut that it's Matt, all concerned. Don't have to look, just know it like I know that that woman's still cooing softly to her little bag of mush. It's called love, not that I'd know anything about it.

"So get your jealousy under control," he huffs. "That's how dating works."

Dating? I don't know dating. I know possession, ownership, claim. I know throwing my knife in the dirt for someone and if I win, taking them until Jack said I was finished. But Jack isn't here. I frown. If Jack isn't here, and I never threw my dagger in the ground, then what hold do I really have over her? I told her I wouldn't force her...I told myself I wouldn't.

"How are you feeling, by the way?"

Feeling? I glare over at Mo, wondering how the air can be so hot and cold at the same time. We're all sweating out here in all our layers, yet the wind that passes feels like fall and tastes like an enduring winter.

"Fffff-fffine."

"You were shot — a couple of times. How can you be feeling fine?"

"I've got Mmmmikey's blood in me."

"Not enough to cure Luke, at least not fully. Can't be doing you many favors, can it?"

I shrug and roll my right shoulder back in the socket. It stings a little bit, and not all the bullet holes where Matt was rooting around in my body have completely healed over. They've closed, but the scabs are still there. All last night and this morning, I could feel them pulling.

Worth it.

I glance back again and see Pia still locked in debate. Can't hear the words from here, but I don't like how her face is all blotchy and red, or the aggressive way he stares her down. Don't give a shit that he's her dad and she's his daughter.

"Wwwounds are fine. L-l-lead them," I order.

"Lead them? Why? Where are you going? Diego," he says as I stop and turn and the crowd parts before me. "It's family business."

Too bad I don't know what that word means either.

The people around me start to slow and whisper, looking nervous when I turn back, but Mo urges them to keep going.

"He's just having a fit of lunacy. Don't mind him."

I stomp over the grasses, hear them crunch beneath my feet in a way that's oddly satisfying, before I get to Pia and her dad. They both quiet when I approach and, falling in line with Pia, I feel a little stupid, not sure what to say now that I've arrived with a mouthful of complaints and insults.

Luke grimaces. "Pia, leave me and Diego alone for a minute, would ya?"

"Dad, I'm not going to…"

"I wasn't asking, sweetheart." I don't like the way he looks at her, don't like the way he talks to her, don't like the way he orders her around. She's *mine*. I feel my fists clench.

And then she says, "You are so annoying." She turns to me and huffs, "Sorry about this. He's being ornery and dumb. I'd blame it on his being a dad, but I really think he was born this way." But she doesn't look…mad.

She was talking to him like she was furious, but now that her back is to him, I can see her smiling just a little. I don't understand this.

Maybe it would help if I had a father or understood the thing called family but all I ever had was Jack, and all I ever wanted was to kill him.

"Are you okay if I go up with Mo for a little bit and let him do his whole macho-dad-what-are-your-intentions-with-my-daughter-routine? Even though I *thought* we already did this once." She says that last part loudly over her shoulder and rolls her eyes, cheeks flaring pink.

"I can hear you, Pia," her father grumbles at her back.

"I'm well aware. That okay, Diego?" She blinks and places her hand on my arm and I can deny her nothing. I find myself nodding, even though I don't know what was agreed on.

"I'll see you up front when you're finished then." She starts towards Mo at the front of the crowd, but doesn't make it far, choosing instead to stop and talk to every single person she passes like she knows them. Like she cares for each and every one.

It's weird. Probably going to get her killed if I let it, but I won't.

"Diego," comes a heavy drawl, stained in a southern accent that's thicker than Pia's. I look at his face and up close, I see that he looks bad. Real bad. The guy next to him is holding most of his weight and I feel rage fire into my bones.

Doesn't matter what he was about to say, because I fire off first, "Y-y-you c-c-can't f-f-f-ffffucking walk."

His bushy eyebrows come together over his hook nose and he takes another awkward, cantering step forward. "Can walk just fine. And we're not here to talk about me, we're here to talk about you and Pia."

I ignore him and scan the horizon, looking for a warehouse to raid. Some place likely to have a wheelbarrow. On the other side of the road, there's a farmhouse set about fifty yards back. Not ideal, but it's better than letting him walk himself to death. Especially after I gave him Other blood from my own damn vein and could have saved myself the trouble if he's just gonna die anyway.

I growl, "Llllater."

I move away from him, jogging back to Mo and Pia standing beside him. "What is it?" She says the instance she sees me. "What's wrong?"

I shake my head as they both come to a stop and start scanning the road frantically. "N-n-nothing. Nnnneed to raid that farm for a minute. Keep going. I'll c-c-c-catch up."

"Raid that farm?" Mo shakes his head, running his hand back through his inky black hair. He stares at me like I've grown two heads, maybe an even more scarred one. "What for?"

"Wheelbarrow."

"He's being dramatic!" Comes the shout from the back of the crowd. Several people turn around and shush him, which makes my mouth twitch, though it never quite realizes the smile that comes so easily for Pia.

Pia looks between me, the distant farmhouse and her father. "You think he's slowing us down?"

I debate lying, but don't. I nod.

"What will the farm have to fix that? We didn't find any useful medical supplies at the last place, short of baby aspirin. He's already almost finished the bottle."

"Wheelbarrow." Or a wagon. A car would be ideal — how about an RV with a functioning generator big enough for twenty? — but I'd bet my right nutsack that a wheelbarrow'll be the best we can find.

"That makes sense," Mo answers before Pia can. "I'll go with you."

"No. Stay-stay here with the others. Keep them mmmmoving."

Mo hesitates, then nods. He relays orders to the rest of the group while I veer away from them, towards the road. It doesn't take me long to realize I'm being followed.

"Pia," I growl, "g-g-g-go back."

I turn and she's looking at me remorselessly, both hands on her hips. "Cute, but no. You're getting supplies for my father. I'm coming with you."

"No."

"No?"

And then from ten paces behind her, comes her father's low drawl, "You sure you even want one that stubborn, son?" His voice is disparaging cackle. It makes me smile to think that we might be sharing a joke.

"G-g-got you-you to thank for that, don't I?" I call back, joking in return and only for the second time in my life.

Pia gives me a glare that looks about as threatening as a cornered rabbit, but before she can respond, I grab her wrist and reel her into me. "St-stay cl-close. D-d-do what I ssssay."

"I'll stay close, Diego, but we'll have to see about that last part. Now if you don't mind, you can follow me." And before I can stop her, she turns from me and leads the way to the street, then across it.

This farmhouse is in way worse shape than the last one, and despite the fact that any stop is worth raiding, this one's got a feel about it that's all wrong. I hesitate to go inside. Pia must feel the same way because she's the one to suggest we go around back.

The shed isn't locked and when we open her up, I see why. It's been ransacked, the walls stripped bare. But in the very back of the maelstrom, there she is, one perfectly busted up wheelbarrow. And she's got no wheels.

I laugh as I spin the empty husk of a wheel around on its metal rail. Pia has her hand on her chin and her face all scrunched up, like if she just squints hard enough, the wheelbarrow'll repair itself.

"What if we just…"

"No. T-t-too heavy to drag."

She exhales deeply, shoulders slumping forward just a little bit. "Ugh. Sorry. This was a total waste of time."

She kicks a rock out of the shed's only opening while I step up behind her. Alone, even as we are now, there's only one thought in my mind. I wrap my arms around her and inhale deeply along the column of her throat, kissing the spot where I marked her earlier, tasting the chain of her cross pendant.

"Is he r-r-real?" I ask her.

"Who?"

I touch the cross with my free hand. In my other, I carry a saw she hasn't noticed yet. "Oh. You mean God?"

I nod.

She says, "Of course he's real."

"Wh-wh-why of course?"

"Because he gives us these small moments."

I inhale a little deeper, wondering if she knows how precious these small moments are to me. "But what about the b-b-bad ones?"

She exhales as my free hand slides down to cup her breast. I can feel her nipple through her tee shirt underneath her coat and wish we had more time to linger here.

"Without the bad, this wouldn't feel so good." She reaches down to touch my hands — both of them. "What is…"

I grunt, feeling the small moment shake apart, and smile. "Not a wheelb-b-b-barrow, but it's something."

I hand her the saw and she laughs. "What is this? In case I need to make any quick home repairs at the next place we crash in?"

That surprises me. Reaching around her body, I reposition her hands so that one is on the saw's red rubber handle while the other one grips the blunt side just shy of the tip.

"Ssssaws make for good w-w-w-weapons. A little unwieldy, but use-use-useful." I take her hands and, with a sharp slicing motion, show her how to swing a saw for maximum damage. "D-d-don't need two hands, but it helps stabilize you. Always aim for the f-f-f-f-f-ffffface and neck."

"God, you're a psycho." She turns in my arms and smiles up at me, like that's the best compliment in the world. Maybe it is.

I smirk and comb her hair back behind her ear. I search her gaze for a truth I'm not sure I want. But I ask her anyway. "Hhhhhow d-d-does this not b-b-bother you? And my v-v-v-voice?"

She leans back, letting me take her weight — and the saw. Her eyes drink me in. I can't imagine what she sees because she isn't looking at me like I'm a monster, and she isn't looking at me with pity.

"In the World Before, from what I remember of it, you'd have gotten stares." Ice spears my gut, then spreads. But her words are contradicted by the gentle way she combs her fingers over my hair.

"But I don't think you realize that this world we live in now is completely different from the one that ended all those years ago. Diego," she says with a laugh, one that melts the ice and turns it to the most blinding sun, "You are fine as hell. And it's *because* of the way you look. Do you think I'm the only woman in Abel's whole little convoy that wanted you?"

I think about Constanzia and what she said, only this feels different. Constanzia is like me — she's a taker — but Pia is someone who gives. If Constanzia and I had ever done anything, it would have been Constanzia taking. But every second I'm with Pia feels like a gift.

Pia says softly, "I feel like I shouldn't even be telling you this, but the kind of damage you've been through proves that you're a violent man capable of surviving anything. What woman nowadays, in this violent world, wouldn't want a man like that behind her?

"I do." She smiles and leans up and plants a kiss on the corner of my mouth. The fucked up side.

"So you llllllike me b-b-b-b-because I can keep you alive?"

The red in her cheek rises again. She casts her gaze aside. "I'm attracted to you because of the way you're built, yeah. But I don't know if that's why I like you. I..." She hesitates, smiles, gets even redder. "I liked you first because of your voice. I remember the first time I heard you talk, you were... ashamed of it? It was just such a weird thing for me to see. On the outside you're a hardened warrior, and on the inside, you seemed so frightened. You hid away and it made me want to draw you out.

"And then as time went on, I started to notice..." She looks away again, fingers skipping over my shoulders and lightly touching my chest. Meanwhile, my hands are rock hard, curled in the fabric at the back of her jacket.

I've got the saw in hand, so close to her now, it'd be so easy just to slid the teeth across her throat and get her to stop saying such terrible, pretty things. Things that make me run towards a pit of emotion that I won't be able to claw my way out of. A chasm that, once I reach the bottom, will mean she owns me in a way Jack wanted to own me, but never could.

But I don't slit her throat. Instead, I nudge her gently and whisper, "What?"

"I started to notice that you were going out of your way to do kind things for people. Beyond just saving Abel's life when she was attacked, and beyond helping Mo and Matt and Cleo. You were constantly doing small things for me and even for my father. Just like this." She cocks her head towards the defunct wheelbarrow.

"And I'm sorry. I feel so stupid that I didn't tell you before about my brothers. We traveled with you for weeks but we thought we could outrun them."

I nod, knowing from what her father explained. "It's o-okay."

She exhales, breathing out an exhaustion that's just as deep as that chasm I've already fallen into. "You forgive me?"

"N-nothing to forgive."

"And for shooting you?"

My mouth quirks. "D-deserved it."

"You didn't. You were just trying to keep me safe."

I shrug. "Easy."

"Keeping me safe is easy? It should be. I'm not helpless, you know."

I grunt out a laugh. "G-g-getting shot is easy." I wish keeping her safe could be as easy as that. She's not helpless, but she's still exposed and she will be until I can find a way to build a fortress around her.

"Well, I don't want you to get shot again, okay?" Worry. It's hers and it's for me.

I nod as a lump fills my throat and I bow my head, pressing my forehead to hers. She's so warm. Flawed, but good. "D-d-d-do we have time?" I start to press her back onto the workbench behind her and she flails, reaching out to catch herself on my chest.

I cup her core through her jeans and breathlessly, she says, "Diego, we're going to lose the others!" But I feel her body grow slack already in my grip.

I cup my hand around the back of her neck and draw her in so I can press my lips to her lips. I taste her, tongue tangling with hers, trying to remember what in god's goddamn name I was thinking back on the truck when I first saw her.

Why didn't I ravage her then? Why didn't I tear down my heart box, rip out the organ and throw it on the ground at her feet? Why aren't I begging her for mercy? This woman could do whatever she wanted with me.

And I'm going to do whatever I want with her.

I growl into her neck and my hands go to the collar of her shirt, prepared to tear the damn thing off her when the sound of an explosion ruins everything.

I rip away from her, push her to the ground and drop beside her. I wait. In the quiet, I hear screams. My gaze flicks to Pia's and we share the same thought. The horror on her face makes that clear.

She starts to move forward, but I hold her back for one moment more, checking her over for weapons. She's got the Beretta in the back of her pants, but other than that, she's barehanded.

She doesn't want the saw, so I take that and, finding a carabiner on one of the workbenches, attach it to the rudimentary sling I've got looped over my neck and one shoulder, letting it clatter beside the bone spear. I scour the rest of the space, finding a crowbar. That I hand to Pia.

There's a pickaxe and spade, so I take both of those too, shoving both in Pia's backpockets. She gives me a surprised look when I do.

"Stay-stay-stay behind me. D-d-d-d-d-do..." I stammer. Can't get the fucking words out when they matter. Pia said I looked like a scared boy? Well, fuck her. She ain't seen nothing. Because the thought of riding out into battle is nothing new, but the thought of doing it with her on my six makes me sweat bullets and shit bricks.

"D-d-don't be a fffffucking hero."

She frowns at me and opens her mouth, but I don't want to hear it. I grab her arm and jerk her behind me as I make my way carefully out of the shed. There's smoke rising in the distance, about where our group should have been — where they *are*. Because that's me, alright, the goddamn optimist.

I head towards it, cutting straight ahead first instead of taking it at a diagonal. Whoever attacked did so from the road, which means they can't be ordinary scavengers.

Scavengers don't, as a rule, carry explosives, and scavengers don't ever travel by road. It's far too dangerous. Which means it's either a rogue gang, or it's Pia's brood, specifically hunting us. Pia and I hunker down and crawl through the grasses until we're a stone's throw from the road. From our new vantage, I can see boots and tires.

I'm still mulling this over, trying to count numbers and bodies, when I feel a tug on the back of my sweatshirt. I glance back at Pia and softly, she says, "I just saw Kenny and Leondra, but they're with another group. A bunch of men I don't recognize. They look mean, though, and they're well armed. We had a couple trucks, but these look like they're in better condition."

Uncertainty pulls through my stomach like a rope. I hold up a hand, telling Pia to stay fucking put while I edge a few feet closer, and then a few more feet. And as I crawl, my uncertainty turns to unease, which then becomes dread. Because when I catch sight of the twenty-odd men and women gathered around three pickup trucks, I recognize some of them. More than some of them.

And not from the caves.

Laughter threatens to bubble up my throat and Pia gives me a look she used to give me all the time, back before we ran through the woods together, back when I was still a corpse being dragged along by Abel's lifeline. I crawl back to her, brush her hair behind her ear and lower my lips to her feather-soft earlobe.

"Your brothers got p-p-p-partners?"

She shakes her head. "I mean, not that I know of. But I don't think they were chasing Abel's convoy alone. I heard Rico mention needing to wait for some others to get back. I assumed he was talking about the survivors from our community, but it's clear to me now that he was perfectly fine with abandoning them."

"Ssssacrificing them."

Pia winces, then nods, her blonde hair tangling with the dry grasses beneath her, blending into them. Makes me relieved. I want her to blend in as much as possible so that when I leave her and go out there to slaughter the men I recognize from another lifetime, they won't ever know she's here.

And they won't be able to tell him about her.

Maybe he's out there now.

Maybe this is it. The moment where I die if I somehow don't manage to kill him.

"Do you think they're dangerous?"

I grin at her murderously and restrain myself from smacking her in the skull.

She must see something in my expression, because she edges back just a hair and rasps, "Are these…no. This is *your* gang?"

My gang? Fuck her for even thinking it. "J-J-Jack's. I g-g-g-got out, or d-d-d-d-did you ffforget what I looked like when we-we first mmmmet?" I sweep my fingers from my left temple, to my right jaw, following the line of the scar Jack decorated me with. I feel nausea roil through me at the thought of our reunion.

Pia swallows. "I didn't mean…"

"D-d-don't care what you ffffucking meant. If it's Jack, you should already be dead. Jack trades three-three times — just enough to llllearn, then he k-k-kills everyone. Wh-wh-why would he s-s-still be working with your b-b-brothers?"

She chews on her bottom lip for a momentary consideration, then jerks. "I don't know."

But I do. Watching her bottom lip and the red way it glows reminds me of a time Jack was sitting around a fire, trading jokes and liquor with the leader from another community.

It was our third time trading and the guy'd been confident because they outnumbered us two to one. Jack convinced the fuck to go raiding together and only after a successful raid of a gang bigger than both did Jack, sitting there at the fire, slit the leader's throat.

It was a bloodbath after that, but we came out on top because Jack used the leader and his community for its *numbers*. He let the gang cut them down, then lopped their head off and gave what few male survivors there were the choice to die or join us. We grew our numbers, we got all the goods, and Jack only had to do half the work.

"Nnnumbers. Jack nnneeded your numbers to attack the convoy."

Pia's face blanches. "That's why he sent so many? But what was the point? They were so badly armed."

I shake my head, my gut tightening. The nausea's getting worse. "I d-d-don't know." And that can't mean anything good.

Jack's smart. Too smart to make moves that don't make sense. What's he after? What game is he playing at? And more importantly, where is he?

"Is he here? Jack?" She asks in a very small, tight voice and I fucking hate hearing his name in her voice. "From here, I can't see many faces. Just the two."

I don't know. But I'm not taking that chance with Pia. "Sssstay here."

"No way. You can't take them all out on your own."

I want to hit her. I want to slit her throat. Let her bleed out here. Because that's a better end than what will happen if Jack is here and Jack gets ahold of her. He'll recognize her as my weakness, and he'll do unimaginable things to her just to create new agonies, specifically for me.

He loves me just that much.

He hates me just that much.

I don't know how to tell her all this, not when our time is so tight. Not when people could be dying — the ones I promised her I'd protect. I grab the back of her head so hard pain flashes across her face. With my other hand, I grab her neck.

I speak an inch away from the tip of her nose and I mimic the tone that I've heard Jack use on his insubordinate men. "If you so much as mmmm-mmmm…" I bite down through the pain of air jerking out of my lungs. "Make a p-p-p-peep, I will hhhhhunt you d-d-down myself and ffffuck you b-b-bloody. Don't fucking mmmmove."

I shove her against the ground and steal the weapons from her back pockets, leaving her only with her Beretta. I ignore the welling of water in her eyes or the bright red color in her cheeks. That shit's got no place here.

I turn from her, and I start to hunt.

They're dragging bodies out of the tall grasses and onto the road and loading them into trucks. Or trying to. Some folks are putting up a fight. Mo, mostly. Matt is trying to *reason* with the unreasonable fucks. Damn him. Or rather, bless his soft, stupid heart.

Recognizing some of their faces, I have a momentary bout of insanity that I might be able to actually *save* some of the sorry sacks who fought under Jack alongside me, but that's not going to be possible, not alone as I am without a heavy stick to intimidate them. I'm going to have to reduce enough of their numbers for the rest to cower and listen.

Or I'll have to kill all of them.

At least that way, we'd win ourselves two trucks.

I've still got a clip left in the M4 I lifted from Clay, plus a bone spear and a machete. It'll do just fine. And I've got no reason to wait.

Crouched where I am among the grain stalks on the side of the road, I wait until the first body comes close enough for me to reach. Lunging out of my hiding place, I grab the woman and tip the blade of the machete to her throat. She was the dark-skinned woman who spoke up for Clay before.

Clay, Rico, and Adam…where are they so I can shove my fist through their throats?

I don't see the brothers among those scattered before me and bite my front teeth together. Why wouldn't they have sent one of the brothers? That shit pisses me off. But not as much as the thought that Jack didn't come either. I don't know why, but I'm just as relieved as I am disappointed not to see him.

I want it to end. It'll either be his death or mine. And I don't mean the suffering. I'm fine with that. What I'm not fine with is the horrible, debilitating fear I have that Jack will find her and that when he does, she won't just die, she'll be ripped apart and Jack will make me watch the entire time.

The woman in my grip tenses and releases the handgun she's holding when I tell her to. She makes a clucking sound, but she doesn't protest.

"You-you-you d-d-d-do what I say, you might just survive."

I swing the barrel of my M4 around as the first of Jack's dogs looks up. His eyes meet mine and there's momentary recognition in them. "Holy shi…"

I open fire.

Four bodies hit the ground, three are Jack's dogs, one is from the Dixie freaks who started sprinting towards me. They all start to react now, throwing themselves into the surrounding crops and off of the truck. Some plaster themselves to the road while others try to grab other bodies and use them as human shields. It's what all of Jack's dogs do. It's what I'm doing too.

"That's Diego," I hear one of them say.

And then the response from somebody else. "Diego's dead."

A huge weight slams into my side, taking me down to the asphalt. Coming from the tall grasses where I didn't anticipate him, a dog — one hopped up on alien blood — crushes his hands around my throat.

He's trying to crack my skull open on the road, and he might've, had the woman's body not been a barrier between me and him. She's screaming and kicking and writhing and knocking her fluffy hair into my chin and clacking her forehead against the dog's mouth.

I think I recognize him and scour my memories for names, but I can't come up with one. Not that it matters. Among Jack's dogs, we were all interchangeable. Each man as sure to die as the next.

The nameless guy cocks his fist back and hones it on the woman's face. I shove her out of the way and rip my head in the opposite direction so that the idiot beats his fist into the cracking asphalt.

He shouts out a curse. "I know you used to be one of us," he snarls down at me. "If you'd been tough enough, Jack wouldn't have killed you."

I can't pull my gun between us, so I reach down, hand palming the ground until I reach the hilt of my machete. As he reaches into the back of his pants to pull out his Ruger, I meet his gaze, and I tell him a truth that's only just starting to mean something to me.

"Killing me w-w-was the o-o-only good thing Jack ever did for me."

I hack my machete into his neck, pull the gun from his hand, duck behind his body and use him as a shield as a fresh wave of bullets rain down onto us.

They had more than I accounted for and I'm suddenly concerned that this might not go the way I thought. I can hear fighting somewhere near the trucks, but I can't see past the body blocking the bullets to see if Matt and Mo or any of the others are alive and fighting back.

Shit. This might go very fucking sideways.

This *is* going sideways. I'm about to have to do some kamikaze shit, and I start to gather all the weapons I can get my hands on when I hear it on the wind.

A song that makes my head ache, only because I've memorized all the goddamn lyrics.

Do I believe in life?

Maybe.

Maybe only life. *Pia's.*

I start to chuckle under my breath. Goddamn Constanzia... Oh fuck it's Constanzia.

"E-e-e-everybody down!"

I can hear my butchered words repeated by Mo as he roars, "Get to the ground, now!"

The dull thud of bodies raining down onto the asphalt around me precedes the ricochet of bullets that squeal out of Constanzia's goddamn Browning M2HB. I pray to The God in that moment that Pia's on her belly in the grass, because Constanzia is taking out the fields too. And they call *me* the psychopath...

Cries of pain are punctuated by the gunfire's explosion, and spliced with lyrics to a song that's got no business screaming through Population...And then the more horrible sound of a human voice singing over the music, "Do you believe in love, fuckers?"

"Goddammit, Constanzia, we got it!" Mikey shouts over the woman.

Covered in blood as I am, I can't help the ragged laughter that chokes my throat.

The bullets stop raining down a few moments later, but the song continues for another goddamn eternity until it reaches its finale. The thing that pisses me off? I'm starting to stutter the goddamn lyrics under my goddamn breath.

"D-d-don't nnneed you any-anymore..." Goddammit!

"Goddammit, Constanzia!"

"There," comes her voice, followed abruptly by the sound of the truck's engine powering down, zapping the music with it.

I glance up at the pickup as it rolls in close. Mikey and Constanzia stand in the cab behind the massive tripod-mounted machine gun while Roderick mans the wheel, the Other called Laiya in the passenger's seat next to him.

Mikey is searching the road with the barrel of his M16 and when he finds me, he grins. "You still alive?"

I return his expression and, careful not to let the body shielding me slip too far out of place, I rise up onto my haunches and glance around it at the scene to see who's left. Turns out, most people.

Constanzia must have shot above them — my gaze snags on two dogs lying in a pile on top of two other dogs near the right side of the road, where they'd evidently been trying to flee — for the most part.

Everybody else is face down on the asphalt. I rise and quickly make my way over the bodies to where Matt and Mo lay side-by-side.

"Up," I order them, giving Mo a gentle boot to the arm. "Ffffriendlies."

Mo takes a haggard breath then tips his head back enough to see. He grins when he does and it's an infectious thing. "Wow. You make quite an entrance."

"We thought Abel might have forgotten about us," Matt says, rising up to stand alongside his husband...boyfriend... person.

Speaking of...where's mine?

I swivel towards the dead crops where I hid Pia, only to see her making her way onto the road. She's almost at the pickup truck now, heading to the driver's side window. I frown at the contact between her hand and Roderick's. It's only a fist bump, but still. I don't want anyone fucking touching her.

"We ran into trouble on the road. Reunion with some old friends." Constanzia's mouth hardens as she narrows her gaze on the dogs that are still alive. None of them are stupid enough to have moved yet from where they lie prone.

"Everybody alive?"

"Yeah. We had a pretty good idea of where they were — Star and I have been tracking them — so we only saw them when we were driving up. They didn't follow, but I'm damn sure they plan to…"

"You're all dead!" A body surges out of the tall grasses on the opposite side of the road. He's got a gun on him and points it at Constanzia. Bad idea.

He must have been delusional, because I can see his mistake in the expression on his face as the barrel of his gun dips a half inch. Constanzia fires. Half a dozen bullets take him off his feet and throw him back into the grasses where he came from. I wince as the sound of the gun going off rings even after Constanzia pulls her finger off the trigger.

Mikey spits, "Goddammit. Why do you humans have to make weapons so goddamn loud?"

My heart beats a little harder until I see Pia straightening. She drops her hands from her ears and looks at me. She's alright. So I'm alright. But there's something weird about her expression. Her lips are pursed and her cheeks are pink, but not like they were the night before.

I take a jerky step towards her. "You h-hurt?" I ask her, tone spiking just like my pulse.

She balks, "How could I be injured when I'm stuck on the sidelines listening as people I care about are killed?"

I don't understand. It's like she's saying something, but she means something else. I shake my head and stalk towards her. She tenses and edges back, balling her hands into fists like she's going to attack. I freeze.

Is she afraid of me? No. My heart's beating hard and stonily. I feel a breeze flutter through my hollow soul. She isn't afraid of me. She's not supposed to be. She wasn't before.

"Are you fu-fucking afffffraid of me?"

Her eyes get all red. She makes a wild gesture with her hands. "Why would I be? After all, you only took all my weapons away from me and threatened to fuck me bloody."

"Jesus Christ," Mikey shouts.

Constanzia swings the muzzle of her Browning towards my chest. She lifts one slender eyebrow and says, "You for real?"

Roderick shakes his head. "That's fucked up, man."

"I don't have to explain mmmmmyself to y-y-y..." It doesn't come. You. I repeat the word over and over in my mind, but it fails to manifest. You. *You.* You. It just doesn't.

They all stare and me and wait for me to finish and fail. The urge to kill sweeps me. Nothing makes me want to kill more. Behind my back, I hear the carnivorous laughter of one of Jack's dogs. "Fucking freak," he growls.

I pivot on my heel, remove my bone spear from my sling and throw it on easy motion. It hits the guy in the gut and he falls, further impaling himself on the road. A body — a woman, one of ours — rolls out from underneath him just in time to avoid being gutted.

She squeals as she scrambles to her feet and joins Matt and Mo by the pickup truck where Matt's tending to some of the wounded. Pia's dad sits on the roof of the cab, his feet propped up on the edge of the truck. He meets my gaze but his eyes aren't staring at me in horror or fear, but in shame and I know I've disappointed him.

My stomach hurts. Killing that guy did nothing. Miguel. Shit. I knew his name. One of the few.

Miguel liked beating other men to death. Maybe he didn't like it. Maybe he just did it to survive. He wore a cross around his neck like Pia does only his was silver and hers is gold. He always spoke in quotes from movies I'd never seen. He missed his mother and a woman called Mary. Sometimes he'd speak to her at night with his head bowed and his eyes closed, but only when Jack wasn't looking.

And I killed him.

I shouldn't have done that.

I turn back around and meet Pia's gaze. She looks away from me and asks Roderick and Laiya if she can ride with them in the cab. Away from me.

From above, Constanzia says, "You don't have to explain shit to us. But to her? With the way you look at her? And the way she's looking at you right now?" She shakes her head, her long, dark hair spilling over her right shoulder and pooling there. "You *might* want to consider it. But later."

She turns to the crowd. "Who's a part of Generation One and who's with Jack and the Dixie brothers?"

"Generation One?" A woman says — the same woman who still holds little Jack by the hand. He's watching me again. Don't like that. Don't want anyone watching me now. Wanna go back to the old days where I was just Jack's monstrous shadow.

Except I don't.

Pia doesn't live there.

"Yeah, that's what we're calling ourselves. We're committed to establishing the first generation of humans and Heztoichen who live, work and build together in a safe territory called Brianna. Closely linked with the Diera, the eventual plan is to wipe out Population altogether and bring the borders of Diera and Brianna together so that the whole of North America can go back to being a safe space for us."

"You keep using this word — *safe*," a cold voice cackles. It's fucking Ken. He's kneeling in front of the pickup alongside three dogs — the last that are left — and the six other Dixie people who attacked us that are still breathing. "That doesn't exist out here, sweetheart."

He licks the outside of his teeth as his gaze holds on Constanzia. She swings her Browning around and I wince away from the impending sound, but instead of firing, she pulls a throwing star out of her back pocket and launches it at the man, hitting him in the shoulder.

Ken grunts and hisses. He rises up, like he's stupid enough to attack her — or try to anyway — but she holds up the rest of her throwing stars, fanning them like a deck of cards, and he settles back down onto his heels.

"Anybody else? No? Okay then. Now that that's settled, divide up the ones who are still making up their minds across the three pickup trucks. Make sure that they're outnumbered."

As people begin shuffling to obey her commands, Roderick looks out the window. "Who elected you leader of this here outfit?" He mimics a southern drawl, like he's imitating somebody, but I don't know who it is.

"Yours truly," comes her reply. "Just kidding. It was Abel." She reaches down and hauls a body up onto the truck. One of ours. The woman and her small Jack. I help them load the rest. As I push and haul and drag bodies up onto truck beds, I can sense the urgency in the air. Something's coming.

"Something's coming."

I'm up on Constanzia's truck, standing beside her as it revs. She's looking out towards the mountains and the trees growing out of them. As we take off, putting them at our back, she looks over at me. Her hair whips around her face. Mikey's got himself planted on the edge of the truck, his knee in some fuck's spine who didn't want to come along for the journey. I thought we should have killed him, but I've already done my fair share of the killing for one day.

"You saved a lot of people, Diego," she says, but it means nothing.

"You ready for the battle we're about to have? From what Star and I scouted, Jack's numbers are triple what they were six weeks ago. He's been recruiting ever since Abel first started out towards Brianna."

"Hhhhee wants her d-d-dead," I grunt.

She leans casually on the receiver of the machine gun while her hair whips around her face. Her naturally slanted eyes slant even further towards her temples when she smiles. "That has something to do with you, doesn't it?" I don't answer. "I've heard the story. You're a hero."

I bang my fist on the hood of the cab. Roderick sticks his head out the window and, when he sees it's me, flips me the bird. I shake my head. "N-n-no, I'm nnnnot."

"Yeah, I guess not," she drawls. "Hero gets the girl." The beat in my chest catches. "And he doesn't usually tell her he'll fuck her bloody." My stomach drops through the soles of my feet.

I growl, "C-c-can't let her g-g-g-get hurt."

"I know. Can't imagine how threats must sound to her, though. She just got out of a cage."

"I'm not a ffffucking D-D-Dixie."

She just shrugs and it's an infuriating gesture. "Just saying — they love her too."

"So what's the plan?" Ken says from my feet. His got his gaze trained on Constanzia in a way that makes my blood heat, even though she's not even the woman I want. She's too much like me — me, but with heart.

"And why should I share it with you?"

He says something to her then in complete gibberish, but it makes her posture relax. Her smile blows open wide. "You speak Mandarin?"

"I do."

"How?"

"I'm half-Chinese."

She nods. "Me too."

"I figured. What's your other half?"

"Black. Yours?"

"Vietnamese."

She nods again then heaves out a sigh, "Well, in that case, the plan is to mount a last stand."

"Sounds about right. It's gonna be a last stand. Have you met this guy? Jack? He's insane."

Yes. Yes, he is.

Constanzia just nods. "Oh yeah. I've been tracking him for a long time, trying to find the right moment to off him. And I didn't mean our last stand. I meant his. We've got a good base, we're well armed, and we've got Others. All he has are numbers from the Dixie brothers."

So I was right. It is all about the numbers. Probably doesn't hurt that they share a common mission. Does Jack know that? If he does, he probably doesn't even remember it. The only goal Jack ever sees is his.

I frown. We might have Others and arms and, if what Constanzia says is true, even a base to fight from, but Jack's got more than she's giving him credit for. He's got numbers and a will to sacrifice every one of them. He has no weaknesses. We have too many.

Ken shakes his head. "You might think you've got this under control, but Jack plus the Dixie brothers? You don't stand a chance. They're going to do anything they can to get her back."

"What do they want with her anyway?"

"A ritual."

"A ritual for what?"

Ken has the audacity to look away then and grumbles under his breath, "I don't know."

"You don't even know? You killed for them and you don't even know?"

"I did it for their family. Their mother was a good woman."

"And their ffffffather?" I choke out. I can't stand the lies he tells himself in order to be able to rationalize this for us.

His gaze jerks up to me and blazes with a heat he didn't offer Constanzia. Ohhhh yes. This fucker's mine. He's gonna die before the end of this. "He wasn't fit to lead. And besides, it doesn't matter. Y'all will all be dead by morning. Strung up in whatever forest or on whatever road you think you've found out here in Population to defend."

To that, Constanzia's lips jerk into a smile that makes my skin crawl. I bark out, "Wh-wh-where are we h-h-headed?"

"Wall." I wait, because I don't know what the shit she's talking about. "It's a drug store."

Chapter Fourteen

I t takes a couple hours to get there, but not more than that. On our way, we pass a host of signs advertising the same thing and with increasing frequency. Even though I can't read them, that's fine Constanzia reads them out loud and laughs at every single one.

"Wall Drug — free ice water! Can you believe that?"

"Wall Drug — hot coffee five cents…ugg. I'd give my left tit for a cup of hot coffee…"

"Wall Drug — seventy-two miles!"

"Wall Drug — refreshing! It's cool here."

Quietly under her breath. "I need time to move on. I need a love to feel strong. Cause I've had time to think it through, and maybe I'm too good for you, oh!" Then much louder, "Oh — only twenty miles!"

"Wall Drug — the ice water store. Next two exits."

"Wall Drug — half a block away." She pauses. "Do you think they really have ice there?"

By the time we do the sun is dark, stomachs are grumbling and I'm shot. I don't miss being a leader of sorts, but I miss not having to talk to anyone but Pia.

Now Abel's got me in some kind of a meeting and Pia's standing on the opposite side of the long stretch of table between us, far down. She's as far from me as she could get.

The woman with a bandaged jaw called Cleo passes by her and they exchange a few words before the Cleo lady looks across the table and gives me a little wave that I don't deserve. I hurt her. It could have been worse — she attacked me — but I still hurt her when I could have tried to be more gentle. I didn't know gentle then until Pia opened for me, though. Does she know that? Does she forgive me? Do either of them.

I give her a nod in return and she turns to lead a dozen other men and women towards the kitchens of this strange, enormous place.

It used to be a restaurant, I guess, but there's little to recommend it as such, now. A few busted tables and chairs have been salvaged from the scraps that Abel and her people have pushed to the far edges of the room.

Now, I stand almost directly under the only free-standing thing left in this dusty, wooden space. A cluster of statues are fixed around a huge pillar. Carved out of wood, Native American Indian figures face out, their faded black eyes and hair looking down on us in a way I should probably find disconcerting, but don't.

They're calming me.

They can't speak of the unspeakable things that have happened here and they can't pass any judgment — not on me for what I said to Pia, and not on anyone. And still they somehow don't give off sadness, like most things in Population do. They seem strong.

Or maybe that's just the way I feel standing side-by-side with twenty-some odd beings, each of us strapped to the nines. Maybe it's because each person whose gaze I meet returns my own with a confidence that says that we might just be able to win this, take out Jack and the Dixie freaks, and make it to Brianna in one piece.

This isn't like meeting around the pit with Jack's dogs where, no matter what the meeting was about, no one could be sure they'd make it out unscathed, or even alive. The only surety we had was knowing that, if it came down to it, we'd each throw our daggers into the soil to kill our brothers in defense of our own lives. And often, we had to.

I look past Pia at Mo standing beside her. Laiya stands next to him, shoulder-to-shoulder. Then comes the SEAL team with Star, Avery, Zala, Marine and Constanzia. Ashlyn, Sandra and Matt are missing, taking care of Luke and the other wounded. Abel stands flanked between Constanzia and Kane. The Others Hila and Feron fill the space between Kane and me. Calvin stands to my other side, looking small, yet fierce. Gabe's been patched up and stands on his other side, and on his other side are another two Others, then Mikey at the foot of the table. Finally, Roderick stands by Pia.

She hasn't said anything to me since we unloaded the trucks, locked the bad guys in the freezer and gathered here. And I haven't said anything either. Is Constanzia right? To get the girl, will I have to be the hero?

"I'm glad you're all here and that you all made it."

A whoop goes out — Gabe's — followed by a low drumming of fists on the table. I find my lips getting lopsided at the sight. There's a strange energy here I've never felt before. It's warm and enveloping, and for all my hate, I don't seem to be able to claw my way out of it.

I might not want to.

I glance at Pia again and this time, she's looking at me. She looks away quickly, but not before I see pink rise in her cheeks.

"There are some serious thank yous that need to be said, so I'll start. First, I've gotta thank Constanzia and Star for doubling back and forth and risking their lives a dozen times over to keep tabs on Jack." Jack. There it is, his name acknowledged out in the open. Like an old friend. *Or even a lover...*

"And I also have to thank Hila and Feron for getting the second truck up and running after it almost got burned to pieces. Without that, I'm not sure how we'd have outrun them with just the one eighteen-wheeler." The two Others tip their heads forward in acknowledgement.

"And of course, Diego." Me? She's talking about me?

All eyes turn my way. "When Matt and Mo volunteered to go back for you and Pia, I expected that they'd maybe be able to get all four of you out. Turns out, y'all managed to leave with twenty-three extra bodies, all of whom are eager to join us in Brianna. I talked to a few of them, and they thank you for that."

I don't move because staying frighteningly still is the next best option to running. And I've got nowhere to run. Luckily, Abel doesn't leave the spotlight burning on me for too long. She glances up at Kane.

"I also have to thank my hubby here. He called the Lahve and convinced him to send reinforcements. We should be getting twenty extra Heztoichen warriors within the next three hours."

Kane breathes out of the side of his mouth and slides his arm protectively over her shoulder. "There is no thanking me for this. You carry the first ever human-Heztoichen child. The Lahve is bound to protect you. If Brianna weren't in such a chaos from how Elise left it, he'd have come himself. As it is, he can't spare any more warriors defending the territory from scavengers and gangs. They're a goddamn infestation…"

Abel claps her hands together and smiles around at us, speaking quickly over her husband even while she gives him an elbow to the ribs. "And on that positive note, let's talk tactics. I'm not a war general, so I'm open to suggestions from any of you on where to keep the new converts, the ones who won't be fighting and the wounded, where to fight from and where to defend.

"We've only got a few more hours until reinforcements arrive, but we've also got to hold out until then, and according to Constanzia and Star, they could be here any minute."

"An hour and a half at our last estimate based on their historic speed of travel and what we calculate to be the amount of fuel they have left," Marine pipes up.

I grimace. That isn't enough time. Jack will have already had a plan. Jack will always find a way to surprise us.

I watch as Mia, Zala and Roderick plot out a crude layout of the structure that they call Wall Drug — some kind of sprawling series of shops that seem to be structured around two city blocks with what they call a "backyard" in the center. It's open air. Got some kind of giant sculptures in it. And while most of everything else has been run down, it's clear that some kind of group used that center backyard for something in the past, because it's reinforced now with only one way in...one way out...

"They won't concede while they have numbers..."

"Jack's confident, I'll give him that, but he's not stupid enough..."

"He's a psychopath. You can't be sure *what* he'll do."

"I can't, but Diego can." My name in Abel's voice pulls my attention up. She gestures down at the table, crudely laid out with shattered sticks and wooden blocks. "Tell us. What's Jack going to do?"

Not even I know that.

But.

I do know one thing...

I step through the people blocking my way to the table and place the tip of my finger in the center of the open ring. "Hhhhere."

Abel squints down at where I'm pointing. It's Kane who says, "Luring them to their deaths would be optimal, but I don't see a way we can successfully do that without hiding and hoping they slip past us and stumble into the backyard all on their own — an unlikely scenario — or without having a ringer. A hare we're sure their dogs will chase."

But we do.

My stomach pitches and my jaw clenches and I fumble through the words, but I say them knowing that if things go my way, she'll be safe. In my plans, Pia is always the most protected woman in the world.

"P-P-P-Pia," I finally hack out.

All eyes turn to her, including mine. She's standing with her arms crossed over her chest, her hair sinking around her shoulders, eyes bright. She hasn't said much this strategy session. I wonder why. Is she remembering what I said to her before? Is she scared I'll say it to her again?

"You want to use *Pia* for bait?" Abel asks. Her jaw hangs open and, with her palms planted on the marble tabletop, her arms look like they're the only things keeping her up.

I frown and my spine straightens. My core muscles clench. "The D-D-Dixie brothers will ffffollow her anywhere and Jack will t-too." I swallow, lick my lips, look at everyone and no one. "When he s-s-s-sees what sh-sh-she means to mmmme."

If I was uncomfortable by the attention before, I'm damn near skinned alive by it now. This immolation lasts and lasts and lasts. I glance up at Kane. He's the only one who's looking at me like he *knows*.

"You are certain that Jack will follow you? Last I heard, it was Abel he was after." His grip tightens around her shoulder.

I nod. "Hhhhe wanted Abel to suffer be-be-because he wanted me to bleed. When hhhhe sees I don't give a shit about Ab-Abel, b-b-b-b..." Breath. Try again, "...but would die for Pia, h-h-h-he'll come.

"This is his love." I take another breath and gesture to the lines crisscrossing over my face and neck, the visible backs of my arms.

"This is his hate." I say those lines without stuttering once. I wish I had. It would relieve the fire chewing its way up my body, eviscerating my lungs. I can't breathe. What did I just admit? And why did I have to admit it to everyone?

Don't be an idiot. They already knew.

Everyone knew.

Does Pia? I can't look to see her face right now, so I concentrate on Kane and Abel. They share a glance. Abel chews on her lower lip.

"Pia. What do you think?"

"How would it work?"

Abel points to locations along the ramparts of this Wall Drug compound, but I'm already shaking my head. Wrong, wrong, wrong.

"What?" She mutters when she catches my expression.

I reach across the table and move her arm away from one of the dozen entrances and then away from the drugstore altogether, out, out, out to the road. "If we wait for him to come here, he-he-he-he wwwwon't attack. He'll wwwwait and g-g-g-get organized. You c-c-can't let him get his feet planted. He'll rip us a-a-apart."

Abel's gaze widens. "You want us to leave Wall Drug after we've finished fortifying it and wage war out in the open? Meet him on the road?"

"Meet-meet him on the road."

Abel exhales heavily, then looks around at the rest of the folks gathered. "Any other suggestions?"

No one says anything, until Roderick grunts around his toothpick. "It's a good plan. I'm with Diego."

Around the table, one at a time, folks voice their assent. They say my name and I feel my skin start to itch. Pia nods when it's her turn, but doesn't speak up.

I'm still watching her when Abel says, "Looks like the ayes have it. We're with you, Diego." I look up. She's smiling. "And I'm really glad you're with us."

Chapter Fifteen

I pause at the entrance to the store and take a breath. It's got a glass door and through it, I can see Pia talking to Constanzia who's showing her how to load and shoot a crossbow, of all things.

I pause, taking just another moment with my hand on the doorknob, feeling its slick bronze exterior. The glass panel in this door is still intact, and beyond it, most of the leather goods that were once here are still here.

I guess, in Population, the market for cowboy boots doesn't seem to be so demanding. I notice Pia's wearing some. She looks cute in them.

So cute, I'm losing the air in my lungs.

"Like this?" I hear her murmured words as Constanzia stands back to admire her posture.

"You got it. Now let 'er rip."

Pia pulls the trigger, but nothing happens.

"You remember the safety?" Constanzia asks her.

"Oh shoot," she whispers, flips the safety...but her finger's still pinned to the trigger. She pulls and the arrow goes wide, shattering something I can't see. I rush through the door as the recoil tips Pia's arm back and she trips over her own two feet, falling into a clothes rack.

Panic makes me burn, but laughter douses it just as quickly. Pia's laughing in that light, breathy way she does while Constanzia howls. Goddamn, that woman has an ugly laugh…

Half-snort, half-chuckle, Constanzia throws her head back as she offers Pia a hand. "Remind me never to stand near the target next time you're experimenting with new weapons."

The bell on the door rings as the door whispers shut at my back. Constanzia looks at me and she doesn't share the same surprise Pia does. "Was wondering when you'd show up. You've got five minutes before we need to ride. Y'all are in Roderick's truck." She hefts Pia up to standing and as she stalks towards me, gives me a rough slap on the back.

Without saying anything, the bell dings again and Pia and I are alone. My skin is crawling and my feet won't stop shuffling to the left and right. Is this what it is to be nervous? Ugh. Disgusting.

I try to squash the emotion, but I realize it's getting worse the longer I stand here staring at her. Because she doesn't say anything. She's just watching me expectantly — *insistently*. Makes me want to run. Should I? Nah. I've never run from anything in my life. Least of all a fight.

"You up-up-upgrading to this?" I pick the crossbow up off the floor and hand it back to her.

She takes it, but sets it aside on top of a pile of shoe boxes. "I was considering it, but I'd rather stick to my Beretta, thank you."

"You still got it?"

"Always."

"Got bullets?"

"Enough." She pouts up at me and damn, if her lips don't look soft. I want to trace them with my tongue.

She inhales, pushing her tits out to the edge of her tank top beneath her jacket. My gaze strays to them before moving to the crossbow. "Are you…"

"Are *you* going to tell me what you're thinking? Anything at all? Because right now, I could not be more…" She inhales, then exhales just as deeply, "…frustrated.

"You've got so much going on under the hood, and you never share any of it. And then all of a sudden, in a day, you tell me you're going to fuck me bloody, then you tell everyone else you'd die for me? I don't get it, Diego. What do you want from me?"

Frustrated? *She's* frustrated? I've been nothing but frustrated since I first saw her. Since before.

I inhale deep, but the second I open my mouth, the words bunch together at the gate of my teeth and refuse to pass it. I turn away from her and kick a pile of shoe boxes, sending the cowboy boots within them scattering.

I shake my head.

She makes a small, tortured sound. "You say horrible and beautiful things, but none of them are true. What is true, Diego?"

"I c-can't."

"Don't give me that as an excuse. I don't give a shit if every word tears you apart. You owe me this. If nothing else, you owe me one truth. Just say one thing that's true. Just one and I'll stop asking."

One truth. Should I tell her that I once used a man's skull as a bowl? That's a truth. Should I tell her I once cried over a woman's body I ruined? Or should I tell her that I did it when no one was looking? Should I tell her that one night with her has made me a greedy man and I'm not going to give her up? Should I tell her that, even before that night, she turned me onto the most dangerous monster out here in Population? That when she held my hand and took me to the river and let me touch her face with just my fingertips, I tripped and fell and face-planted into love?

"I love you," I blurt, and it comes without consequences — without any *physical* consequences. Just one perfect sentence. One lonely truth.

I start to turn from her, too terrified to read her reaction, but her fingers snag on the opening of my coat. She pulls me back to face her and with her free hand, traces the line of my scar from my left temple, across the bridge of my nose to my snarling upper lip.

Time holds.

"This isn't love," she whispers.

Time releases and so does the breath in my lungs.

She lifts up onto her toes and I flinch back, but she firms her grip on my coat and pulls me in close, close, closer. Her too soft lips trace the path her fingers had. As she delivers small, fluttering kisses across the line of my scar, she says, "Love is the whisper of a kiss, not the whisper of a knife. Love isn't revenge or retribution or threats."

She settles back onto her heels and the ethereal, almost magical tenor to her words fades. She stabs her finger into my chest. "When you fought me in the woods with everything you had, that's when I fell in love with you. But when you threaten me because you're worried about me getting hurt? You cut the legs out from under me, Diego. Don't do it again."

I think my heart has just stopped because I sway on my feet when she spears me with her finger again. "What?"

"Don't threaten me again or I'll cut your junk off while you're sleeping."

Laughter bellows out of me, hot and fierce. I snatch up her hand and start to push her back. Her eyes light, then sizzle. "N-n-not that. What you s-s-s-said before it."

"I know what you want to hear," she says, her voice a low drawl that brings out the south in her accent.

"Then s-s-s-say it."

"What makes you think you deserve it?"

"Nnnnothing. B-but I want it anyway."

She smiles up at me, though I can tell she's trying not to. Her chin tips up as I smash her against a wall crowded with frames of Indian chiefs I can't name. "I love you too, Diego."

I know it probably doesn't mean as much coming from her — someone built to love, someone who actually can define it. But in this moment, it doesn't matter. I can't hold back.

I sweep down at the same time that I pick her up. Her legs spread around my hips and she lets my erection settle in her warmth. I bow my head over hers and kiss the top of her head. Kiss. Not used to it, but I'd like to be.

I feel a little shaky knowing that she feels this love thing for me...

...and that I'm about to take her out and dangle her like roadkill in front of a vulture.

"I don't-don't know what it would d-d-do to me if I lllllost you."

"Hey! Fuckers, I'm waiting," Roderick's booming voice cracks into the space. I hadn't even heard the door ding open.

"We're c-c-coming," I shout over my shoulder.

"Now! Constanzia's already rolling!"

Fuck. I lower Pia's legs to the ground, but she takes my hand, forcing me to look back at her for one more moment. Her eyes are tender. That tenderness doesn't belong here. Jack will shred through it. Jack will...

"I won't let him hurt you. Not even through me." She gives my hand a squeeze and smiles at me lopsidedly. "I promise. But don't ever underestimate me. I've had enough men do that already in my life. Do you understand?"

I nod, hating myself for agreeing, but she's right. Constanzia was right. Maybe she's right, too. Love can't be a cage. Love can't be the rage-filled stroke of a knife.

I open my mouth like I'm gonna say something profound, but Roderick bangs his fist on the glass panel so hard, the bell above it goes haywire. I wonder what I would have told her as I follow Pia and Roderick out of the door and out of the drug store towards one of the trucks.

We never did get that free ice water.

Somehow that's all I can think as we pass by one of the signs advertising this place and Pia points it out. The wind is hot on my face, despite the fact that it's not hot out here at all. Maybe it's the fact that Pia's standing next to me that makes me feel like I'm burning up. I want to get her alone… in a bunker…somewhere a thousand feet underground where none of Population's nightmares can ever find her.

But that's not reasonable. Mainly because it'd take me too long to build a bunker like that…and even then, I doubt she'd get into it.

We ride in the pickup behind Constanzia's. She and her goons lead the charge in their modified pickup with the Browning tripod. Their goddamn playlist is ripping through the quiet.

Above the sound of the rushing wind, is a male voice shrieking, *"Where are you? And I'm so sorry! I cannot sleep, I cannot dream tonight. I need somebody and always…sick strange darkness comes creeping on so haunting every time…"* And of course, all five women are shrieking along with every word.

Every. single. one.

"You think if Jack and your brothers catch wind of this, they'll just make a break for it?" Mikey asks Pia over the roar of the wind from his position seated on the edge of the truck.

It's Calvin who answers — though why he got saddled with our group, I've got no idea. Maybe just so we can keep an eye on him.

"By break for it, you mean jump off the trucks they're driving and hope the fall kills them?"

Pia laughs. "I think it's a possibility!" But when we take off again, I can see her mouthing the words along with the melody. *"I miss you, I miss you…"*

Zala, driving, lays down on the horn in front of us. Roderick follows suit, and I sweep my gaze back at the six other pickups that have fallen in line behind us. It's everybody we've got, including some I'd rather not have. Ken, of all fuckers, and the dark skinned woman who I nearly gutted a couple times — Lenora or Leona or some L name — somehow convinced the others that they were trustworthy enough to join this mission.

Abel's got them in teams entirely made up of Others, but that doesn't make me feel any better. I don't trust them and would rather we left them locked up in the freezer with the others. Then turn the freezer on and let them claw each other to pieces.

"Y'all ready?" Calvin asks. He's got a shotgun hanging on a sling around his neck. His grip firms around the stock.

I nod, checking my own M16. Happy to be reunited with it. I've also got a Ruger in the leather holster around my belt, two hunting knives, a butterfly knife, and twin smoke grenades attached to the same belt.

I also snagged the crossbow Pia was using. Just in case. It hangs down my back and when I check it, Pia rolls her eyes. "Yeah, we're ready."

"Good. Because I think they're here."

I glance over the top of the technical in front of us and my pulse starts to beat in time to the rapid beat of the song blazing through the world in front of us.

From where I stand, I can see a convoy of jalopies headed down the road coming towards us. Most are pickups, but there are two massive SUVs and at the very back, a bright yellow Hummer. Jack is likely to be somewhere in the middle. I know better than to try to anticipate which truck he's in. Little about him is predictable.

"You know the p-plan?" I say to Pia.

She nods, the color in her face holding while her brown eyes scan the convoy headed our way. "I know the plan. Let Jack see us. Then you take over the truck and drive like hell back to base. Hope he follows."

"Hhhhe will."

"And so will my brothers." Pia looks like she'll say more, hesitates, then checks her Beretta again. "I...should have told

■ 205

you about my brothers before. I should have told all of you."
She looks from Mikey to Calvin, back to me again. "I'm
sorry."

"Ain't nothing to be sorry for," Mikey says.

Calvin nods his agreement and so do I.

Pia still doesn't look convinced. She swallows hard. "I
should have also told you why…what my brothers want with
me. They um…Oh God." One of the worst curses I've heard
Pia say, I feel tension, knowing that whatever comes next, I
might not want to hear it.

She reaches up and touches the gold cross in the hollow
of her throat. She seems to pointedly avoid my gaze as she
says, "My brothers lost it after my mom died. And we came
across another group of scavengers once…they were after
our water. We fought them off and my brothers wanted to
kill them all, but I persuaded them to try to integrate some of
them. There was a woman. She got in close with my brothers
— slept with all three of them — and she convinced
them…"

"About the rrrritual," I say when Pia doesn't.

She looks up at me surprised. "Did Luke tell you?"

"Yeah. In the c-c-cages."

"Did he tell you what the ritual was supposed to be?"

I shake my head. She closes her eyes. "Oh God," she
repeats.

I brace, but the impact is surreal when she says to me,
"She convinced them that my mom would reincarnate if I
gave birth to a girl…with Luke."

"Jesus Christ," Calvin says.

Mikey rubs his hand down his face once, looking a decade
older when his hand falls. "And people went along with that?"

She shakes her head. "They knew that there was
supposed to be some ritual, but no one knew about the…
reincarnation."

"Why didn't you tell them? Matt and Mo and others I'm
sure would have done something…"

I blink, the words slow to sink in. I can't quite process. But when her face twists and she looks away, ashamed, I get it. Every move she's made. "You w-w-w-were wwwworried, they'd believe her."

Pia cringes. Her cheeks flush. "Yeah. I thought they'd be desperate enough to try. People aren't — weren't — *sane* after my brothers took over. You can see that they aren't. They attacked your convoy with no weapons. They teamed up with Jack and his gang."

She shakes her head. "I couldn't risk it."

"Damn." Calvin shakes his head.

Mikey looks up, straightening a little at the sight of the cars closing in. "We better look alive, kids." He raises his newly acquired M4 — also fitted for his left hand.

I turn forward, but just before I do, I touch Pia's throat over the mark I made there. "You d-d-did the right thing, every sssssstep of the way."

She looks into my eyes, as if seeking answers or something. I've got none for her and nod just once. Weirdly, afterward, she looks reassured.

And then come the bullets.

"Ohhh I wanna..." The song has changed and this time, the woman's asking a question — no, she's delivering a bold, bawdy statement about wanting a goddamn dance. With somebody, anybody. Why this song was added to the list beats the shit out of me. I don't think I've ever seen anyone dance in a decade.

"I wanna dance with somebody!" Tacktacktacktack. The thunder of bullets as they're traded between the pickup in front of us, and the convoy advancing. *"I wanna dance with somebody..."*

Thuthudthudthud. They hit the front of Zala's truck. Constanzia's at the Browning again, both hands on the trigger while Marine ducks behind the cab and fires her own M10 and the woman blaring through the speakers demands love.

There's that word again.

Do I believe in love?

I feel Pia's heat so close to me now...

Fuck yeah. I may believe in nothing else, but I believe in that.

The women's pickup veers off the road to the right and almost immediately, Roderick peels us to the left. Pia's exposed here and I have to choke back the desire to grab her, shove her to the floor and throw myself over her to make sure she doesn't get fucking shot, but she's doing a decent enough job of hunkering down behind the reinforced siding of the truck. Then she glances back.

"Diego, get down!" She barks, just as a bullet goes whizzing past my ear.

She turns before she can make sure I've followed her order and starts returning fire. It's hard to hit a live target as they're on the road and we're rocking all over the place on the grassy yards flanking it on both sides.

It's weird, looking at us. There are houses infrequently dispersed on either side of this street. Yards with structures for kids to play on. Weathered awnings providing shade to front doors that stand ajar, like the owners of the houses have just gone inside and haven't locked up yet. Meanwhile, we're an army of trucks — six on our side, five on theirs — trying to tear each other apart.

We didn't know how well armed they'd be. My guess had been 'better than we should expect,' but I was wrong. They aren't very well armed. The realization shocks me and fills me with a warm hope. Something greedy and cold snakes through it, but I don't dwell on it, but focus instead on the fact that they've got a dozen handguns between them and fewer machine guns than that. No technical vehicles but the hummer, and when Star pulls a slingshot out of her pack and fixes a grenade to it, then lets it fly...it lands in the hummer's open sunroof, promptly taking care of that.

Screams shake the grey overhead as bodies burn and shrapnel flies. I duck over Pia as bits of flaming debris sail through the smoky sky in our direction, catching a hot ember against my back. I shake it off and tip my head up, searching…looking…it couldn't have been so easy, could it? Could Jack be…d…

"Diego!"

My blood turns to ice. My even pulse lurches along like an angry drunk. I look up. In the center of the road, surrounded by a ring of cars, Jack lounges out of the sunroof of a black SUV, looking like he's right at home. He holds a handgun and nothing more and when he meets my gaze, he smiles at me.

I grab Pia instinctively and pull her behind me. I'm not even thinking about our plan at this point. I don't want her to see him, to be infected by the same poisonous drug I was. He's a devourer of souls, Jack, even if mine might not have been much to feed on.

Jack's gaze flashes to Pia, behind me now. "Diego!" She's trying to get the barrel of her gun past me, so she can shoot, but I've got her pinned to my side.

With my other arm, I lift my M16, point it at Jack's chest and shoot. My shot lists a little too far to the left and pegs Jack in the shoulder. His body slams back against the sunroof, but he right himself and laughs. Hopped up on Other blood, that shit probably has no effect on him. I need a headshot. And then I'll take his head just to be sure, cut him up and burn all the pieces. There will be no coming back. There can't be. I'm done with him fucking haunting me.

"Diego, I am so thrilled to see you," he roars at me over the sounds of the chaos. Everything seems to dim behind his words. The roar of the burning hummer, shattering glass, bullets and the tinny sound they make as they hit metal, and the duller sound they make as they thud into bodies — all of it fades to white noise until there's just me and Jack.

Green eyes meet mine, looking brighter than I remember them even as they denude me to nothing. Until I'm just a little boy standing outside of a diner, wishing…wanting…

Jack's the only family I ever had, and in my own sick way, I loved him. I still do.

"Diego!" Pia stares up at me from where I've shoved her flat onto her back on the floor of the pickup.

She's still talking, but I don't hear her. All I see is her face and all I can feel is the trickle of her fingers over my scars, as she touches each one with a gentle care a monster like me doesn't deserve. I don't deserve her. But I love her.

This isn't love. I hear her voice in my head as loud as if it were Jack's. Replacing him. No, replacing him means that she'd have to somehow step into the Jack-shaped hole that's there in my chest. It's as if she…as if she fills up the hole with little kisses until the hole ceases to be a hole anymore… as if he ceases to exist.

This is love.

"You mean ev-ev-everything to me," I growl down at her, before wrenching her up by the neck and brutalizing her mouth with mine. I'm breathing hard when I pull back, and sound returns to me louder than ever now.

"Avery's hit!" I hear Zala yell. "Pull back!"

"They're retreating!" Comes a voice from one of the Others with us. "Follow them!"

And then Jack, "Bring me Diego!"

And then goddamn Rico, "We want Pia first!"

And then Pia. "Diego."

I grin down at her and she blinks, startled. A barrage of bullets slams into the side of our truck. "Let's ffffinish this."

I pound my fist on the cab of the truck and the truck lurches ungainly back, and then forward as Roderick pulls the truck around and we start to retreat. I can hear the roar of engines at my back first dimming, then growing louder.

"It's working," Calvin whispers.

I look over at him and see he's got blood all over him. "The fuck happened…"

"It's not mine." He points his rifle to Mikey, who's holding onto his chest like his heart's trying to stage a rebellion and break free.

Mikey grimaces at me. "Your boy Jack's got a good aim."

"A g-g-good memory." He hasn't forgotten Mikey either, of that I'm sure.

"Jack shot you?" Pia says.

She crawls over to him, but bullets thud against the truck and she flattens herself to the bed. We ride like this for some time, and when the lull is long enough, I dare a glance up to see what's happening.

"How's it look?" Pia says, panting. Her hands are sticky with red now, but Mikey keeps waving off her assistance.

"I'm fine."

"I was talking to Diego."

"They're fffffollowing. It's wwwworking."

Calvin whoops. Pia beams. But that cold snake that sits in the middle of all my plans keeps slithering, and growing and when we finally reach the drug store, he's a turbulent fucking cobra sinking his fat fucking teeth into my face. Something is wrong with all of this.

Walls rise up on either side of us as we make our way towards the entrance of the backyard. Reinforced steel is mixed with sheets of tin and pallets of wood to create a well-fortified container. Once we get Jack in here, the Lahve's aliens will surround him from the rooftops, Abel and Kane will close the exit and we'll…

The music blaring in front of us cuts off in one blazing explosion. There are screams. Screams from *our* people. I'm already starting up on my knees to see what the fuck is going on when I hear Roderick, from the cab, roar, "Oh shit!"

The car goes sideways. Spirals through the air. Doing dips and dances. We fly forever. We fly for seconds. When we land, I'm face down on the cold ground and something heavy's lying on my legs. My ears ring.

"Diego? Diego!" Pia's voice becomes distinct, but it takes a while and it echoes in a way that's unsettling.

I blink my eyes open in time for her to roll me onto my back. She exhales in a rush when she takes me in and sees me alive. The relief on her face hurts worse than the fall...at least for the first second. Then I breathe.

"Shh..." Pain spiderwebs across my back and chest as I struggle for air.

Pia's got her hands under my armpits and is dragging me back...where? There's a huge white wall in front of us...only it's a carving? Stone? It's got some faces in the front of it I think. I remember seeing it before. Between the sculpture of four white faces and the wall, there's a narrow space of about six feet.

Pia drags me into the shadowy safety next to Roderick. He's sitting up on his heels, sweat dripping down the sides of his face as he stares down at the body below him — Calvin's — and presses both hands to the bloody spot on the front of Calvin's shirt.

"Don't you fucking dare..." He growls under his breath.

But Calvin is wheezing. I slowly roll onto my side, and then push myself up. Pia's gone and I'm still shaking out my head.

"Pia," I growl.

A roar. It's deafening. *It's Kane.* And if Kane's making sounds like that, it could only mean one thing. No. "Pia." My heart catches in my chest, but my gaze focuses as my adrenaline pushes me to action and I swallow in gulps of air like a drowning man.

"I'm here," she heaves, Mikey's massive body in her grip as she saves his life, just like she saved mine.

His middle name is agony in this moment, and I can see the shrapnel that's embedded deep in his left side and on the right side of his chest.

Pia's fingers start to pick at it, drawing shouts of pain from him every time. "Just hold on, let me..."

"Diego, did you really think you could beat me!" Jack's voice calls out and it's loud and cold and enveloping. How? How! I don't understand how he beat me when I thought I anticipated everything.

Moving past Roderick and a broken Calvin, I crawl to the edge of the sculpture and peer out at the scene. It is one of pure carnage. The destroyed remains of both trucks block the backyard's only entrance, preventing any more of our people from getting in.

Or out.

And in the center of the space beside a maniacal-looking statue of a rabbit, there's Jack and the Dixie brothers — Clay with his one arm, Adam with his dark hair, and Rico lording over the rest of them — and there's also someone else...

He stands taller than the humans beside him, his skin as dark as the rest of their's is light. His hair is sheared tight to his scalp like mine used to be and he wears battle armor — black, military-like — but what's most shocking about him are his eyes.

All the way from here, even with smoke wafting between us, I can see their alarming color. Bright lavender, they beam like neon, emitting their own light. And it's horrible. Unsettling. Carnivorous. He definitely isn't human, but he doesn't really look like an alien either. He looks like something worse.

Coughing draws my attention to the bodies before them. Human bodies, and Heztoichen. Abel and Kane kneel side-by-side with Laiya, Gabe, Luke, Matt and Mo, looking like they're ready to face the music that's long since finished.

To the far left, Constanzia is kneeling in the shadows of the wreckage blocking the exit. There's a body lying face down in front of her. Zala is at her right side and Marine is at her left. They're all hunkered down trying to save the life of someone who, by the slump of their shoulders, is likely already dead.

My heart squeezes. Avery? The happy one?

That seems so wrong. Except it isn't. Did I forget where I was? The good all die painfully in Population.

"Did the Lahve's people betray us?" Roderick asks, gasping over Calvin's body as he props Calvin up on his side.

Mikael speaks around his wounds. "Can't be. I mean, they're dressed just like his fighters, but his fighters are loyal to the Lahve above anything, and he's loyal to the Notare, above anything. They aren't authorized to harm humans. And did you notice the mark on these guys?" Mark? "Some have it on their wrists, others have it on their necks. It's the same thing we saw on the Others — the *Heztoichen* — who tried to kill Abel. They had those ticks on her necks."

"Do you recognize them? Are they the same ones?"

Mikey shakes his head. "The leader, I don't recognize, but I think I saw one male that looks familiar. I'm not sure though..."

"Diego, come out and bring your new pretty friend, why don't you? Send her over here to this big, fat rabbit." I can hear the hollow thunk of his hand against the big plastic rabbit with horns.

My mind is racing. I take another look and count our odds. Bad. They look fucking bad.

"Diego, the longer you make me wait, the more likely I am to kill the one I already started on, first. Your little leader here is looking mighty tempting..."

Kane's roar rattles me down to my intestines, which twist. I look at Pia and hallucinate the sight of her flayed alive, like Abel once nearly was. Only Pia doesn't have any Heztoichen blood in her, to save her life. She's just a human. So fragile.

"I can't let them kill her," she says, shuffling towards me. "Even if it only buys us some time. The Lahve's guys still have to be coming...don't they?" She's pleading with me, even though I've got no answers. "And the others. They'll be able to find a way through, once they pick off everyone outside."

"Wwwwe don't know how mmmmany they brought. And I'm not let-let-letting him torture you."

A gruff voice I don't recognize speaks. "This is taking too long. Our agreement was your lives in exchange for the human Notare. She is the only one we want."

"Blasphemous," someone spits. I peek again and see another Other standing just behind the first. Dressed all in black, like the first, she's got freckled cheeks, light brown skin and wild, unruly brown hair as well as the same frightening lavender eyes as the first.

"What are we waiting for? Kill the false Notare, now, brother."

"Silence," says the male. His alarming gaze switches to Jack, who looks unfazed. "We want the pleasure of ending the Notare's life."

"You sacks of swine," Kane writhes. He's being held down by two Others. "The Lahve should have killed you when he had the chance. When he arrives…"

"When he arrives, the human Notare will be long dead and we will be long gone. Tare will select another *worthy* of it, and balance will be restored," says the violet-eyed male. "The Lahve cares little for life. Even your precious human whore's. He cares only for the Tare. Do not delude yourself into thinking he cares for you."

His female counterpart snarls, "We are correcting nature's imbalance. You will thank us when it's over, Notare."

Kane shouts an insult in his own language, but the other two don't rise to it.

"You have been confused. We are helping bring you clarity," she answers.

Mikael is holding his chest together with his hands, but is still trying to stand up on his own two feet, like he's going to throw his body between the female and the woman he's in love with. Knowing him, he will. Even if she is pregnant with his brother's kid.

Pregnant. The word hits me and sticks, demanding something from me. A plan? But what is it?

"We just want our sister," comes Rico's blunt voice. He sounds so petulant, like a child, next to the weight of words spoken with age and brutal force.

I can see Jack roll his eyes, all the way from here. "Which one is she? If she's one of the ones still trapped outside, then we can't vouch for her."

"She's here. We saw her on one of the trucks."

And that's when I feel it, all of the answers clicking together. My opening. Oh fuck… I'm not going to be able to use my weapons. I'm going to have to *talk* my way out of this one.

I glance over my shoulder at Pia, knowing how we can kill them. Because Constanzia was wrong. I'm not supposed to be the hero.

Pia is.

I was wrong, too. This whole time, Pia's been telling me the right thing — giving me answers I was too stupid and blind and proud to accept — it's not my job to protect her. Correction — it's not *just* my job to protect her — she's strong enough to protect me too and she's definitely strong enough to protect herself.

I've still got her trapped in my gaze as I roar over the sounds of the Dixie brother's answer. "I'll never let you have her, Jack. She's *mine.*"

"Oh Diego, Diego, Diego… Did you learn nothing in our time together? Everything you have is mine. Now let me see the pussy you've lost your mind to. I'll give you another three-seconds before I start to get too jealous."

"Nnno!"

"Enough!" The Other shouts.

"No!" Jack roars in reply. "You will wait until I have decided you can have her, or else her death will be mine." I can hear the click of a safety going off, a gun's hammer being cocked… Abel doesn't have much time.

I look at Pia, grab my butterfly knife, grab the front of her shirt and shove my butterfly knife between her tits. Jack doesn't like the shape of a woman. It's the one place he won't check. While Pia's hands flutter, confused, as I relieve her of the rest of her weapons, I grab the back of her head and wrench her ear to my lips.

"Ssssave us. I know you c-c-c-can."

I pull back from her and kiss her hard, memorizing her taste. Earth and water. Wind and the sea. My nerves are shot to fuck, but I can't pull back from this moment, from this plan or its uncertain trajectory. She meets my gaze and she seems to *understand* what's required of her, and what's at stake should everything go to shit. But, like Pia would, she smiles in the face of it.

Silently, she mouths, "Thank you," without saying anything at all. What the fuck is she thanking me for? Sending her to her death? Sweat breaks out over every inch of me. My stomach lurches.

I'm going to be sick as she shouts at the top of her lungs, "Diego, let me go! I'm not going to let them kill her!"

"No!" The agony in my voice as she runs out from behind the statue into the center of the backyard is the only thing about this moment that isn't fake or forced.

I throw myself out from behind the safety of the structure and trail after Pia as I watch her approach Jack with her hands raised. He flinches when he sees me and for a moment, I worry I've miscalculated everything.

His hand on his gun is shaking. He's got the shakes. Must mean he's been feeding on his dogs for days. Human blood makes Jack crazy — crazier than usual. Right now, the others to his left are looking at him like they've drawn the same conclusion.

"That's her. She's our sister," Rico says, taking a step toward Pia, causing Jack to swing his gun up to Rico's head.

"Don't move. This woman's mine."

Rico frowns and his fists clench. "That wasn't our agreement."

"That was before I realized that she's taken something very precious to me."

"Jack," I bark, "P-p-please. She's p-p-p-pregnant…"

Rico and Adam and Clay all speak at once, seething. They break formation, stepping out of line with the bad guys to descend on Pia.

Pia looks at me over her shoulder, her hair whipping back and forth, looking like moonlight in the grey. Her cheeks are red and her eyes are blazing, but I can see a trust in them that I don't deserve, but that I'm going to try to earn right now, and every day after this one. Because this is not the end of our story. And guarded with that knowledge, I'm not afraid of Jack. Not anymore.

"Get away from her," Jack seethes at the brothers. "She is mine now."

Rico is closing in on Pia and when he arrives in front of her, he slugs her across the jaw. I start forward, rushing the brothers, who turn to me in unison. They each draw arms.

"You defiled our sister."

I nod. "You can't have your m-m-mother back. I t-t-t-took Mmmoira from you."

"And my fucking hand!" Clay is the first to fire.

The bullet hits me square in the chest and I hear Pia scream. But Jack's scream is louder. "No! You stupid fuck! Diego belongs to *me!*"

He lifts his gun as I drop to my knees and he opens fire on the three brothers, sending them all to the ground. Rico's still alive, still coming for me, even as my consciousness fades in and out.

But I don't care about Rico. I pull my M16 around my body and I pull the trigger.

The Other with the dark skin and the female beside him look at me as my bullets push them back. Not sure if they're dead. Knowing the rules of Population, probably not.

"Sing it with me girls," Constanzia roars, followed by a chorus of screeches tearing through the world as they belt out, *"Belieeeeeeeeve."*

I'd have shouted for everyone to get down, but there's no need. Pia drops. Laiya drops. Mo and Matt drop. Kane throws himself over Abel and plasters the both of them to the ground.

Tacktacktacktacktack. The Browning M2HB joins in the chorus and sings and it sings loud.

Returning fire lights up the grey and I hear the thud of a wounded body — more than one — behind me. But someone — at least one voice — keeps singing. It's Constanzia. Her voice jerks with pain, but she doesn't give up. I don't know her yet, but I know that she's like Pia. She never will. "I'm strong. I really do think ladadadada…" Tacktacktacktacktack.

"Bring her down!" The female Other with the wild hair shouts from her position hidden behind the weird horned rabbit.

A blurry figure rushes past me. He's got blood all over his white shirt, but he's running — he's fucking flying. Mikey throws himself at the Other woman, who grunts as he collides with her. I lose track of the two of them as Kane — and Abel — sever the connection. They're charging some of the other Others now, both weaponless.

"Abel!" I roar.

She whips her head to look at me, and I remove one of my hunting knives and let it skate over the ground until it knocks into her feet. She picks it up, spins and stabs just as an Other lifts his own blade and tries to bring it down on her throat.

I don't see the rest of the fight. I just follow Pia with my gaze. She's on her feet, circling a man — a monster. He's injured, clutching his stomach which is dotted with red, but for Jack that means nothing.

The woman I love is fighting the man that I hate.

Agony rips into me. Love too. I think about Pia's God and I pray. I may not believe in him. But she believes in him, and I believe in her.

"Pia! You ruined her." Hands are on my legs, pulling me down to meet Rico's rage.

I turn to face it and drag some rage of my own out from the depths — the same rage that's keeping me breathing. Just kidding. There is no dragging. It's always there and I use it to scrabble over the ground until I eventually win the upper hand.

My stomach hurts, like I've been run through with a bone spear, but I continue to drag that fire from those depths as I straddle his chest and find his neck with my fingers. His hands are slick with his own blood and mine and he can't find purchase in my skin. He pulls at my tee shirt, but it's a piece of shit and it just gives.

Eventually, his movements slow and his face turns from white to purple to blue and his arms go slack and it's just as his eyes roll into the back of his skull and my own thoughts begin to disperse, that I remember what Luke once said. He may be a bastard, but his life is up to Pia.

Pia.

I draw my arm back and slug him hard enough to silence him. I need to get up and get to Pia, but when I try to move, it's hard to do much more than lurch off of his body. My stomach. Something's wrong with it. I look down and see the blood without understanding how there could be so much of it. Also, why is it slowing me down? I have to get to Pia!

A grunt pulls my attention up, because I recognize it as Jack's. He's still fighting my girl and I can tell he's injured her because she limps where before she didn't. Fucker. I want his head. I want him dead on the ground below me! But more than all those things, I want her safe. With my injuries, all of those things won't be possible, I know that.

But...

...what if we fight him together?

The thought is strange and alien for someone who's spent so much time living and fighting and dying alone, but it sticks.

"Pia," I try to say. Try, but nothing comes. So instead, I say, "Jack."

He looks up at me as I lurch forward, falling and catching myself on one arm. He laughs. "Oh Diego, please look up. I want you to see this."

His gaze flashes and it's full of satisfaction. He's going to kill her. He's going to make me watch.

She grunts and his gaze refocuses on her. She spins and kicks, connecting with his thigh. He catches her foot so easily…but she seemed prepared for that, so even while my soul leaves my body as he swipes for her chest, ripping her shirt apart, she slashes.

It looks like such a small thing, the way the knife flutters in her hand, catching the light seconds before Jack's head tips back, his throat open, blood pouring out of it. It's darker than it should be. Black mixed with red. How much of them did he drink?

Pia jumps back as he roars out his rage, but with one hand clutching his throat and the other reaching for her, he's not in a position to defend himself when she swipes again. She repeats the same move — spin then kick. She connects with his leg this time and as he goes down, she brings her blade with her and whips it into the side of his head, piercing his temple.

Jack's torso jerks. His knees hit the concrete about ten… twenty feet from where I'm kneeling. Now he's kneeling. Like this we're at eye level. His gaze holds mine and he's seething, blood seeping out from between his teeth. He wants to live. He wants it more than anything. Even more than he wants me.

"Diego!" Pia shouts my name and I feel her shoulder slide under my armpit a moment later.

But why is she coming to me? Why isn't she running?

"The Lahve's forces arrived. The Others who were with Jack ran. Abel's alive and so is Kane. Mikey's running around trying to revive everyone on our team. Everyone else is dead! You did it!" She gives my side a small squeeze, but my gaze still hasn't left Jack's form, now prone.

"Not yet. And n-n-n-nnnot…" I can't finish. I want to tell her that this wasn't me, but I can't find the words, not as I stagger forward the few feet it takes for me to arrive at Jack's side.

He hacks up a lungful of blood. And then another. "Diego, how could you?" He sighs, sounding strangled by his own blood. He smiles up at me and through slack, bloody lips, he lies to me and it's a lie that, up to recently — maybe even this moment — I thought was true. "I loved you."

I shake my head, things getting hazy and switching out of focus. I can feel Pia's hands on my back. I can hear her shouting for help. But right now, I've got something to finish. My life. Because when I close my eyes, I don't care if Jack takes me with him, but there's going to be a world without Jack in it when I wake up. One where Pia can be safe from him and his horrors.

My voice is hoarse and I can taste metal on my teeth as I whisper, "This-this is-isn't love." I sweep my fingers from my temple to my torn lip, remembering the way he'd looked at me as he'd delivered it. He'd looked at me enrapt, with pure devotion and revulsion.

I jerk my second hunting knife free of the scabbard and show it to him. Fear flickers in his face as I bring it to the hand covering his neck. I want him to feel the cold of the blade and feel the words on my lips down to his wicked soul.

"This is love." I say without stutter at the same time that I sink my blade through his hand, through his throat, through his spinal column, severing it in one stroke.

So much more than he deserved.

His eyes roll back as heat fills mine. I don't know why. Maybe I did love him. If love and hate can live together, I'm sure I did. But mostly, I think, I want to cry out of relief.

It takes me some time, but I'm not interrupted as I finish removing Jack's head from his body. I don't want there to be any chance he'll come back, not even as a spirit.

When I'm finished, I fall, landing hard on my side next to his body. The smell of him — rich metal and hard sulfur — disgusts me. I don't want to touch him. I try to pull away from him, but I can't really move. I want to close my eyes.

"Don't even think about it," comes the hard crack of a woman's voice. It reminds me of a voice I've heard before. But she's a woman Jack strung up in a kill box. No way she could have survived. I should know, I almost died trying to give her a shot.

And then another voice, one that's softer, one that has no business being in Population at all. "Diego, you're going to be alright."

And even though nothing's alright and nothing will ever be alright out here in the shit strange world called Population, I blink up into warm brown eyes and I believe her.

Then I sleep.

Chapter Sixteen

L istening to the sound of voices, I wonder if I'm dead or asleep. I have to guess at alive, considering how loud they all are, and the fact that I'm finding it grating. But other than the discomfort of hearing their chatter, their laughter, their god awful singing, I feel pretty good. There's no pain, no agony. Nothing.

"I think he's awake," a male voice says. I open my eyes and groan at the sight. At the *angle*.

"Je-Je-Jesus Christ," I groan. "D-d-d-didn't expect to see your ug-ug…" Inhale. Exhale, "Ugly mug first thing."

"Ha," he chokes out, tilting his chin up so I see even more chin and neck and blonde stubble, plus the insides of both his nostrils. "Hate to break it to ya, but you're no beauty queen yourself."

"Don't I kn-know it." I feel my mouth pull up into a grin, the sound of the truck's engines filling all the empty spaces Mikey's voice doesn't. Back in the eighteen-wheeler bunker, then. That must mean we're back on the road. But who's we? Who made it? Who didn't?

My heart catches, expanding through the room that once caged it and it feels so damn full. It's worry that does that to me, because I've suddenly got so many feels for so many people. Matt, Mo, Calvin, Roderick, Abel, Kane, their baby, Constanzia, Star and their whole gang, the woman and her little Jack, Luke…

"Pia," I breathe.

Mikey's smile doesn't shift at all, but spreads. "Don't get your panties in a twist. She's right here. Pia," he shouts over his shoulder.

A second later, pounding feet and then I see slender fingers cupping Mikey's shoulder and pulling him out of the way. Pia appears in his place, looking disheveled, her hair mussed on one side and her cheeks flushed.

"Diego! They made me go to sleep. I didn't want to. I'm so sorry I wasn't here when you woke up. I wanted to be, but you've been asleep for two days. Are you okay? How do you feel?"

She lowers herself onto the edge of my cot and her hands move to my neck, my bare chest, my face. There's a sheet covering me, but it doesn't present much of a barrier against the sudden surge of blood to my crotch that hardens my cock to a tire iron.

I lift my arms, surprised to find that they work, and snake them around her waist. I drag her down to me, and then under me and then my mouth is on her mouth and I'm pouring myself into her whether she knows it's happening or not. I want her.

Need comes over me swiftly, like death, and my hands start pulling at her tee shirt and jacket while my mouth moves from her soft, swollen lips to her jaw and ear down her neck.

"Jesus Christ. Stop the truck!" Mikey's voice shouts.

There's murmuring. Abel's voice. Kane's. Somebody else's too. Then Abel says, "Fucking psycho." But she's laughing. "Why not? He deserves it. So does she. Everybody out!"

Stomping feet, giggles, whispers. One that says, "Thank God Luke is on the other truck..." The rustling of fabric as people make their way past us. But I don't look up at any of them. I don't look at anything. I'm all feels. All hers.

"Diego," she whispers, "I was so worried. You were dying." Her hands are threaded in my hair, which desperately needs to be shaved, but for right now I like it. I like the way she pulls me around like I'm hers to do whatever she wants with. Fuck it. Maybe I like having hair, after all.

I rear up and knock the back of my head on the underside of the bunk above me. I curse and Pia barks out laughter that's long and loud and high enough for me to float on. I grin in response and snarl as I find the buttons on the front of her pants, undo them, and yank them down over her ass along with the panties she's got on underneath.

Her laughter fades on an inhalation. I push up her shirt and free her tits from the bra she's got on and she lets me.

"Diego, are you sure you're okay?"

I shake my head. "Need you."

"I'm yours for as long as you need me."

"F-f-f-forever."

"Forever then." She smiles.

I'm naked and that comes as a welcome surprise when I get her legs out of her pants in the cramped space under this bunk and cover her with my body. I reach down between her legs to make sure she's ready for me and find that she's wet. I'm not confident she's wet enough, but when I pull back to taste her down there, she loops an arm around my neck while her other hand reaches down between us and lines me up with her hot opening.

"I want you too, Diego."

"I lllllove you." I slam forward, driving home like a madman.

Pia's body jolts, so I hold her fixed, wrapping my arms around her like a coiled snake while my hips pump to a frantic beat. "I love...love..." She doesn't finish. Her voice breaks off and I feel the unimaginable sensation of her pussy pulsating around my length. It makes it hard to think, hard to focus, hard not to nut right there.

Fuck it. What am I holding back for? We've got days. Eternities. Forever to do this. Because I'm not letting anything get between us again. Not gangs, not Others, not scavengers, not psycho family members, not the ghosts of monsters, not even me.

Not even me.

My chest is aching as I breathe into her hair. "Want-want-want to nnnnut in you."

"What about getting pregnant?" She says. And that's not a no.

My chest sparks. The thought of coming in her has my cock pulsing. I can feel precum already leaking out of the tip and into her body or maybe I'm just imagining it, but whatever it is, it feels so freaking good. And not just the weight of her wet walls shivering against me. But the thoughts that they bring. Watching her get round like Abel's already starting to. I picture Kane's face when he looks down at his woman and damn if that doesn't look like a man who has everything he wants and wants everything he has.

I want it too.

"I wwwwant it with you. Want ev-everything with you."

Her hand slides back up into my hair and she pulls me down, her lips finding mine and prying them open with very little effort. Our tongues clash, a battle I don't stand a chance of winning because I lost a long time ago. Over that first bath in the river. Over that fight in the woods. The first time she looked at me and made me feel like I was anybody, and like I was somebody.

"Fuck it," she says between my lips and she laughs. "Fuck me, Diego. And don't hold back."

The haze grips my mind and lasts and lasts. I'm completely lost in her. I think hours might pass or it could just be breaths. But when I come to, there's that creeping heat lighting up toes and throttling through the backs of my legs. My back arches up. I bite my lip hard enough to draw blood, but I don't feel it. All I feel is the movement in my hips and the sudden fire exploding out of the tip of my cock and into her body as I fill her up, up, up.

She yelps beneath me and I feel her body start to shudder a second time, shivering like she's cold, even with the sweat on her skin and my body wrapped around hers like a glove. But I know she isn't. She might be wet as morning dew, but she's also pure flame.

"Fuck," she says, laughing as I push myself off of her.

My head is in the clouds, but I still manage to stay grounded enough to work my way down her body and spread her legs with my hands. I slide two fingers into her opening and spread her wide so I can see down her channel. White semen sits there in the midst of so much pink and my stomach clenches, my abdomen jerks, my thighs harden.

I look up at Pia and a momentary fear flashes in her eyes. She should be afraid, because I'm nowhere near done with her. I wrench her towards me, cover her again and begin the process anew and I keep repeating it until I've wrung her out and she lies wasted on the cot and my own muscles have turned to soup and it's all I can do not to crush her as I flop down beside her.

She's covered in my cream as I'm covered in hers and I look down the length of her body at the mess I've made of it and grin. "I h-h-hope you d-d-do get pregnant."

"You do?"

I nod. "I was wwwwrong."

"Hm?"

"On the rrrroad, I thought I wanted to d-d-die. But life is w-w-worth living. It's worth fighting for."

She smiles and nuzzles her nose against my jaw as she twists on the cot to face me. She wraps her body around mine and I feel like a man made anew, stripped of all my scars and rendered whole.

"You're worth fighting for."

I blink, feeling heat grip the backs of my eyes. "You fffought for me. You k-killed Jack."

She traces her thumbs over my eyebrows. It feels good and I lean into the feeling. Her hands on me, causing pain and not pleasure. Who would have known such a thing would be possible? I wouldn't have six months ago. I couldn't have even fathomed it.

"You trusted me. You knew that Jack would try to kill me, but you also knew that my brothers wouldn't let him."

She shudders. "You knew Jack wouldn't let them kill you either, but you sacrificed yourself when you let them think I was pregnant with your baby. You knew they'd shoot you the moment they thought that Moira was taken from them."

I nod at her retelling, then frown at the worry lines that have appeared between her eyebrows. "Are they d-d-dead?"

She blinks at me, surprised, then shakes her head. "I forgot you don't know. I was coming to tell you, but you distracted me."

She punches me in the shoulder lightly, playfully. A word I didn't know before her, but that I now cherish.

"Mikey brought you back with his blood and after, went around and offered his blood to a dozen of our people. He saved Star and Zala, who were almost dead, Calvin too. He also gave his blood to Luke.

"He was too late to save Avery, though. And Marine too. They died along with three others from our side." Her voice grows distant and melancholy, as if she has truly not known loss before in her life. As if, in her eyes, all lives are special and worth something. Because in her eyes, they are.

"Evan, Ellen and Rotran. They were with me in the caves. They were with me and my family from the beginning."

She starts to get distant from me, but I quickly bring her back. I touch her cheek gently and coax her into returning my gaze. When she does, I whisper, "But how many did you ssssave?"

Her frown tilts back up into a flat line, before one edge of her mouth curls up, just a little bit. "Fourteen. And it wasn't just me, but we managed to keep just fourteen of Jack's guys alive by the end. That's in addition to the dozen or so from the caves and from the attack on the road, who were locked up in Wall Drug before. Most seem to be adapting to the change of leadership pretty well. We were worried Jack's guys would rebel, but they seem more relieved that he's gone than anything."

"Your b-b-brothers?"

She winces. Looks away. "Rico…didn't make it. Mikey could have saved him, but…he's more a danger to others than the other two are. I talked to my dad and we…we decided he shouldn't be saved with the others."

Shoot. That's gotta hurt, even if I'm not sure about her assessment. Clay seemed dangerous too, even with one arm. I tighten my grip around her and wait for the tension to bleed out of her body.

"You d-d-d-did the right th-thing. They hhhurt a lot of people."

She exhales, "I know. But he was my brother. I just…I wonder what mom would have done."

"She ssssounds like a good wo-woman. She'd have done the ssssame thing."

I don't know if Pia believes me, but she lapses into a silence that I allow, for a time. She needs time to grieve. Hell — *heck* — we both do. She lost her psychopath brother, same as I lost mine.

"And-and the Oth-Others?" I finally ask, after some time. It's hard not to fall asleep right here, but I know we're not out of the woods yet — literally — and we do need to keep moving. I just want to tally my opponents and my odds first. Who's still left among the breathing? Who's still hunting us? Who are we hunting?

"Apparently the ones who attacked were part of that same gang that attacked Abel on the road. From what different people remember seeing, they all had the same marks. And they all ran when the Lahve's backup showed up. Kane, Laiya and some of the others seem to think that they share ancestry with the Lahve and that they come from his same breed of Heztoichen? But they aren't sure. The Lahve is supposed to be the only one of his kind here."

I frown, unsure of what to make of that. All I do know is that if they're all still alive, headed by that dark-skinned Other guy and the light-skinned Other chick, they'll keep coming until either Abel's dead or they are.

"We're closing in on Brianna. Only a day or two away. Kane thinks that Abel will be safe there. Apparently, they've heard from the Lahve and he's agreed to stay until the birth of Abel's child or until the Heztoichen gang is destroyed. Whichever comes first."

This guy comes with a lot of promises. In my experience, promises like safety usually come with too high a price. Jack taught me that. But…

Jack's not here. And I'm free and I've got my arms wrapped around the most beautiful woman in the world — left in the world — and she claims to love me and I believe her because I love her back.

I kiss her instead of answering and she's smiling when I pull away. Too quickly, though, her smile turns to something else. I can't quite read it, but I know I don't like it as much as the lazy way she was looking at me before.

"Will you do something for me?"

Anything. Everything. Lay waste to the whole world. "Y-yes."

Her eyes go distant. She starts to sit up. "They found a girl in the trunk of one of Jack's cars. She's um…she's in real bad shape."

"A g-girl? That's not J-Jack's usual MO."

"It doesn't sound like he was using her…that way. She had Other blood in her system. It looks like…"

"He was d-d-d-draining her." I feel my throat clench and the blood drain out of my face. I've seen Jack do that that to Heztoichen they've caught before, but I don't know what draining would look like on human skin.

"Wh-wh-what can I d-d-do about it?"

Pia's putting her clothes back on. Sh...shoot. I try to snatch away her tee shirt, but she's quicker and pulls it on over her head in a rush. "Get dressed. I think we've taken enough of the group's time already." She winks at me. "And I think you could try to talk to her. You've been a victim of Jack's before." A pawn. A son. A prodigy.

Begrudgingly, I put my clothes back on and follow her to the edge of the truck. Right before she pulls back the flaps and jumps down, she looks up at me, her eyes ever bright in the dark.

"About the girl. Abel knows her somehow. They met on the road apparently a few months ago. Abel wants her to live."

I suck in a breath. It hits me like a punch to the stomach. I understand now why Pia wants me to talk to the girl.

I am that little girl. And that little girl is me.

She's another one of Jack's victims left out on the road like carnage for carrion to feed. And Abel, like some merciless winged angel has struck down to place one warm hand on her cold, dead chest, every intention of resuscitating the unwilling.

"Sh-show me."

Pia pushes the tent flaps aside, and I notice that somewhere in the maelstrom, she's managed to arm herself. She steps out before me like a bodyguard, looking ferocious. Her shoulders rolled back, her gaze sharp as she canvases everything. How could I have ever thought she was the one who needed so much protection? I grin and she relaxes, but only after a moment.

"Wow." The slightly southern drawl pulls my attention to the left. Seated on top of an ammo chest is Roderick, polishing his M4. The toothpick perpetually in his mouth slides to the side when he smiles up at me. "Bold, my friend. You are one bold-ass mother fucker."

I sidle up to Pia's side, slide my arm across her shoulder and with my free hand, return Roderick the middle finger he showed me once, not long ago, in kind. The rest of the group is seated in small clusters close to the edge of the trees lining the road, eating, drinking, talking, even laughing, like we haven't just recently battled our way out of hell — or a drug store.

We've somehow managed to make our way back to forests again, pine trees glowing in shades of dark green to copper, like it's fall. Like it's fall before The Fall. It might just be my imagination, but even the sky looks a little further recessed, as if the Grey is giving us space to breathe again.

I see Constanzia's group farthest in the back seated in the bed of a pickup, but frown when I notice that the women are just three now, instead of the five that they were three days ago. They're still singing through, even if it is a sad song sung more quietly than they ordinarily would.

Even though it's a sad song, it does something to me to see that they're still singing.

Every community I've ever come across can be defined by a word. Maybe two. Jack's was bloodthirsty, the Dixie brothers were desperate, the Others with the slash mark scars were determined, but Abel and her crew?

Resilient.

It's a beautiful thing to see. It buoys the soul.

We round the first barracks and make our way up to the second parked a little farther down the road. The pickups are dispersed like they always are — in the front and in the back of the convoy. Luke's sitting with Matt and Mo in one of the pickups and, seeing us, frowns.

I walk a little faster, leaving Pia to trail slightly behind. Mo and Luke jump down from the truck while Matt stays seated. Matt covers his face with his hand and shakes his head. He looks like he's laughing.

I shove my hand out to the center of Luke's chest and he jumps back, I think expecting me to punch him. Instead, I say as clearly as I can, "In l-l-love with your d-d-daughter, sssir. Thought you sh-should know."

"I think we all *heard* how much you love Pia a few minutes ago," Matt mumbles. Mo shoves Matt's shoulder, sending him toppling off of the edge of the truck, landing with a bang on the truck bed. He laughs. They both do.

I can't help but smile. Luke evidently doesn't find it funny. "I've seen you in action, son. I know you'll keep her safe. But if you ever hurt her, I will kill you."

"You w-w-w-won't need to," I whisper.

He glances over my shoulder, likely at Pia. The severe lines crossing his face flatten just a little bit. He rolls his shoulders back, shakes his head and sighs, "Then alright. But no more of this shit." He waves his finger at the trucks and the road and even Mo cracks with a little laughter as he does it.

I smile. "Yessssir."

"Excuse me, but I don't think that's for you to decide," Pia says, taking my hand and pulling me away from the group. "Or you either." She gives my palm a little squeeze.

Matt and Mo both laugh outright then, while Luke mutters, "Good Lord." My back is to Luke when he calls out to me and I turn. His crisp green gaze reminds me of a time before. A time when I looked into the diner windows and saw fathers sitting with their families, only now this one feels, strangely, like my own.

"You're alright, son. Don't give me any reason to doubt you."

I nod, swallowing down a lump. "I w-w-won't."

We make our way to the back entrance of the truck and Pia pulls back the makeshift covering — not canvas, but a series of tarps, crudely stitched together — back.

Near the entrance, Kane's sitting on an upturned crate and looks at us with worry carved into his expression. Strange to me that, looking at him now, he doesn't look like Jack at all.

His gaze switches back and forth from Pia to me before settling. "You can try," he offers, pulling back the tarp and allowing me space to enter.

I hold Pia back, asking her to wait as I step up and inside. It's dark in here. The tarps don't let in any light. There are just a couple electric lanterns hanging from some of the bunk beds to light my way down the aisle. Reminds me too much of where they'd thrown my body, strung out on pain killers and Mikey's blood, like some junkie, for days.

Halfway down the aisle, I can already smell the blood. My steps falter as I hallucinate *me* in another life, like if I just keep walking, I'll step into the past and have a chance to meet myself after they hauled me up off the asphalt and forced me to breathe when I wanted to die. And if I could just take that step into the past, I wonder what I would have told then. I wonder if the me back then would have believed any of it.

I walk to the bunks at the end of the row. Abel's sitting in one, staring at the bunk across from her. She looks up, but it takes her a while to actually see me. Her brow scrunches up. She's got tears in her eyes. She opens her mouth, but I stop her.

"Out." I cock my head to the exit.

She stands up and comes close to me, getting all up in my face in a way that's almost, but not quite intimidating. Would have been more intimidating had her hand not been covering her belly, which pokes out through her jacket just a little bit.

"Candy can't die," she rasps under her breath.

I nod, knowing, but only because I've seen that manic look before in Abel's strange, blue eyes. And whatever she sees in mine must sway her.

She quiets, pulls in a breath, then exhales more evenly. She nods once and slowly slides past me and I wait until both she and Kane or gone before taking the place Abel once had. I brace myself and hold a breath before I open my eyes and look at the human-shaped thing laid out before me.

It's a grisly sight to behold and I have to wonder if this is what Pia first saw when she looked at me. A nightmare made flesh, a flayed soul.

The girl Jack tortured is white with red hair whispering around her cheeks in soft curls. It's long and almost blends in with the marks covering her neck. Angry slashes decorate her skin from just below the jaw to just above her clavicles. They crisscross over one another. Some looking swollen, others looking infected, all looking painful.

Her arms boast the same cruel slashes and I can tell that some were made with Jack's favorite serrated hunting knife, but other cuts are smaller, more scattered, more faded too…

Jack may have eviscerated her, but he wasn't the first. The thought makes my fists clench and my bones ache. Jack could do this to *me* because I know I can take it. I'm big, and I was always mean, but this girl is young — too young — and skinny — damn near emaciated. She looks like a goddamn corpse. So white underneath the blood crusted to her. It's clear someone tried to clean her up in spots, but she refused. That's my best guess. Because that's what I would have done if I were her, too.

She's got a dress on that's stained red around the throat and the crotch. Don't know if it's from rape or if it's from Jack draining her thighs, but in either case, I know she's in pain and that she's just waiting it out. It's not that easy, though. Not here.

"You d-d-d-don't get to die if Ab-Abel doesn't give you p-p-p…permission."

I watch her wince, and then wince again at even that slight movement. Her eyelids twitch, her lashes long and copper colored. At least, that's how they look in the light of the lantern hanging from the end of her bed.

"I d-d-d-don't understand it myself, but I think sh-sh-she's got one foot planted in the sssssstream of the uni-universe." I plant my elbows on my knees and lean forward so that I can smell the metallic blood emanating from her skin more closely. It smells all human. I wonder how much Other blood she's got left in her, if any. Doubt Jack would have given her that luxury.

"You can b-b-b-b-beg for d-d-d-death, but it won't come. I should know. I've t-t-t-t-tried." I pause, watch teardrops roll from the corner of her eyes to wet her hairline, and curve back behind her ears.

"Look at me," I tell her.

She doesn't move.

"J-j-j-just want you to see what Abel ffffforced me to live through. I lllllook j-j-just like you."

It takes an eternity, but the woman's eyes flutter open and she tilts her head about a millimeter, just enough to take in the sight of my face. She closes her eyes quickly after and more tears come. There's a slight hitch to her breathing.

I know that Pia or Abel or any other human-like human would reach out and touch her right now to try to give her comfort, but I know how much comfort can hurt when you're hurting like this.

"Jack cut me into p-p-p-p-pieces…" I inhale, struggling through so many sentences strung together one after the next, but I power through it. Because Pia asked me to and I owe it to her. I also owe it to myself. "He r-r-r-raped me. T-t-t-tortured me. He ffffforced me to do the same to other p-p-people. I didn't deserve to live when Abel found me. D-d-d-d-didn't want to either.

"B-but Abel didn't give me that-that choice. She and Ashlyn and Ssssandra and Mikey shoved me b-back together and ev-ev-every day ssssssince has b-b-b-been harder than the last and I thank G-God ev-every day for Ab-Abel and what she did to me.

"If she decides you have to lllllive, it's b-b-b-because the universe has something g-g-g-g-g-good waiting for you."

Her cracked lips part. She croaks in a voice so low, it's nearly incomprehensible, "There's nothing good."

"If it we-were that easy, I'd k-k-k-kill you myself, b-b-b-but it's true."

I shake my head and watch as the trickle of tears in her eyes grows more forceful and then turns to sobs. And I wait, without moving, without touching her, offering her absolutely nothing but the stony, sorry truth until eventually her sobs fetter out.

"I'm sssssorry, but that's just the way it is. You've g-g-g-got to live."

She whispers, "But it hurts."

"It w-w-w-won't hurt ag-again. I swear on my life."

"How do you know?"

How do I tell her that, looking at her like this, I see myself in her? Or stranger, that I feel responsible for what Jack did to her? And because of that, she's as akin to me as a sister? I don't have the words for it, and even if I did, they wouldn't make sense to her. They hardly make sense to me. So I tell her an easier truth.

"I k-k-k-killed Jack, and I'll kill anyone who f-f-f-fucking touches you." I stand abruptly, feeling strong emotion swell in my chest. It burns and I can't decide if it's hate or if it's love. For too long I've lived with both.

"Now my w-w-w-wife, P-Pia..." I choke, unable to continue for a moment.

Strange that it doesn't piss me off this time, the fact that I can't even have that — her name — come to my tongue as easily as I'd like. No, this fucked up, slow way of talking is just another part of me. It could be a piece of the good part, or it could be part of the more monstrous side of me that's going to slay dragons to keep this girl — one of Jack's other battered, broken children — alive.

Happy, hopefully.

But it's a piece. And Pia loves all the pieces with her soft, perfect little heart.

"P-Pia's going to come get you cleaned up,' I say, starting again, "You can't stay llllike this."

As I stand, I watch the girl's eyes open. She sees me and though her expression is tortured, I can see a necessary resignation calm her. Her muscles settle, growing soupy. She exhales a shuddering breath.

"Don't let them give me drugs or…or blood," she stutters herself.

I shake my head. "Not on mmmmy life."

She nods, trusting me as I turn away from her and leave her there, condemned to life, just as I once was. It's a brutal prison, but I wasn't lying when I said that it wasn't her choice. Out in Population, no one has a choice either way.

I make it to the end of the truck, feeling a resolution in my bones that wasn't there before. An extra desire to protect. Jumping down and out, I land on the concrete and immediately, a body barrels my way.

"Abel," Kane grumbles, as she wraps her deceptively strong arms around me. She's got my own arms wedged against my sides and heat lights up my cheeks.

"Thank you," Abel whispers against my chest. "Mikey told us what you said."

I glance up and see the brute standing just behind his more menacing-looking brother — the one who's still glaring at the contact between me and his wife. Not wishing to get my face caved in, I carefully disentangle my arms from Abel's and tell her the rules I set for the girl called Candy. No drugs. No blood. No touching, except for Pia. I send Pia inside with a bucket and water and when she returns some time later with a muddy, bloody bucket and a rag that's got to be burned, she steps up close to me and looks up into my eyes.

"Wife, huh?" She smirks.

"Yeah." I shrug.

"You know, you're supposed to actually ask the woman about this first."

I wrap my arm around her waist, and lift her off the ground, pressing my lips to hers. Somewhere nearby, I hear a man groan. Others cheer. Someone curses.

"T-t-t-too risky," I say against her cheek.

Pia laughs into my mouth and kisses me once, even harder, for good measure. I squeeze her ass as I lower her back to the ground. "In that case, I guess I have no choice but to accept."

My heart swells a little wider and soon I'm not sure there's anything else left but a heart and emotions that are willing to do a lot — not just for Pia, either, but for every one of these crazy psychos around me, still fighting for humanity and its first new generation.

I kiss her once more, tuck her hair behind her ear and look over my shoulder at Abel and the damaged truck carrying delicate goods that have been so badly damaged. Goods worth keeping safe.

"Let's lllleave P-P-Population now. Let's go hhhhome." To a home I've never seen before, in a territory once known for brutality against the human race.

Abel laughs and slides off of Kane's lap where she'd been perched. She glances around and claps her hands together once.

"For real. Fuck this place. Population is the worst."

Chapter Seventeen

The way into Brianna is anticlimactic. Feels like it should be more than just a large silver gate built into a large silver wall, sliding open, but that's exactly what it is and all that it is.

About a block later, we pick up a tail — a couple big SUVs carrying the Lahve and his guards, whoever that its, but that's what Mikey tells me and I believe him because he's a good guy — hopeless, and an alien, but good.

The SUVs follow us down the highway for another hour before we reach a destroyed city — big from the looks of it, and full of ghosts — and then proceed more slowly through quiet, residential neighborhoods.

Ashlyn, Pia and I try to distract ourselves by playing cards, but soon, I've got my knife out and the little hole I ripped in the canvas covering by my bunk is now a face-sized portal big enough for the three of us to look out of.

I don't know what any of us were expecting — or what I was expecting — but I'm not expecting to see *people* milling about on the streets, carrying baskets from some places to other places, trying to cut grass with big machines, trying to repair wood and brick structures with small machines.

"Smells like pine," Pia says, taking a deep breath.

"There are kids," Ashlyn says, eyes bugging out of her head.

Pia gives her shoulder a squeeze in that fond way she does that makes me smile because I like that touch and the way she gives it to me. It makes me feel safe. Like everything will be okay. I also have to remember that Ashlyn's the only kid here.

"When's the lllllast t-time you saw someone your age?"

She winces when I ask her that, and shakes her head. "There were some in the Diera, but I...I didn't get along with them."

Pia seems to understand what she means better than I do, because she says, "They'll understand you better here. They've lived through Elise and survived it."

Ashlyn looks at her and nods and I don't miss the way she fingers the gun shoved into the holster on her hip. It's the same Glock I handed her, back before the caves. I'm surprised and strangely touched that she kept it.

"Alright, this is it!" Abel stands up at the back of the truck and the energy shifts from one moment to the next. Before it felt like a rising crescendo. Now it feels like the moment before all-out war. The moment that the trucks are rumbling and we're riding out to meet Jack. That uncertainty. But this...this is better than that.

This feels full of hope. Promise. Expectation — and not of being ripped apart, but of putting something together. Of building. Of rebuilding. Of wholeness.

I glance at Pia sitting next to me on my bunk, her fingers cupping her knees. I take her hand. She looks at me. I pull her to me and am about to cup the back of her head and bring her in close, when Abel's voice breaks the tension between us.

"I want to introduce you all to the Lahve. He is the mediator between all of us Notare and was kind enough to scout ahead and secure Brianna from the chaos that had claimed it in Elise's wake. He's got some info for you before you get out. Lahve." She gestures with her arm and steps to the side.

Rising up in the back of the truck is a man with dark skin and darker hair that falls in locks to his pecs, but it's his eyes that shock me. Just like the lavender-eyed Other, they shine with their own light, orange this time. It's freaky as shit, but not quite as freaky as his wicked sharp teeth.

I tense as the temperature in the truck drops by ten degrees. I glance across at the bunk on the other side of me. Candy's bunk. She's still lying down, asleep or not asleep, like she's been for the past few days.

Pia and Ashlyn are the only ones she'll let near her. Maybe because they look young. Maybe because they look at her without expectation. She's been eating though — at least a little — and she's dressed in jeans and a clean shirt that are too big for her, but they're clean. It's also got a high neckline and long sleeves.

I don't like that she can hide her scars so easily, because looking at her, you wouldn't know that she's a warrior, even though she is. Just as much as me.

"Welcome," comes the creepy, cool drawl from the back of the truck, swiveling my attention around. "You are currently in Elise's compound at the heart of Brianna. My soldiers have swept the area and the other humans that were found — Elise's blood slaves — were released. Many require rehabilitation, but some are functioning and are attempting to clear the rest of the homes so that they are...habitable, for each of you.

He pauses for too long — longer than a human would — before continuing. "The compound is about thirty square blocks and it is safe. I recommend however, that you remain central. A makeshift marketplace has been established. Certain homes have been designated for certain manufacturing centers. There are no maps, but the humans that you meet in Brianna can explain the layout to you in greater detail.

"As for your new sleeping quarters. A home adjacent mine has been deemed fit for Notare Kane and Notare Abel. For the rest of you, you are free to select among the remaining homes. All houses that are unfit for habitation have been marked with a star. Those that are safe to enter have been left unmarked. Are there any questions?"

Silence. Dead silence. There's something *wrong* with him, and I feel my hackles rise when I notice that Kane's got his body angled between the Lahve and his wife. If even *he's* uncertain, then I know that I should be.

"Alright then, everybody out! There's a lot of work to do, so we'll reconvene tomorrow at the marketplace on Starlight Avenue. Just ask around, you'll find your way," Abel shouts, but still nobody moves. She whispers something to the Lahve that I can't hear and he disappears out of the back of the truck so quickly, I don't see him move.

He's there one-second, the next...poof.

"Did y'all hear me, or would you rather live on this damn truck forever? Last one out gets to sleep here for the night." She bangs her fist on the edge of a bunkbed and suddenly everyone is in motion.

Descending from the truck into the fresh air that smells like pine, according to Pia, but really smells more like exhaust and body odor, Pia and I walk with Candy and Ashlyn to find a home they can share. Constanzia, Zala and Star offer to take them in, which they do.

A big, brick house is where they find their final home, but we've spent so long with them that most of the other houses are taken by the time Pia and I begin the hunt for one of our own.

I cock my head towards the hill marked by a sign that Pia reads out as Glengary Way. By the time we turn up, I can't tell what time it is, just that the sky is the color of terra cotta. The hill is a steep climb. Steep enough to keep most from following us — or at least that's the plan. I want Pia alone, all to myself.

Glengary Way dead ends at a cul-de-sac though a sharp right at a massive weeping willow takes us up to a second cul-de-sac called Glengary Court.

There's a corrugated tin wall separating the residential area from the highway. Must be the same wall that surrounded the entirety of Elise's compound. The wilderness up here has all been cut back and cleared, making it look strangely like the war of the Heztoichen and the humans never touched it. Even the wind smells like honeysuckle and the air is wet and warm — different from the cool, grey north.

There's more varied vegetation here and the clouds overhead are lush and full and emit a red glow and never break. No rain here. No wind. Just stagnant perspiration and all tension releases from my wrists.

I glance over at Pia as we stop in front of a brick house with a red door. I grin at her and she grins back. This is it — even if it does have a white star spray painted on the front door.

"There aren't many houses left," she says, glancing around at all the other white-starred houses ringing the cul-de-sac. "Should we try anyway?"

I nod. "Af-af-after you."

The sound of Pia chambering a round makes me grin. I've still got my M16 strapped to my chest and pull it around my body, pointing it forward and following the path it makes inside.

As we wade through the house, I have to wonder why it's got a star on the front when everything looks so goddamn suburban. Big, open kitchen, granite countertops, stainless steel appliances, hardwood floors shiny enough to see my ugly silhouette in.

The living room furniture is covered in plastic tarps, likely left by some rich family that thought they'd come back later after the apocalypse was over.

We try the upstairs and find three bedrooms with more plastic-covered furniture. The master bathroom is big enough to play baseball in and I try the water. Hot and cold, it works.

I'm too tense to be properly surprised as I stare down at the porcelain basin, watching murky water drip from my scarred hands until it clears. It's only then that I suck in a quick breath, turn the faucet off and look up.

It's the first time I see my face in more than just the warped reflection of a building's dark window, the surface of a glass of water, the thin sliver of a blade.

I look grim.

A scar begins in the center of my forehead, cutting clean across it to halve my right eyebrow. It's a bright, furious pink against my light brown skin and in the dim light, shimmers silver. Skipping over my eyelid, the scar carves a shallow groove through my cheek before curving around to meet the right side of my upper lip so that I'm trapped in a perpetual half-smile.

The scar on my neck begins where the one on my face ends. A few millimeters beneath my bottom lip, it forms a jagged line from my jaw to the collar of my shirt.

In the reflection of the mirror behind me, Pia approaches, coming closer and closer and closer…

She lowers her handgun, wraps her arms around my chest and pulls our bodies flush together. She doesn't say anything. She doesn't need to.

She just holds me.

And I just hold her.

And we keep holding each other until, at the same time, we peel apart. Just before I turn from the mirror, I smile at my own reflection.

I've got scars.

So what?

The most beautiful woman left in the world doesn't mind, so I don't give a shit.

I follow her into the basement even though it hurts my bones to let her lead the charge into potential danger. We take the stairs cautiously, keeping our guns close and ready.

The lights are out down here but I find an electric lamp by the door that has batteries that still work. It throws an unnatural fluorescence across the room we find at the bottom of the stairs.

On the lefthand side of the large space is a work bench covered in glistening stainless steel tools that are dust-free and sparkling clean. Clearly used not too long ago. On the other side of the room is an enormous steel cage.

One-part torture chamber, two-parts prison — this is why the house had a star on it?

I sigh, tension releasing from my shoulders as I inspect the equipment and Pia inspects the cage. I glance over at her standing in the prison's open doorway. She shrugs. I shrug.

Then we both laugh. How and why I couldn't tell you, but there's something about this shit that's so damn funny — so *darn* funny.

Pia shakes her head and when she straightens, she flips on her safety and puts her Beretta away. At least, for now.

"Y-y-you like it?"

"It's perfect for us," she says, and I agree in her assessment, but only because she said it.

I step in close to her and press her body against the bars of the cage. I reach for her neck and the fading mark that she wears on her shoulder. I kiss it softly.

"I want you to h-have wh-wh-whatever you want."

She takes my hair and wrenches my head back by it. When she kisses me, she bites my lower lip hard. Brutal, and so soft. Perfect for me.

"Good thing I already do." She reaches for my pants, unbuttons them and draws the zipper down.

My head drops back and I wrap my arms around her shoulders, pulling her close. Home. That's what this is, isn't it? I look into her eyes and brush my thumb over her cheek. I smile. My cheeks are hurting with how much I've been smiling these days.

"Home sweet hhhhome, Pia."

She smiles up at me and circles my cock with her fingertips.

I moan.

She whispers against the scar winding its way up my throat, "Home sweet home, Diego."

IMMORTAL WITH SCARS

POPULATION SERIES: BOOK THREE

Preview

_____

Chapter One

It is seven-thirteen. It is the evening, I suppose, though the sky betrays no difference in color. On Sistylea, it would be bright pink by now, perhaps deep purple should the clouds have resumed their cover, failing to burn off entirely before the night renders the world dark.

Here, in this world, there is no dark. There is no fluorescent pink. There is no indigo. There is only a flat red-orange that is not so much red or orange as it is grey. There are only the clocks that the Notare Abel and her *council* have elected to simultaneously set, describing a time that they have agreed upon that makes no sense to me and the time that I have long since learned to live without. Or perhaps, the time that has learned to live without me.

These numbers continue to count up and then down and then begin again in a ceaseless rhythm. *Strange, though functional.*

I rise from my seat and stride slowly to the door to my study. At precisely hour twenty the Notare Abel dismisses her council and retires to the comfort of her home with the Notare Kane.

She is heavy with child now, but she still seems intent to perform the inspections herself and she continues, despite protest from said council, from her mate, and from all other humans and Others unanimously — including from myself — to perform manual labor. Each watch she takes is strain to Notare Kane.

His affections for the female intrigue me and I have spent much *time* contemplating it.

Time.

No, I have spent much of my own *energy* devoted to thinking about their relationship. His fascination with her is fascinating in itself. He has existed for hundreds of their earth years, while she has existed for very few. She is penetrable in ways he is not. So quick to temper. Easily riled. Impetuous. Impulsive. Passionate.

Yet, he cherishes her as if she were an extension of himself.

It is a funny thing and reminds me again that Heztoichen are as different from humans as I am different to Heztoichen. A momentary grief flutters through me, one I have not devoted much of my energies to until the recent whispers reached me that there may be one of my own kind on this planet — a *female*. It is a pity that she is among these impassioned rebels who seek to destroy the Notare Abel, despite the fact that she carries true Tare. Were she not, I would have most certainly considered seeking her out. Together, we could continue our species, at least for one more generation, had we together the stomach for it.

I straighten up where I stand at the window, looking out. The clock now reads twenty-one forty-eight. Much time has passed. Time, this inconsequential thing. As inconsequential a concept as grief.

"No, the rebels must be rooted out and slaughtered." I say the words out loud. Hearing them always serves as a means of solidifying truth, lest my mind attempt to stray. "They have lost their way."

It is with a certain...acceptance that I exhale that fleeting, ephemeral desire and return to a truth that is as lonely as I am: I am the last and the last, I must remain. For my kind was doomed from the moment we sacrificed ourselves when Sistylea fell. We chose to stay behind, all but one. Myself. I wonder every so often were my purpose here not so necessary, if it were perhaps, not too great a sacrifice not to die alongside the rest.

Instead, I must remain here, in this wretched world, as the last of my kind, dedicated to my purpose until the Tare shifts again and life itself fades. I will watch these Notare fall as I have watched them fall for the past three millennia until, some millennia from now, I too return to dust.

And that will be the end of the role of the Lahve.

Three thirty-four. I move back to my desk and continue to pour over the correspondence I have received from the Notare around the world. Seven regions. The Diera. Brianna. Carata. Hviya. Molthanithra. Strentara. All regions are functioning as well as predicted, short of Carata, across the ocean, where Notare Tanen continues to pillage and burn and destroy. I attempt to reach him on one of the few communication devices still functional in this new world — a thing the humans call *computer* — but the connection does not go through. I do not believe he uses this or any other technology born of this world, unless it is to destroy.

And I understand why he has chosen this path, even if I do not approve.

I wrinkle my nose in distaste at the thought of returning to that part of this globe to negotiate with Tanen directly. His region holds the manufacturing plants necessary to create these communication technologies — as well as other life-saving harvesting equipment — that other regions do not. If the humans fall beneath his attacks as he advances further and further east, then it will all be lost. And, if these humans here in Brianna do not get their small, frail hands on those technologies soon, they may no longer have enough food to sustain their rapidly increasing human population. They are a species much like a virus. How greedily they consume.

I sigh and repeat my thoughts out loud, "Tanen will need to be dealt with soon."

Yet, before I can cross the world, I will need to root out the rebels here who disgrace the Tare with their attacks on Notare Abel. That it was given to her, a human, matters not. They disgrace themselves by attempting to interfere, forcing the Tare's hand as if it were a mortal.

No. The Tare chose and it chose a human called Abel and though I myself never dwelled much on the matters of humans — the primitive, brutal race that occupied this planet before our arrival — I am merely the Tare's incarnate. Neutral, above all else.

Five fifty-four. Night has long descended as I have ruminated at my desk. I leave the brick structure I have claimed for my manor and walk the streets of Brianna alone, members of my guard lurking at a respectful distance. The sky remains light, even through the night. A longing for our home world sweeps me — the sprawling violet fields, the luminous cities that spiraled high among the clouds, the rural dwellings carved directly into the mountainsides...

Here, I pass by squat homes, mostly brick, though some are constructed of wood. Stars mark the front doors of the houses where, only a few weeks ago, Elise and her Heztoichen supporters kept and tortured humans for their own perverse pleasure.

It angers both Notare Kane and Abel that this practice was undertaken, however, what they do not know is that it is a common practice among several of the other regions as well. That, however, remains the problem of those Notare. It is not my place to give voice to the Notare on how to govern themselves, merely on how they must interact with one another. I will intercede only when Notare Abel summons her humans back home, for it is certain that many other Notare will not be so willing to lose their blood supply. It will..create friction. It already has. Through these gangs of defilers and betrayers that dare to call themselves Heztoichen, it has already begun.

That however, is a matter for another day. Another *time*.

The suburban streets come together in a cul-de-sac at the end of a road marked *Starlight*. Here, a marketplace already begins to see its earliest activity, with those that harvest bringing their fruits and vegetables to long wooden tables. Bakers have stands where they keep bread. The aroma is pleasing.

Other humans have begun crafting — creating plates and cups from fired clay, weaving baskets from dried reed grasses, even concocting soaps and perfumes from animal fats and herbs.

Primitive though they may be, they are resourceful and inventive, these creatures.

As there is no coin here, goods and services are often bartered. When they are not, paper tickets are exchanged for more valuable goods, however this system is badly flawed. Alcohol, above all else, is the greatest currency. People have begun concocting all manner of foul beverage to trade with one another only to drink themselves into glut on the days labeled "weekends." Often, on these weekend days I find men and women passed out on the lawns surrounding each house, or occupying one of several buildings at the end of Starlight called *bars* and *restaurants*, though these restaurants are distant relatives of Sisylean restaurants, at best.

I remember what it was like walking through wide archways in all the trappings of glamour. Eyes roaming my body yes, but never touching. They know better than to attempt to touch their Lahve.

It is eight-twelve and I find myself passing through Brianna's steel gates. Four humans attend the gates at all times, while twenty-two additional humans stand as sentries at intervals along the steel walls that surround Abel's territory.

The territory is tight, the need to expand strong, particularly given the rise in attacks…

While the compound itself has not been raided, groups attempting to travel to Brianna often find themselves under siege. Survivors have told us of bleak attacks by humans *and* Hezoichen. Families have been lost that Notare Abel would have saved. Discussion has commenced over whether or not the humans of Brianna are prepared to build outposts, however, there is doubt over their ability to adequately protect them…

Hmm.

I still. Up ahead, a tree catches my eye. I advance towards it, changing my trajectory by a few degrees, my swordstick held lightly in my fists behind my back. My shin-length coat flutters with my steps, but there is no wind out here beyond the perimeter in what the humans call Population. Though this territory is still classified as Brianna according to my maps, there is no marker for it and too many feral humans reside outside of the walls in these cannibalized cities, in these forgotten woods.

Coming to a stop before the tree, I tilt my head to the side and inspect the sign carved into the bark. I narrow my gaze, flipping through a long list of languages both old and newly acquired, but there is no meaning in this sign that comes to me. My fingers twitch around my swordstick.

My gaze pans out, widening and absorbing everything rapidly. I take in the entirety of the woods before me clearly, precisely and in the blink of an eye, I spot three other signs nearly one hundred paces away, all equally foreign.

Alien.

Nine forty-two. The Notare will be awake by now.

I close my eyes and seek out her husband. Using my rheach, I prod into him. I cannot speak to him telepathically, but I can alert him to the fact that I seek him. I feel his conscience ping in acknowledgement.

Out loud, I say, "Yours and the Notare Abel's assistance in the woods is requested." It is not a request and he does not treat it as such.

Some moments later, I hear the loud crunching of feet through the undergrowth and moments after that, the Notare of Brianna and the Diera appear flanked by a small battalion of soldiers.

Notare Abel's stomach proceeds her as she walks — waddles — behind it, grumbling grumpily under her breath, "This is ridiculous. We don't need forty guards accompanying us wherever we go."

"Correct." Notare Kane nods. "That is why we only have fourteen."

Notare Abel growls, "It's too many. They're crowding me."

"They wouldn't be able to guard you properly if they were far away."

"I don't need guards."

"Of course not. They're here for me."

He looks down at his wife with a grin that disorients me. Standing together as they are, I can feel their love as a tangible body between them. When we arrived on this planet, I had no expectation to ever see such attachment between one of our kind and one of theirs yet here it is, in defiance of my predictions. I am rarely wrong. Never.

Only once.

Because of the human that stands before me, golden light beaming from her chest like a torch in the Antillian desert right at sunset. The lights of the sky would reflect off of marbled sands, turning the dunes to a charred black — but if one held a torch or light a flame right at that moment — the contrasting reflection would send rays of light scattering in every direction, in millions of colors. It was…incredible.

And now it is lost and the only beauty to be found here is none at all for, in Population, beauty itself is a foreign concept to these humans. There is only survival.

"You're a liar, Notare." Abel throws her hands up in the air and when they land, they land on her belly, drawing eyes from several of the guards flanking her. Mine as well. Fascinating. My curiosity to see the first child born of an inter-species union is strong and helps to break up this thing called *time's* perpetual monotony.

"To you, Notare? Never." He turns to face her and tips her chin up with just his fingertips. Her eyelids flutter and she leans in. Before they can partake in their embrace, I clear my throat gently, to alert them of my presence.

"Lahve," Abel says, stiffening and spinning to face me, her pronunciation aggressively horrible. She says my name like the human word for *lava,* rather than LAHH-vey, as it should be correctly said.

Kane must hear it as well, for he manages some contrition as he bows from his waist. "Lahve," he repeats, correctly emphasizing the *h.*

I bow to each of them in return. "Notare. Notare."

"What's going on? Why are you out here?"

Brash as ever, I have learned to accept this unfortunate style of communication as I have learned to accept the faults of many other Notare before her. "I make it a habit to patrol the perimeter daily."

"By yourself? Out here? You could get ambushed."

The thought is amusing. As is her concern for my well-being. It is…quite nearly…endearing.

"I do not think the Lahve is in any position of risk out here alone, Sistana," Kane says, tucking a strand of unruly hair behind her ear. "And he isn't even alone. His guard is two hundred paces behind us. We passed them." He kisses the top of her head.

"We did?" Heat rises in her cheeks that I can feel even from where I stand, so many feet separating us. "Alright. Well, we still could send patrols out here. You don't have to do this. I know you have a lot on your plate."

"The safety and wellbeing of Brianna is within the scope of my charge, Notare." I give her a slight bow, to let her know that I am not offended by her remarks. Her eyes grow large.

"Oh. Yeah of course. Shit. I mean shit. Fuck." She stammers.

Her mate cracks with light laughter. "We appreciate your assistance, Lahve. Did you find something?"

"I did, indeed." I turn from them and gesture at the tree and the marking decorating it. "At nine forty-one, I came across something I have not seen before. I had hoped you could correctly identify this marking and let me know if one of your own people had made it and, if so, for what purpose. Further, should this be a mark made by one of your scouts or under your direction, I will need to rheach through the one responsible so that I may have a thorough understanding of all marks. I do not wish to alert you each time I encounter one." *I do not want to rely on humans for anything, not even a Notare. I am Lahve. I must know all.*

Notare Abel shifts uncomfortably as she speaks, gaze flashing to my sharpened teeth. She blinks many times before switching her gaze past me and strutting towards the tree carved with that alien carving that unfortunately eludes me. Her face scrunches up, emotions so easily betrayed as they often are for these humans, who are paper thin in every way.

"No, that's not one of mine. We don't leave signs like that. We use the radios — the six that actually work, " she snorts. "Either that or the council just shares info by word of mouth with the guards that need to know. Only gangs use marks like these. Sometimes as warnings. Sometimes as a way to communicate within the gang. Sometimes to communicate with other gangs."

"And can you read them?"

"No. I never spent time in any gangs and I never paid attention to the markings when I was out there by myself with Ashlyn and Becks." I do not miss the way Kane's fingers tighten on his Sistana's neck. "Can one of y'all go back and get Diego? He's one of the best at this stuff."

"One of, Notare? Should we not procure *the* best among your people? These signs could be drawn with malicious intent."

"Of course they're drawn with malicious intent," she snaps, then blanches when she meets my eye. "Sorry. It's the baby, I swear. I'm not usually so irritable." I do not believe her, but I offer her a conciliatory nod nonetheless. With that small creature in her stomach, she is afforded every liberty.

"I think…I mean, Diego will be fine. He's the second best. He lived his whole life in a gang."

Second best. I find this phrasing curious in its precision and her deflection. But no matter. I nod.

Time. Too much of it is needed for the human male Diego to be retrieved. He watches me warily as he approaches the group and, atop his jacket, I notice his sling is covered in weapons fit for battle. I also do not miss that his left hand reaches for the nearest among them as he eyes me.

"W-w-what's up?" He says, his speech distorted for some reason. As is his face. He bears gruesome, painful-looking scars. And then I remember rheaching through members of that wretched human gang and reliving the spliced hallucinations from so many memories accompanied by so many sensations…

Throat pain as a man is stabbed. Pain lancing up his side as he's stabbed again. His eyes fluttering as he struggles to his knees. He watches as Diego — with his pale brown skin and eyes the color of the crystal ice caves on my home world — circles another man who looks remarkably like Kane.

Jack.

I know of Jack. I know of him through this rheach and many others. He still haunts this weary world even though he is dead.

The knife in Jack's hand as it comes down across Diego's face. He is unable to avoid the strike as he's outnumbered and surrounded. I occupy the body of the man as he moves onto his feet. He fights Diego and they nearly lose, all four of them. But they don't. Not when Jack cuts Diego down.

How, with Diego's injuries, he was able to flee from this and survive is a story I learned from other witnesses, but I am…*impressed*. It is not a sentiment I experience often toward these humans. But from this battle, both Diego and Abel proved remarkably brave and alarmingly resilient. I doubt many other humans would have survived such assaults. *Any* other humans. And from the account that I witnessed myself through a read of the Notare Abel, I know that this male received these scars in defense of her. For this, and no other reason, I hold him in slight elevation from the other human creatures crawling this camp.

"Can you read this?" Abel says, pointing up at the tree.

He approaches with his head cocked and I find myself momentarily forgotten as the two humans debate this sign.

"Could it be the sign for refuge?"

He shakes his head. "Nnnno. That's got a hhhhook at the top. This is three st-st-straight lines and an X above them. It could be a w-w-w-warning."

Abel grunts and shouts at me over her shoulder. "Did you see any others?"

Sometimes, I believe she forgets that I am not human and that we are not friends.

She looks at me when I do not answer immediately and her cheeks heat once more. She curses under her breath then stutters almost as badly as Diego does, "Sorry. Didn't mean to uh…shout."

I nod, accepting her contrition, and lead her one hundred paces further around the perimeter wall where three thin trees stand clustered together, each one bearing a different marking carved at eye-level — a human's eyes, not my own.

Diego curses when he is within sight of them. "I d-d-d-don't know these, b-but you can see here that this one matches the one b-b-b-back th-th-th…" He cannot finish his sentence, at least, not right away. A moment later the word bellows out of him. "There." Other than the way his pulse beats slightly quicker, he gives no indication that this speech bothers him. Curious.

I look him over once, from his scarred face, to his sling stacked with weapons, to his build which suggests he knows how to use them. Perhaps, confidence then, can explain it.

There is a long silence, one that is filled with a tension whose provenance I cannot place, before Abel finally says, "Should we…"

"*Nnnno.*" His voice is laden with emphasis, communicating a meaning that frustrates me as I do not understand it. On my home world of Sistylea, there were no things I did not understand. Here, in Population, there are a few. And that is far, far too many.

Her fingers twist together. Abel huffs, "This seems kind of important and she's the best. She has a better shot than the rest of Brianna combined."

"Sh-sh-she won't come," Diego hisses.

"If you go get her…"

"You-you want me to ab-ab-abuse our rrrrelationship like that?"

Abel's eyes widen, but her tone does not betray the racing of her heart. "If it means ten minutes of her being uncomfortable against her being ripped from her bed by a bad guy looking to take Brianna, then I'm going with the latter. The former, I mean. Ugh. Whichever it is." She stomps her foot. There it is. The childlike stubbornness that both reminds me exactly why she is leader of her humans, and confounds me in equal measure.

But I am not here to judge. At least, not out loud.

Another long silence stretches, while Diego seems to weigh a decision on a scale that's tipping towards no. Then Kane says, "Pia lives in Brianna too, Diego."

Diego stiffens and levels an icy glare at the Notare — one that would have gotten him flayed had it been up to me, and had we lived in an earlier era. "That's lllllow."

"It's true."

Diego groans, "Ffffuck. I'll need human g-g-g..." He struggles through the word. It comes out in a bluster. "... guards."

"Whatever you need."

Diego trudges away and again, time passes. I stand immobile, looking at the carvings in the trees while my guards push forward into Population. They hear it, too. Far, Teera and Nethral. Just over six miles away, the sound of humans speaking with one another is clear, though their words are muted and mumbled at this distance. Still, their presence is significant.

I ask my guard under my breath to confirm their numbers and, finding them in line with my estimates, I return to the present with a lurch and inform Notare Abel of the presence of two humans. She diligently makes notes in the small pad she carries with her everywhere to combat an affliction of the memory that she calls "pregnancy brain," though I have yet to investigate the validity of such a diagnosis.

She speaks with Notare Kane and some of the guards, attempting to devise a plan to retrieve these humans. I remind her gently that, perhaps they could be retrieved in combination with a plan to build the first outpost and she hastily agrees and thanks me many times for the part I've played in this recovery and many others. She comes towards me, she stumbles, trips and catches herself on my arm and, even though there is fabric between us, I still catch a glimpse of a memory — *her* memory — I would rather not have.

Cold. The sensation comes over me quickly and I shiver all over, even though my body has never felt true chill before. *Desperate. Looking at two faces — both women, one older and one very young — debating leaving a building that had running water while chewing on the fetid, stale remains of dog food. Then going out onto the street and having to run.*

"Oh my god, I am so so sorry!" She wrenches away from me and I extract myself from her thoughts.

With great pain.

I straighten and say nothing at all. I merely clench my lips together and allow her memories to slough off of my skin like an oiled shield under the rain, worn down but not ruined by it.

Notare Abel continues to curse and apologize while her husband coddles her to his chest, looking warily at me, just as the human Diego did. He fears for his Sistana in my presence, which does not trouble me, even though it should. It is always better to be feared just the right amount.

Crunching boots betray faces moments later when Diego returns, three human females carrying guns and a slight, unarmed female with him. He shows the unarmed female the first marking on the tree as they approach it and when she nods, he continues, bringing her forward to show her the rest.

"Anything, Candy?" Notare Abel says to the slight, youthful-looking woman standing among the others.

She pinches her eyebrows together and pulls her shoulders in as she sweeps her gaze among the Heztoichen crowded near her. Her gaze seems to hitch and stall on me and as our gazes lock, she begins to tremble.

The right amount of fear. I would be satisfied had her fear not been slowing our progress.

Diego glares and a vision of flogging him returns. Deprived of such an outlet, I feel remiss and long briefly for Sistylea, then return to the present where the world smells of wet leaves and human scents. Diego turns his back to me, blocking me from view from the small red-haired woman with the dark, blank eyes, and asks her to concentrate on the signs and ignore the rest of us. He promises her in low tones that she's safe here and that none of the Others have any intentions towards her. That she'll be bitten only over his dead body.

Very fragile, this human, and utterly unlike Abel. It is a mystery to me as to why she was summoned until her soft as ash voice says, "This is where they're going to try to break in."

The humans and Heztoichen stir and I blink once, twice in quick succession. I am pleased that the others present did not notice.

Notare Abel moves in line with Diego. "How do you know?"

"The marker back on that tree." She points to the tree one hundred or so paces from us. "Diego was right, it was a warning, but not to us. It's a sign to them, warning whoever will break in that there's a shift change at three am."

"You got all that from just three lines and an X?" Notare Abel says.

I shift slightly so the female comes back into view. She nods and presses her fingertips to her lips. They are very pink those lips. Her bright red hair that I suppose is really more orange than red falls all the way to her waist in tangled tresses. The rest of her is pale and clenched.

"Three lines for three am. If it were three pm, they would have drawn the X under the lines, not over them."

"Shit," Notare Abel curses at the same time Notare Kane does. Diego rubs his hand roughly over his head. His hair is short and uneven around the scars that cross over his skin.

The little red-tressed human says, "This tree has the same mark, but the one behind it has a hook with a circle under it. That means there's a breach point somewhere here."

"And the third tree?" I glance to the tree in question and the sign mutilating its natural state. A five-pointed star with two circles connected by two lines just beneath it.

"What is it?"

"The Five Point Gang. The one that Jack was working with. That's the star anyway. Five points for the five lines they wear." The ones I branded them with.

The humans hiss. I struggle to maintain a neutral expression while inside, I feel a strange…guilt.

Hm.

Prior to Notare Abel's arrival, I culled Brianna of the Heztoichen I felt were…unfit to cohabitate with humans. There were many of them. Each one, I marked with a series of scars as a warning to humans. Already, several of these Heztoichen attacked Notare Abel and her contingent of humans and Heztoichen on the road.

One of my soldiers, Laiya, killed two who attempted to murder the human doctor, Sandra. *Perhaps, I should have killed them.* I feel my mouth twitch harder with the desire to frown.

"The one under it, I think is the sign for another human gang — they call themselves the Disciples. They work together sometimes." She shudders at that. "But I'm not totally sure. It might be a warning from the Five Point Gang to the Disciples that they've claimed this territory, or it could be a rallying beacon. I'm not sure," she repeats. "I don't know." She shakes her head, hiding once more beneath her hair. "I'm so sorry I can't do better."

"No — no, of course. You've done great." Abel curses again and continues to curse until she notices that the red-haired female is shivering properly now. I do not see how she could be given that the air is warm and she wears more clothing than anyone else — a grey misshapen turtle neck that stretches all the way up to the underside of her jaw and down past the tips of her fingers, a pair of equally large grey pants that are so large they drag when she walks, and a dirty apron to cover both.

"Shit. Sorry, Candy," Abel concludes. Candy, I think, not for the first time. What a foolish name. Abel reaches out as if to touch the other female, then balls her hand into a fist and brings it back to her side. "Sorry," she says again. "I hate to

16

ask, but would you be willing to hang out here a little while longer and see if there are any more signs you can read?"

The Candy human closes her eyes and though I have never been adept at reading body language — with my gift, I have not had to be — her grief is clear.

I speak. "There is no need. If *Candy*…" I say, tasting her name for the first time and finding it odd. "…would allow me to touch her, I can pull the information I need from her memories and her services beyond the perimeter walls will no longer be required."

Abel grimaces. She hesitates. I wonder absently, what for. I do not like to wonder. She looks to Candy. "Candy, would that be alright with you?"

Candy shakes her head and closes her eyes and tightens so stiffly together, one push would surely crack her down her rigid center.

"It's really not what you think. He just needs to touch your arm or something, then he can like…download the information from you. All you have to do is think about the symbols — try to picture them in your head. It will take a minute max."

"Seconds, at most," I coo.

It takes some more time. Time. It just wastes away. These humans squander it, and I wonder if they do not realize how little time they actually have here. I can already see the dust that their corpses create drifting through the breeze. Their bones will litter these fields.

Eventually, the female extends her arm. Her eyes remain closed and I find myself momentarily offended, then I move past it. She's just a human.

Abel looks to me and nods and I enter the orbit of the human female's heat with every intention of making this unpleasant trip as quick for the both of us as possible.

I straighten and cut off my next inhale so that I am not too distracted by the smell of the dew beading under her arms and along the soft hairs between her mane and her forehead. The scent of her sweat is oddly pleasing. She smells like earth, like clay, and a little like the bright sky of Sistylea after a rain. My nose wrinkles and I frown so slightly I doubt any of these humans would notice it.

"This will pass quickly if you concentrate on the symbols you know and how you know them," I rumble in a voice that attempts to be soothing in order to speed this process along. It does not seem to matter though, because she flinches all the same. Infuriating...

...is what I would think were I base enough a creature to allow emotion to rule me.

But fortunately, I do not.

I brace, steeling myself for the onslaught of what is sure to be a barrage of emotion and memory and visions and hopes and wants. It is inevitable, given that humans have very poor control and, even when directed, often open themselves to me too much.

I take hold of her forearm.

When rheaching through memories and time, it has happened that I run into walls. Only the very strong Heztoichen have the ability to keep me out. Notare Elise was one of them. She was, perhaps, the last of them. And even with her thousand years, she was no match for me. Using Abel as a vessel, I was able to damage her mind and rip out the mental barriers she'd erected without touching her at all. It was, as is the case for most things, merely a question of time as to how long it would take for her mental blocks to crumble like dry sand castles in a monsoon.

Even the virgins of Syth, who are trained in this art form, fail more often than not. For all the luxury given to her, the female selected to mate with me still was not free of desires of her own. She still had wants that made it impossible for me to couple with her, no matter how pure and strong and beautiful she was or not.

And this female is none of the above. She shivers like a leaf in the wind. Her eyes are closed in fear even though sightlessness has never been an effective defense for any creature, no matter their species' planet of origin. Her skin is pale, her color weak. There is pink in her cheeks that makes her skin seem nearly transparent. She *is* transparent. My thoughts tunnel through her body without any barriers at all to stop me. There is nothing there at all.

There is nothing there at all.

I glance down to my fingers and confirm that I am, in fact, at the present moment, *touching* her tattered grey sleeve. However, where there should be sensation and memory and feeling and horror and terror and blind, white hot pain, there is only a cataclysmic void.

Nothing.

I free-fall through empty space and the longer I touch her, the longer I fall, and there is no bottom against which to shatter. My stomach does not lurch up into my throat. My body is not ruined at the bottom of some well. There is only the purest emptiness. But it cannot be mistaken for *loneliness.*

There are no things. There is only the pure perfection of their absence.

Now, I feel a new sensation, one just as foreign as this nothingness. I feel *sweat* building between my shoulder blades and beneath the curtain of hair that shields the back of my neck. I flick my gaze to meet hers, but her eyes remain closed. I focus on the shape of her eyelashes, their gentle curve, on the smooth slope of her nose between her eyes, on the soft brown color of her eyebrows.

I dig my toes into my hard-soled shoes and I push into her mind with my own. I claw, bite, gnash and tear my way through her thin, transparent exterior and I sink into the bleak emptiness of her mind over and over again because here, there is no gate, no fortress, no moat, no castle to plunder. There is no army. She is not my enemy.

There is only a field, a peaceful jungle where I might lose myself if I'm not careful…

Confused and terrified, I attempt to retreat but I find that I have already lost my way. The thoughts and words and emotions of the others that had been so near to me moments before become muted.

I can no longer hear the two hearts beating inside Abel's body. I can't hear blood pounding through Diego's veins. I cannot feel the fear radiating off of the human guards — a fear that they cannot hide in my presence, no matter how tough their Population-hardened exteriors or how hard they attempt to cage it. I can't hear the two humans hiding in their small cove anymore, still so far away. Two humans who do not even know that Abel will attempt their rescue and that they may soon be saved…I can't even hear the voices of those in the compound, or standing two feet from me…

I can only hear her breath. I can only feel her pulse. Her blood moving underneath her thin skin. The pilling fabric of her cotton shirt beneath my fingertips.

In an effort not to alarm the humans present — and to keep calm myself — I allow myself a single inhalation. It is, in retrospect, a mistake. I can taste her scent in my mouth and it tastes like that jungle, a rich fragrance perhaps enhanced by the scent of wet earth smeared all over her apron. She must work in the greenhouses. She smells like earth… She's sweating more than she was, but it smells like bark from the trees around us. It's…it's *confusing* me.

I cut off my breath. Swallowing thickly, I slowly maneuver my swordstick into the scabbard inside my cloak so that I may free my second hand. I marshal my tone before I speak, being very careful with my volume, pitch and treble. *They cannot know.*

Know what? What is this? What's happening?

"I will pull your sleeve down so that I may touch your arm directly," I tell her. I am already in motion, but she jerks back.

I shame myself — I do not let her go — and wrap my long fingers around her thin wrist, my thumb and fingers overlapping by inches around her very much smaller limb. Her eyes fly open. She looks over her shoulder at Diego.

"Diego," she whimpers.

"Hey," he barks. He steps forward. I hold up a hand.

I do not like the sensation that moves through me and I willfully push it back and refuse to identify it by name. "Apologies. I struggle to...decipher her thoughts. Touching her skin directly will help guide me and provide much-needed clarity," I say and it is...*a lie*. Hm. I return my attentions to the female and say, "I will only touch your fingertips and only for a moment. The briefest instant." I'm begging.

First, I lied.

Now, I've begged.

Hmm.

Distaste sours the sensations rippling over my body and I do not want them soured for they are so very precious. In three millennia this has never happened before, neither to me nor to any of my kind. There is no mention of this in our recorded history and I would know, because upon arriving to this planet, I copied each volume that I memorized into books by hand.

Distracted as I am, I miss the words exchanged between this female and Diego.

I return to the present world to see Diego squaring off to face me, his hands on the weapons on his sling — what has he chosen for me? *Hmm... A grenade. Smart man.* Shoved directly into my mouth it is the only weapon he carries that might kill me. He should hope it does, because my feelings towards him are surprisingly...lethal.

"Mm-m-m-mmmmake it qu-qu-qui-ck-ck."

"It would help if she would focus on me." *Another lie.* This one has origins I, again, refuse to acknowledge.

Still, she looks up at him, eyes wide and afraid but trusting *him*. I do not like that. I do not like that at all. I believed that he already had a female. Pia. I watched them together through the memories of others. So, what is he to her?

He stands with his feet spread to hip distance and glares down at her in a way I do not understand, but that seems to calm her. "You-you-you're alright. D-d-don't pull your sleeve down, just let him touch what he c-c-c-can already sssee now, then you nnnnever have to d-d-do this again and we can keep everyone in B-B-Brianna safe. *Y-y-you* can."

As she visibly relaxes into his gaze, my hands harden and I have to extend concentration slightly beyond usual measure so as not to break every bone in her wrist. Human bones are so fragile, temporary, weak. I pull her sleeve down to reveal her fingers. Her nails are short and badly bitten. I frown.

I drop her hand so that it falls against my palm. I brace. And then, when nothing happens, I wait but there is only more *nothing*, that endlessly calm and magical jungle. There is only *her*.

Her fingertips have their own weight, each one. Her bitten nails are crusted with dirt. There are calluses on the small raised parts of her palm just below each digit and fully covering the heels of her hands. They are red and look like they hurt her.

I do not know why it is, in looking at her dirty hand of all things, that I begin to feel the makings of something I have not felt in a long time. So much time that, though I know it has happened before, I cannot remember it...

Arousal.

My otherwise dormant erection begins to shift in my trousers, cock stiffening against the zipper, bulging against it in a way that is entirely undignified and unacceptable. I panic — *I. Panic.* — and release her. This red-haired human with a name that is nonsensical may be the weakest creature on this planet and I am the strongest one. I *cannot* be aroused by her, least of all by her dirty hand that makes me hallucinate madness.

Her. In the jungle. Naked. Reaching for my hand.

Me. Following in a silence that is spellbinding.

Her. Smiling.

Me. Lost.

I drop her hand and put a healthy length of space between us. Leaves crunch beneath my feet, sounding like shattering glass. I swallow and my pulse rushes like a strong wind through my ears. I stare down at her, shocked and horrified to find that the female has finally granted my request and is looking up at me.

My heart beats hard. A hammer against stone. *Which will crack first?*

Thunder washes over me. I urge to maim, to hunt, to kill. An ancient tribe, it is said that our abilities were borne over millennia of hunting the icy plains of our pre-Frost. Being able to touch the few living creatures that roamed the planet allowed us to discover their migratory paths, where they laid their young, where we might find more prey. It came at a price. The *feeling.* The *rheach,* that was the name for it that the oracles gave. Having studied it from the males of my line before me, I always had the most profound respect for the *rheach.* Respect, and even admiration. But in this moment, I fear it. For what I have seen upon touching the female…what I smelled, what I heard…

Nothing.

Her lips move and I am distracted by their color. They flower an obscene red color and I am distracted by the thought that she is a living creature with blood pumping through her body and that, though I cannot rheach her face or her body, perhaps I could rheach her blood if I drank it directly from the source.

I glance at her wrists and then my treacherous gaze drops to her upper thighs and I feel a dagger in my gut twist as my cock decides to swell without provocation at the thought — *no, the premonition* — of tasting the blood running through this female. Savoring it. Sucking her dry through her upper thigh, like a good little blood whore.

She says something, but I am too tangled in the web of my own thoughts that I do not understand her.

She waits and I have no reply.

"Lahve, are you finished with Candy?"

Notare Abel's voice grates, but I do not look at her. I cannot. This female with the ridiculous moniker holds me bound. *Unacceptable.*

"C-C-C-Candy, get aw-aw-away from him."

I look up at the male called Diego and my left foot, the mutinous beast, jolts forward. *Kill him.* No.

Candy gasps and I freeze, holding everything inside of my body together as I watch her swallow several times — *she could take my cock down her throat and swallow and I would not have to endure the pain of her memories at the same time* — and backs up until her shoulder brushes Diego's chest. He steps away from her quickly, making sure to keep space between them. The sight of that space is what causes her to relax for him. *What is she to him?* The thought rushes up on me again moving with the speed of emotion — a human's, not mine — and it has no business here.

Because I do not feel emotion.

"You got what you needed...sir?" She asks me.

"Lahve," I respond, the reply automatic.

Her voice. It is... "Lahve," she repeats, pronouncing it wrong in a way I don't like. It makes me want to offer her something else by which to call me. "Are you finished?"

I would laugh at the question had I an answer for it. I take another step away from her, but my hand twitches, reaches for *her.* It has not done such a thing before. I take another step and my mouth dries. A third and the fresh sweat coating my body instantly cools.

I will my erection to subside, but it takes more energy than I have to force it down completely. This is...a physiological response I am unprepared for and unused to. The female does not notice. She does not look anywhere but at my face, if that at all. But Diego clears his throat and angles his body between mine and the female's. *Candy*.

"Yes. We're d-d-d-done here." He gestures for her to walk and she does and when she does, he follows and I fight not to follow and tear Diego to pieces, rip the skin from his body, what little of it that there is left. Make a necklace of his scars. *He is taking her from me.*

But she is not mine…

I swallow the thought again and again, repeating it with force, though I don't dare say it aloud. There are Heztoichen present and I want none to hear of this, to know of this, to ever be made aware of my interest in someone like her. And not just because she is so beneath me, but because I am the strongest being, impartial, and I do not want. I do not feel.

Abel glances between the retreating Diego and I and crosses her arms, a peculiar look on her face. "You did get what you needed from her, right? Sorry, I didn't hear you answer."

I did not answer. I should have, but instead I allowed Diego to speak to me with flagrant disrespect. His disrespect was not even among my thoughts. There is no space for it in my mind with how hard I was and am concentrating on the sound of her footsteps. One step more. And then another.

"Yes," I say stonily. "I got from her what is required," I lie. But there is no other truth I can allow. That I am ready for.

―――――――――――

Continue reading anywhere print books are sold.

For more information on where to purchase and to stay up-to-date on new releases, visit <u>*www.booksbyelizabeth.com*</u>*.*

All books by Elizabeth

Berserker Kings - Enemies to lovers. With magic.
Dark City Omega, Book 1 (Echo and Adam)
more to come!

Population - Battles and Heroes that Bite.
Lord of Population, Book 1 (Abel and Kane)
Monster in the Oasis, Book 2 (Diego and Pia)
Immortal with Scars, Book 3 (Lahve and Candy)
more to come!

Twisted Fates - Mafia. Brotherhood. Murder.
The Hunting Town, Book 1 (Knox and Mer, Dixon and Sara)
The Hunted Rise, Book 2 (Aiden and Alina, Gavriil and Ify)
The Hunt, Book 3 (Anatoly and Candy, Charlie and Molly)

Xiveri Mates - Aliens. Heat. New Worlds.
Taken to Voraxia, Book 1 (Miari and Raku)
Taken to Nobu, Book 2 (Kiki and Va'Raku)
Exiled from Nobu, Book 2.5, a Novella (Lisbel and Jaxal)
Taken to Sasor, Book 3 (Mian and Neheyuu) *standalone
Taken to Heimo, Book 4 (Svera and Krisxox)
A Very Xiveri Christmas, Book 4.5, A Novella (Svera and Krisxox)
Taken to Kor, Book 5 (Deena and Rhork)
Taken to Lemora, Book 6 (Essmira and Raingar)
Taken by the Pikosa Warlord, Book 7 (Halima and Ero) *standalone
Taken to Evernor, Book 8 (Nalia and Herannathon)
Taken to Sky, Book 9 (Ashmara and Jerrock)
Taken to Revatu, Book 10, A Novella (Latanya and Grizz) *standalone

Made in the USA
Columbia, SC
21 April 2022